CURSE

"I predict that you will be dead, sir—within the next 45 days!"

Grady's guileless grin stayed in place until somebody in the studio's small crowd emitted a faint scream. Then he looked up at the towering mentalist, reacting as any person might have. "You're putting a *curse* on me? You can't threaten me like that on television, you bastard!"

"I did not say I would harm a hair on your head, Mr. Calhoun," Rajelis said when the murmur subsided. He had raised his long, pale hands dramatically; he was smiling, almost benignly. "It is the persons *around you*—the innocents—who will suffer for you, sir. Suffer, and go on suffering, in diverse ways—until, Mr. Calhoun, you have but a single option—one course—open to you."

J.N. WILLIAMSON

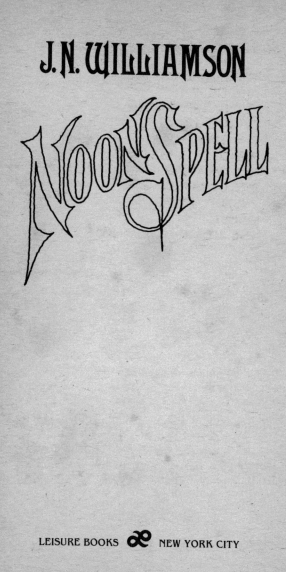

NOONSPELL

LEISURE BOOKS   NEW YORK CITY

Her ideas, during the outlining of this one, were so effective that Mary T. Williamson, my wife, deserves solo thanks. Because she's who and what she is, she may not mind if I also mention Robert Bloch, Stephen King, Jane Yolen, and Gene Wolfe —with thanks.

"Live well. It is the greatest revenge."

—*The Talmud*

"Everything we do is based on fear. . . . Mainly love."

—Mel Brooks and Carl Reiner,
The 2,000-Year-Old Man

A LEISURE BOOK

Published by

Dorchester Publishing Co., Inc.
6 East 39th Street
New York, NY 10016

Printed in the United States of America

BOOK I

"I am reckless what I do to spite the world."
 —Shakespeare, *Macbeth*

"Let me live out my years in heat of blood! —and *let it then be night!*"

 —*John Neihardt*

Prologue

"Forces"

When he was quite small, thin and pale like a matchstick, she made him stay in the front closet of the old house for long periods of time. It was black as pitch and smelled of other people's yesterdays before he was born; it was lonely in there, and she always locked the door.

It wasn't because he was bad, or because she didn't love her only son. It certainly was not because he was a boy; no, indeed! She was as clear as only Mother could be on that point. She assured him that she had no urge to stifle his "natural vigor," his "quintessential aggressiveness." And he believed that. After all, Mother admired power more than anything else, and her whole life she'd yearned to an extent that was almost crippling to be male, herself. So she might experience that proud sensation of nearly feral command that she imagined real men experienced whenever they entered a room. She'd longed for masculine competition, and combativeness, knowing she would excel. Because bending others to her will was the second most important thing in Mother's life—after magick (Mother always put the *k* on the end of it, just the way the Ancients had).

So he became ten, then 11, understanding that Mother saw him as her conduit to a vicarious sharing of his masculine privileges. And as time passed, it appeared likely to him that she fully intended to make him everything she had longed to be and never had been. That touched him; he thought of it as tragic that she had never had the same opportunities. If her attitude was not exactly selfless, it started with him, of necessity. She sought for herself what she wished him to have first, and he accepted her insistent, repeated declaration that youth was only there to be shaped and molded—that a parent's duty was to make of a boy or girl what Mother wished—accepted it without question. Because she had explained that those who went willfully off on their own were the failures and malcreants of society, outsiders who grew like mindless weeds, and who were capable of becoming *anything*. Anything at all. She'd told him that the only escape from such a life was for the mother to select his path in the current incarnation, then consecrate and devote his body and soul to the Forces.

So he'd held back his fearful tears, bobbed his boy's head, accepted what she wanted for him and soon came to know, even while he was very little, *why* Mother made him stay in the closet—so long that he often made number one, and squatted in his own chilly mess for hours; that he soon feared the blackness and circumscription of his closet cell so greatly that, for the rest of his life, he was bound to be frightened when day died and night assumed command of life. Although he sometimes bawled like a baby, although he sometimes begged to be released from the closet, he knew *why* he had to stay there:

Only when he was locked up in one small, snug place and incapable of fleeing from their whispered preachments was it possible for Mother to summon the Forces of Suffering and send them in after him.

Not that they had come for him immediately. Mother's magick was efficient, knowledgeable; she possessed all the individualistic arcane skills, from telepathy and clairvoyance and clairaudience to psychometry and telekinesis; she knew the proper spells, and consistently offered the suitable sacrifices, however disgusting or personally humiliating or murderously violent they had to be. He took enormous pride in her. She was nothing like the other mothers he'd met: pretty, empty-headed creatures of the passing moment, who clucked over their sons' clothing and meals and fretted over their report cards. His mother taught him how to use nature, itself, to his own advantage. And he knew she wasn't there just for the moment, for his childhood, either. He knew that Mother would *always* be there, for him. One way or the other.

Yet even when it came to the matter of questing for sheer evil and making pacts and contracts, even though she had been dedicated to the Forces for her entire present existence, Mother was merely a woman. Not the man she longed to be. And a woman's magick was simply never as rich and varied in its potential, as readily acceptable, as a man's. Try as hard as she could, her son knew, Mother couldn't even be as evil, somehow, as some men who hadn't even intentionally banded with the Forces of Suffering!

At first he hadn't understood it. Then he began to grow up and, when he was almost 12 years old, entering puberty, he grasped the fact that any truly gifted sensitive who attempted to summon the Forces was quite literally putting his or her soul at jeopardy—and there were always masculine souls for the Forces to choose, instead. It wasn't fair, of course. They had lusted for her body when Mother was merely a girl—she'd told him all about that first direct contact, the shrinking terror of being attacked and her admitted foolishness in trying to resist them—and periodically whispered seductive, sinister suggestions to her right up to the moment when that fool on television tried to "expose" Mother. But in concerns of enduring evil, the Forces were meta-physically bisexual with proclivities favoring the homosexual and, always, the masturbatory. Which was one reason why Mother had procured certain photographs for her only son when he was very small, devices as well, and encouraged the earliest conceivable excitation of his boyish lust.

Because the sooner he was fit, the faster they might acknowledge her call.

Much of the time, however, what he'd got out of being locked in the stuffy, smelly closet by the front door was leg cramps, pee, acute boredom, and puzzlement over his failure to respond favorably to Mother's growing collection of photographs. At seven, he'd thought them funny, and giggled. It was only in recent weeks that he'd been able to pore over them without amusement and with a certain newly forming interest in what the people and animals were *doing* in the pictures. Maybe that was a reward for his patience; he'd seen clearly how vital it was that he accept evil earlier than Mother had. That provided him with greater time in which to learn not only the elementary incantations and minor spells but the unique nature of *cursing*. Not mumbling a lot of dirty words, which his mother loathed and punished with nearly savage self-righteousness, but how to place the ideal curse upon one's enemy. And enemies he would have, she'd promised him, virtually all those men and women whom he met as a grownup; "because you're rooted in time and intended for immorality, and they'll hate you as much for the favors you bestow as for the misery you bring."

He had been fascinated by the prospect of cursing people since Mother introduced it to him, for his eighth birthday, partly because he saw that she was right. There were kids at school who called *him* names, and he longed for the moment when he could make one of them have a heart attack, turn blue, and die while he watched and laughed. Or caused one of the boys who plagued him to assault and maybe mutilate one of the girls who had also teased him.

But beyond the ordinary, childish amusements, the uses for the little-understood skill of cursing, of jinxing were myriad. They ranged from the fundamental but quite direct power of psychologically manipulating people who stood in his way to far craftier, subtler methods that had appealed to him since he'd thought them up. And methods for acquiring the kinds of power Mother had craved—except that he could *develop* such methods, because he was a male.

He'd fallen into the habit lately of dozing, after school, squatting among the filthy galoshes and discarded shoes Mother tended to toss to the floor of the closet. Distantly, he recalled the father who had hated such clutter, who had kept the old house neat and clean, who'd smiled gently and obligingly even when Mother excoriated him for holding back, for "refusing to cooperate with Cal and me in raising this family to the greatness that is rightfully ours." Father had died without an inkling of warning one winter night when black clouds raged across the skies above their house. That was the very first time when Mother had locked him in the closet, screaming at him above the thunderous sounds of the anomalous storm that his father had "misdirected his faith, his strength, and failed" and said that it was up to her son "to don the mantle of Suffering for all of us." It was a night when the closet's interior was no blacker than the world beyond, and he'd been terrified and tearfully proud simultaneously. At times such as now, asleep in the closet, he tended to dream and remember all the details of the night Father died and he was made the man in the family. That wonderful night. And, asleep, he had no way of knowing that Mother's dark prayers were finally being answered.

The Forces of Suffering were coming for him.

He'd never discovered why Mother called them that, instead of the Forces of Evil, or Darkness, or whether there was any difference or distinction. When he'd asked, maybe a year ago, Mother's answer had been vague, perhaps intentionally so: "Human beings do not dread evil, my little one, although they say they do. Part of what separates them from us is our realization, our acceptance, that Night is coming—the soul's Night, the Night of Death. Thus, others do not fear that time when they will pay for all they have done— because they failed to accept the consequences of their silly evil deeds gladly, joyously, and have lost the opportunity to be counted among those who had prepared. What they dread, and fear, my little one, is that which we bring them as their final warning: the Forces of Suffering."

This afternoon in late autumn, Mother's preparations had not seemed different or her exhortations more passionate, more persuasive. She had stood right outside the closet door, hiding as always whatever it was she did from him; she'd begun in a steady but low-pitched voice and, little by little, worked her way up to a combination of screaming, snuffling, and chanting that—back when she had started all this—made him think she had brought in the neighbor's cocker spaniel and was tickling him, or something. Incense wafted beneath the bottom of the closet door as it always did; when she moved into the living room light and was closest to the door, he made out glimpses of her naked foot and the way she had painted her remnants of toe nails ten different colors. (Mother chewed her toe nails; he'd walked in on her accidentally once, seen the way she curled her somewhat plump, bare legs until she was able to work the toes, one by one, into her avid mouth.) This afternoon, as always, he could tell by the way the arches of her small feet worked, she'd reached the point in her supplications and entreaties when she dropped to her haunches and bobbed up and down, up and down, while her voice fell to a husky whisper and the *drumming* sound began. Who or what made the sound, he'd never learned; it was an increasingly frantic beat but not, he thought, upon an actual drum and not, he also believed, upon the skin of the stomach—though that came closer to describing it.

Unable again this afternoon to see enough of her through the crack at the bottom of the door to identify the source of the drumming sound or to determine if she was naked all over, he'd settled back against the wall of the closet and begun to doze when it happened.

At first it was merely a fuzzy mistiness seeping beneath the closet door, and he'd thought it was either part of a dream or an emanation of his mother's dinner preparations. Generally, they had their private evening meal right after the hours he spent in the closet and, as often as not, Mother was either ashamed of herself for failing to send the Forces to him once more or inclined to blame him, bitterly, for "having that same idiotic resistance your father had." But today, while the haziness that swam before his eyes wasn't in the least scary, Mother's unbroken string of failures had come to an end.

The 12-year-old stared at the mist without fear because it was already so dark in the closet that he knew he wasn't able to see *anything* clearly.

It hadn't occurred to him that the essence floating at the nucleus of the haziness would have the ability to produce its own shockingly sudden, unexpected luminosity! A light formed, startling the boy so badly he struck the back of his skull against the closet wall, and then sent out filaments that illumined every ribboning fiber of the mist. While he gaped at it, simultaneously striving to conquer his fear and telling himself that *this* was what he and Mother had waited for all the years of his boyhood, a cloudy face took shape and hovered just below his eye level as he crammed his back against the rear of the closet. Another color glittered like two sequins—the crimson eyes of the smoky face—and he sensed it was about to speak, *knew* that it brought him commands, injunctions he would be obliged to obey for the duration of his life. He tried to see the face clearly, sought to identify its features if that was possible, but now the tiny red eyes were holding his own terrorized gaze and the power was beyond anything he or his mother had envisioned.

Youuuuuu! The masked countenance in the haze addressed him in a manner that was inescapable, unavoidable. At once it hissed like something serpentine in his small ears and rattled around inside his head like grenades with the pins pulled. It adjusted itself, then communicated in precise English that was no longer serpentine but remained too loud; additionally, the English was so lacking in accent or inflection that the voice seemed unhuman, inhumane. *Your mother has been accepted. And you are chosen. You will learn the ability to curse—the entire world. No one will stand in your way.*

It stopped, then, for a moment, the hammering, accentless voice that had assailed not only his hearing and his nerves but his soul itself. The sudden phenomenon of silence brought his consciousness shrieking to the surface, and he spasmed, jerked when he heard his mother on the other side of the door. What was she doing? She seemed to be lying on the floor, thrashing against it and moaning as if in awful pain, or suffering from some condition of which he understood little or nothing. When the red-eyed mist momentarily subsided he fell to his knees and there made out one of his mother's familiar eyes beneath the door. It was open wide, yet staring; and he sensed that it did not see, or recognize, her only son. It was as if she, too, were locked in communication, or contact; as if her head and body had been suffused with the Forces of Suffering.

You will receive the gift of foretelling. *Of prophecy.* Both crimson eyes bobbed in the hazy cloud, glowed fiercely. *And with that gift, boy, you will bring a special Suffering.*

He nodded but was newly terrified. The light in the living room, he'd noticed with a surge of panic, had gone *off*—and he could no longer tell if Mother was there or not. Perhaps he was alone with this—this *thing* locked in the closet with him; maybe he was already doomed to Hell. His wide-eyed gaze returned to the crimson eyes, compelled to do so. "D-Do you," he asked, scarcely above a whisper, "always look that way?"

We look the way we please, it replied. A whisper was more than sufficient; the thing was so near it was almost a part of him. But it sounded resentful, annoyed; it did not wish to be questioned. *You will prophesy, you will curse and bring a new kind of Suffering. But YOU AS YOU—are inadequate.*

What did that mean; was he to be given a partner? Then the eyes, without notice, snapped shut. What he saw at the curling heart of the smoke was a mouth as immense and ravenous as that of a shark. Desperately, the boy crammed himself against the back of the closet and, without realizing he was doing it, called repeatedly for his mother.

YOU shall help YOU! And the shark's mouth turned up at the corners in a covert, all-knowing hilarity; the laugh that thundered up from its unguessable depths came roaring at the child with the titanic force of alien winds gushing fire across the face of the subterranean desert depths.

And the mouth, the crimson eyes, the smoky cloud vanished, again without warning. At once he scrambled to his knees and was groping with the doorknob, ready to beg Mother to unlock the door

and release him—release him from the
dark of the stuffy, stifling closet and his
chosen status that he knew, that last
instant, he no longer desired.

But to his surprise the knob turned
and the door plunged wide before his
hesitant touch. And *she* was there, as she
always had been in her way, waiting, fully
dressed but perspiring profusely, kneeling
to take him in her warm arms. He went
happily and with relief; he clung to her
despite the sweat, sulfur, and odors he
couldn't identify pouring from each and
every pore of her quivering body.

"We've *done* it, my little one!" she
exulted hoarsely. "It may have cost us
everything, all that mortals seek in this
benighted plane of being—but now, we
shall have it all, together! Anything that
we desire!"

It was just a week later that Mother
went on TV and their plans were dashed—
delayed, in her case, forever.

"You've *seen* your mother's powers,"
she reminded him when she was home
again, reeking this time of alcohol. The
recognition of it scared the boy badly;
unlike some of the mothers he knew, his
mother possessed no vices—or none that
he was mature enough to recognize. "You
know that I can see the future, don't you?"

He nodded quickly; she was telling the
truth. But maybe, just maybe, the thing
with the red sequin eyes had removed her
gift and given it to him. For the life of him,
he could not figure out a way to mention

the possibility. "You know *everything*," he said loyally.

"But that man, that *dreadful* television man," Mother groaned, sprawling on her bed and fighting back tears of indignation, "he taunted me, *dared* me to say what lies ahead—at a time when I was drained, my little boy. Dry; incapable of piercing the veil and seeing the future with my customary clarity."

"What did you do?" he whispered.

"I made it up." Abruptly, she sat bolt upright on the bed, seized his fleshless shoulders until her nails all but pierced his pale skin. "*I made it up,* d'you *hear* me? Do you *know* what that means?"

He shook his head; guessed. "That . . . you're wrong?"

"Of course I'm wrong!" she snapped, tears starting to spill. "And if all that I prophesied fails, my reputation will be ruined! *No one* will come for readings, my little one; we shall starve!"

"But why did the television man do it?" he demanded, quick, as he ever was, to stand by her side and defend her. He perched on the edge of her bed, small fists doubled. "Did he *want* to hurt us?"

"Of course!" Mother cried, throwing up her arms. "He's one of *them,* remember —one of the *others*! To boost his own reputation or stupid ratings, he *made* me . . . guess." She began to cry loudly, tearfully, voluminously, and, since the boy had never seen her weep before, he was at once grief-stricken for her and badly scared. "He could never have perceived that all sensitives, all mediums, are at the mercy of our contacts on the other side. If they do not decide to tell us the future, we're *helpless*!"

In the weeks ahead Mother's non-psychic prediction of personal calamity came true. Only one of her regulars even dropped by, and, after her Tarot reading, the lady announced she had "pressing concerns" and wouldn't be returning.

After two weeks Mother said that she wished to die. He began envisioning the nature of her death, then. Following the passage of another week or better, she told her only son that she meant to take her own life. His first resolution to watch and prevent her was wrecked by fear, but he remembered her shame and desire for death always.

When three further weeks passed Mother confessed to the 12-year-old that she still wanted to end her life but could not bring herself to do it. He nodded, relieved, but did not believe she had discarded her intention.

He remained in a constant state of nervous tension and dread, imagining all kinds of horrible things, at school. Came the time that, acting on impulse and full of a terrible mental movie that had overtaken him and played relentlessly before his mind's eye, he left school at noon on a bright and sunny day to go home for lunch.

That was when Mother had summoned

the Forces of Suffering to put her out of hers.

He never learned what incantations Mother had used to bring the Forces to her in the awful guise that greeted him when he entered his home and, after calling her name, peeked tentatively into the living room. Nor did he know why the Forces had chosen to assume that hideous singularity in order to act as the weapon in his mother's "suicide."

What he saw was the creature's back and the muscular stumps of its bare legs, and—that second when it turned its head only a little—its profile, beyond forgetting. The back seemed wide as the wall; it showed no clothing. Bristling, porcine hairs grew all over it in two-inch clumps. These were divided by the grotesque and scaly ridge of flesh that grew from the base of the skull to the hairless, meaty buttocks, right above the thick, short, twitching tail. All he could see of his expiring mother was one nightmare-mad eye when it hove into view beyond the pink and hirsute shoulder of the thing, and her naked feet, each of the ten toes painted ten vivid colors and curled, now, into taut little knots due to her agonizing Suffering. Mother's feet looked so small, and they jerked, rhythmically.

All the boy saw of the profiled head was a dripping, fat-wrinkled snout and a carnivorous gap of a mouth fixed in a drooling grin.

He ran to the front closet immedi-

ately. Before entering, he glanced out the
closest window and shivered at screaming
noonday, transfixed by the blaze of light
and almost, for another interval, trans-
cended or transformed by it. Then he
squealed in his fright, closed the door
behind him, and—shaking as if feverish—
waited for the Forces of Suffering to come
and use him.

"Is there beyond the silent night / An endless day?"

—*Robert Ingersoll*

1

Friday. March 18, 1988.

Before that night's program and a good
six hours before their individual pre-show
dinner meals, the *Confab* TV cast and crew
enjoyed a traditional weekly lunch together at Grimelda's. In this "let's-do-
lunch" sense, "crew" generally referred to
director   Tom   Simincola,   program
manager Andy Sutor, sometimes Eddie
Aspen from the Channel 61 film library,
and either of two cameramen who alter-
nated Friday lunch as if mutually pledging
the relative unworthiness of their work on
Confab. It had something to do with the
fact that their star hailed from New York,
and the persistent rumor that he'd be
recalled at any moment.

Grady Calhoun, who hosted the late-night Friday talk show and, basically, *was* the on-camera cast, thought such considerations of class and contributions to his program were self-demeaning and silly. But he had never figured out an unembarrassing way to broach the topic directly to the camera boys. Guido, the Italian, was mutely present today.

There was another person present in Grimelda's this Friday; she had barged in, unasked, and the usually quick-quipping Calhoun was rather less certain of her welcome from the other regulars. At 61, as was the case with other stations, people tended to socialize within their own departments.

But welcoming her was no problem for Grady since he'd been sleeping with her recently, any time she allowed it, and he liked brassy, beautiful Bud Rocker more than he had even admitted to himself.

Third-generation Irish, born with a gift for gab and the kind of guileless, crinkly eyes guests peered into and offered up the secrets of their lives, Grady Calhoun might have invited the world to lunch if the station picked up the tab and the world was willing to hear his comprehensive reportoire of old jokes. He liked most people on sight and was inclined to forgive them before discovering their sins, after which he found himself continually apologizing for them. Six feet tall but so disposed to walk in a swift, shuffling slouch that he appeared shorter, Calhoun seemed somewhat fat in person—never on camera—because his body gave the impression of having been stuck together, one rounded segment after another. He often crooned to his audience about his "lake-blue eyes," but confided to intimates about the times in his youth when, before a mirror, he'd practiced until a lopsidedly innocent smile emerged and eventually became natural to him. He was wholly devoted to his career; it was one of the reasons Jean had left him recently. Midway between the lake-blue eyes and tilted grin, Grady had a nose as pointed as a muskrat's; critics—and there were many —marveled that the proboscis came to a point after his years of putting it into other people's business. What irked them the most was knowing that Calhoun was more curious than malicious.

All such knocks, according to the *Confab* star himself, were "music to my fears." It only indicated that his popularity remained high, "that the good burghers haven't forgotten the old ham" —but not everybody warmed to Bud Rocker, Channel 61's fast-rising anchorperson on the *Evening News*. Not even in the way they heated up to the boyish Grady. Not that anyone questioned her ability, least of all the darkly handsome Andy Sutor, who'd loved watching the six o'clock ratings soar with Bud as the anchor. The PM stood like a gentleman as she joined them at Grimelda's bar, but his brow wrinkled in helpless male dismay

above her head, and director Tom Simincola replied with a ruefully comic shrug.

Grady caught the exchange and didn't
like it, but understood. He merely pursed
his lips and frowned, faintly, as the news-
woman slipped onto the bar stool they
made available to her beside Calhoun.
Fundamentally, their custom was point-
lessly exclusive and outdated. Besides,
Bud Rocker was bound to be the last one
to honor an occasion of masculine
camaraderie.

And she was also the only person
Grady knew who was as ambitious as he
was. Shorter than a *Tonight Show* author
interview, proudly talkative about a great-
grandfather who'd been black, Bud had
hurtled herself into television with a
missionary's chip on her shoulder, defying
anyone to knock it off. Her local climb was
mercurial; she'd even changed both her
names, legally. From Amanda Rockwell.
They had begun dating when Bud objected
to a gag he used on *Confab* as being "anti-
Christian"; to Calhoun's astonishment,
the petite and brilliantly self-educated
Rocker was as narrowly, formally religious
as he was ready to believe anything—at
least for a while. In a week, they'd begun
to argue that they wanted one another's
positions, and what made that fun was the
modicum of truth about the assertions.
Grady yearned to be taken seriously; Bud
longed for the freedom of an open forum.
Within two weeks, they'd begun having
sex, and some of Calhoun's completely

concealed misery over his divorce had begun seeping away.

"Have you eaten?" he asked Bud.

"Often," she said quickly, giving the hand-printed menu a businesslike, brief scrutiny. "Twice a day for years."

Grady's back stiffened. Tom had emitted the high-pitched, whinnying sound that passed for laughter in the tall, horse-faced director's case. "Gee, I always wondered where Joan Rivers had lunch," Grady murmured.

"I wish you'd consulted me about the topic for tonight's *Confab*," she said without raising her gaze fro the menu.

Calhoun's rather fine brown brows did rise. "Hey, when have you ever asked for my opinion about what news stories to highlight?" His tone was light, but Bud had a way of saying what she pleased—which he enjoyed—and she often said it regardless of where she was, and he didn't enjoy that.

Bud drew himself up. "My options are limited to the news as it breaks," she said in that melodic alto that might land her at the network before Grady got back to Manhattan. "You select your weekly topics from thin air, pal. And I think the air is gonna be thin as the devil tonight!"

Grady caught Sutor, the program manager, following the discussion with undisguised interest. But Andy was two stools away and remained silent. Grady also caught the bartender's eye, lifted his arm, and pointed to Bud. "Okay, I get it."

He smiled at her. "We're doing 'Prophesy—Does It Work Today?' as tonight's subject, and *you* object to such a pagan topic. Right?"

"On grounds of community standards, perhaps," Bud retorted icily, "and definitely on the grounds that there are hundreds of truly significant themes that practically cry out for public inspection." She had quite wide eyes, with a fringe of tan lashes and a remarkable range of changeable but easily communicated emotions behind them. Her skin was the color of standing coffee laced with two much cream and her mouth was wide too. Full-lipped and as expressive as her eyes. Grady found her beautiful, yet understood that most men could not ignore her candor or tolerate her intelligence.

"I bet I can tell you what you object to the most," Tom put in. He had wound up farthest away, to the right of the silent cameraman, Guido, and he possessed such a refined and polite manner that Grady couldn't recall the last time anybody had become angry with the director. These days, with Tom's wife expecting their first cihld—again—the rangy Simincola was getting by with murder in the things he'd said in his innocuous fashion. "It's the way we've mixed a clergyman with an astrologer and a psychic. I'll bet you object to the tacit endorsement that appearing on *Confab* gives the stargazer and the mind reader."

Grady, watching Bud's lively face,

realized his friend had hit it on the head. But Bud wasn't about to admit she was that easily understood. "There is that, I guess," she said slowly, pausing to order a hotdog with the works and a Lite beer. It gave her a chance to find another way to express her views. "Mainly, though, I don't think you show good judgment in even *asking* that mentalist on the show!"

Andy Sutor reluctantly broke his vow of silence. "*Ms.* Rocker, Calvin Rajelis is in town *this* week, not next nor any other time in the year. He has a *following*. And *he's* why Grady and I chose tonight's topic to start with." He smoothed back rather improbable but genuinely deep black, glossy hair and peered affably at his ratings-winning anchorperson. "Is it a personal thing with you, Bud? D'you know the guy?"

"Thank God, no," Bud replied, feigning a shudder. "But I caught his act when he was in town two years ago, and he's positively creepy."

"C'mon, Buddy," Calhoun began, grinning at her and tickling the top of her hand. Beneath the rim of the bar, his knee nudged hers. "I saw Rajelis on cable and the guy is sensational. There are a lot of experts who claim he's the only one around who can turn on his psychic skills whenever he needs them. That's why so many of his . . . paranormal tricks . . . have tested out."

"Have you seen him *in person*?" Bud persisted. "And don't call me 'Buddy.' I think you ought to chat with him before your show tonight. He's unconventional as hell. He's capable of saying or doing anything."

Grady laughed, but he also withdrew his hand, and his knee. "I don't talk with my guests in the blue-green room," he said. Grady referred to 61's version of the well-known *Tonight* waiting room for celebrities. "You know that. Like t'keep 'em fresh, to form my own opinions about 'em at the same time the viewers do." Calhoun lowered his voice, trying, for once, to keep a part of the conversation confidential. "But I appreciate your concern for me; for the show. Does this mean you'll be there and we can go somewhere afterward?"

"Our date's Sunday night," Bud said, asking the bartender to put her hotdog and beer in a sack and getting to her feet. She patted Calhoun's reddening cheek and started for the door. "News doesn't permit the time for late lunch hours, gentlemen. As for the show, Grady, I simply don't want you ruining it before *I* take it over!"

The primary fascination of *Confab* to its midwestern viewers—even more effective on the subconscious level than the controversial subjects selected by its host/producer, Grady Calhoun—was the fact that the late-night show was done *live*. The weekend, to start with, was customarily the time when people let their hair down and worked harder at enjoying themselves more than they had in pursuit of their weekday obligations. If members of the viewing audience were drinking, by projection they believed that Confab's guests would also be more likely to say whatever came into their minds. Rumor had it that, in one of his first Confab programs after leaving New York under some kind of cloud, Grady had persuaded a guesting exotic dancer to "take it all off," right on the camera. There was no truth to the rumor, except that Calhoun had suggested she do it, then stopped her; but such uncensored antics of live television—real or rumored—had acted as a pre-selling stimulus to the program, week after week.

By the first commercial break of this Friday's show, no measurable portion of Confab's television audience had switched to another channel or turned their sets off. Grady himself sensed that, knew it, as he gazed away from the dead camera and rearranged his notes for the next portion of his 60 minutes. The studio audience had sat in their seats as if transfixed, as if the slightest movement might break the program's spell. Not yet 40, the Irishman from the Bronx had already invested over 15 years in front of the watchful electronic eye and trusted his own instincts in preference to virtually any other knowledgeable source. Maybe he had been too relentless, taken too many hard-bitten, interrogative risks early in his career. Maybe he'd ruffled the wrong feathers, or even, as they had told him at the Manhattan outlet, reached the point of turning some viewers off. But that was history and, the way things looked these days, Grady Calhoun *wasn't.*

Surreptitiously, he glanced around at the others perched on refurbished easy chairs with him on the raised platform. They were consulting their notes too— Reverend Herbert H. W. Campbell, "Minister to the Dying," as he preferred to be called; the aging astrologer from the state's southern quarters, Freida Rehfeldt; Bonnie Modela, the black, dwarflike numerologist Andy Sutor had flown in from Chicago Heights—except Calvin Rajelis, the performing mentalist. Grady frowned and suppressed a shudder. Bud was definitely right about that one, the professional mind reader or psychic or whatever in hell he called himself. Rajelis couldn't be much past his early twenties; he was very tall and so slender he seemed anorexic, and his features were regular and pleasant enough at a glance—

But the more Rajelis said, spontaneously, answering Calhoun's experience-taught questions rather than reciting from his memorized act, the more his *creepiness*—that had been Bud's word for it—became virtually intolerable. That, and the way he exuded arrogance. Surely he didn't behave this way during his performances! Covertly appraising the man, Grady couldn't decide if it was the mentalist's lipless, leonine snarl of a

mouth, the showy dark glasses, or something else Calhoun could only read as
ominous anticipation—as if Rajelis were
biding his time before dropping some
really tasteless remark among them like a
verbal grenade. Then he realized that
Rajelis was *staring back at him*, just as
surreptitiously. It occurred to the television host, who'd met and perhaps
angered many hundreds of other people,
that he'd never before witnessed such
detestation in another man's eyes. But
why?

The psychic spoke without being
questioned and it was as if he'd read
Grady's thoughts. "You've all managed to
deride me so far tonight. And my work." It
was a curiously high voice for so tall a
man, and one Grady found increasingly
ominous, but breathy and reedy. "The
minister who believes all accumulation of
knowledge ceased with the writing of the
New Testament, yet he preaches of a Here-
after that frightens him and seeks to
comfort the impending dead instead of
celebrating with them." The minister
twisted around to speak, but Rajelis
wasn't through. And Grady Calhoun
realized with amusement that, for the first
time in his career, he had missed the cue
indicating that the camera eye was once
more alive. Calvin Rajelis, himself a performer, had not. "Two practitioners of the
pseudosciences who would be at each
other's throats, comparing nonsense to
nonsense and turning to me as if I were

one of their kind." Rajelis's lids rose like wings and the eyes were shockingly all but colorless. *Contacts*, Grady thought promptly. "Yet little or nothing has been done in the way of prophesy, Mr. Calhoun, though it is your topic of the night. How else may one prove oneself?"

"I take it," Grady began carefully— "and call me 'Grady,' please—that you have a few predictions to lay on us yourself?" He saw the nearly emaciated man nod. Theatrically, he had replaced his sunglasses. "Before you do, I'd have to say that Ms. Rehfeldt's prediction of new war erupting in the Middle East qualifies, and that Ms. Modela's numerology chart for Mr. Quadafi is . . . rather encouraging!" The studio audience chuckled indulgently, and two or three people briefly applauded.

"A combination of embryonic intuition, quite rudimentary and undisciplined, guesswork, and a trace of witchcraft," Rajelis sneered.

"Well, I'm not sure about the 'intuition' part," Reverend Campbell rumbled with a we're-all-friends-here-but-I'm-Daddy smirk in the two ladies' direction. "But I'll go along with the rest of that—save, sir, your somewhat snide allusion to me and my Christian concern for the perishing. I'd like—"

"*Will* you go along with me!" Rajelis exclaimed. In leaning toward the clergyman, he seemed to uncoil and grow. "Perhaps you'll inquire of me about the future of your religion, Reverend. Or would you like to know if and when your Jesus is returning?''

Calhoun leaned back in his chair, clasping his laced hands over a raised knee, content to allow the male guests their squabble. While he wasn't a church-goer, and the need for prayer confronted him only when someone he knew died, Grady found himself rooting for the heavy-set, white-haired Campbell. Standing up for the mentalist would be like cheering for AIDS, or forest fires! How sweet his work was when an interesting topic fired up his guests, the audience, the viewers, and the ratings! For the first time since Jean threw him out, Calhoun saw himself the sweet, old way: as one of the blessed.

Until the hour began to run down he was able to keep things stirred up but not quite out of control with a mixture of questions, commercial breaks, and phone-in calls. His real task was striving to involve Freida Rehfeldt and Bonnie Modela in the discussion. It occurred to him with surprise that he'd never hosted a show with guests who were more sincere about their beliefs. The astrologer and the numerologist, Grady mused, knew their subjects so thoroughly and worked from such detailed bodies of ancient knowledge that it wasn't easy for them to offer brief, off-the-cuff remarks.

He'd begun to wonder if Calvin Rajelis just as earnestly believed the things he was saying—90 percent of it had to do with his own accomplishments, all of which the mentalist said could easily be verified—when Rajelis, just as experienced with the television construct as he was, turned to face him and to seize the closing remarks. The sunglasses were off again, the tall man's face was near his, and a combination of the colorless but challenging eyes and the worst case of bad breath in Grady's memory rooted him in silence.

"If you'll permit it, Mr. Calhoun, I will make a prediction your entire viewing audience can witness for themselves. May I?"

The people in the studio fell absolutely still. *If I don't let the SOB do it,* Calhoun thought, *this'll be the* Calvin Rajelis Show *before Monday!* "I'm sure we'd all be tickled pink, Cal," he said aloud. "I look lousy in pink myself, but go ahead!"

"Thank you." Rajelis instantly stood, the motion smooth, as if he lacked joints. Grady smiled with apparent anticipation and mentally swore at the man for upstaging him. "What follows is only the first part of my prophesy, Mr. Calhoun. Tonight, you made a joke linked to how hard it is for people even to consider the fact that they must die one day. It may assure your viewers to see your renowned sense of humor tested, publicly." He did not look toward his host but stared fixedly into the camera; and Calhoun, just as interested in dramatic effect, motioned Guido to close in on Rajelis's hypnotic eyes. "I predict that you will be *dead,* sir—within the next 45 days!"

Grady's guileless grin stayed in place until somebody in the studio's small crowd emitted a faint scream. Then he looked up at the towering mentalist, reacting as any person might have. "You're putting a *curse* on me? You can't threaten me like that on television, you bastard!"

Now the show audience began to recover from their collective shock and to mumble their disapproval. Grady saw Tom Simincola, his director, white-faced, giving him the cue for the final break, but Grady knew time had not expired.

"I did not say I would harm a hair on your head, Mr. Calhoun," Rajelis said when the murmur subsided. He had raised his long, pale hands dramatically; he was smiling, almost benignly. "It is the persons *around you*—the innocents—who will suffer for you, sir. Suffer, and go on suffering, in divers ways—until, Mr. Calhoun, you have but a single option—*one course*—open to you."

With the expenditure of huge effort, Grady was in control of himself once more and standing, trying to minimize the image of authority a standing Rajelis grasped. But the mentalist remained inches taller than he. "Hold on; let me get this straight." The old reliable Calhoun poise and charm were again in place. Narrowly. "You are predicting—not threatening, just *predicting*—that my loved ones are going to suffer so much that, within 45 days, I'll have no choice except . . . to kill myself. Right? Have I got it?"

Rajelis went on staring into the unblinking camera eye until, for Calhoun, it was as if some sort of magick duel was starting to unfold.

Still, the psychic answered Grady. Obliquely. "It is correct that I have not threatened you—nor have I threatened *any* human being, individually. And I have not said anyone is going to die, except you—at *your own hand.* But because I can look into the future, and do so unflinchingly, some others . . . will." He lifted his long arms while maintaining the level of his voice as well as his stare, and simply emphasized certain words in his thin, fluting intonations. "This is my last prophesy tonight: that all the misery *your* existence provokes, Mr. Calhoun, will be done . . . in *the light.*"

A sweating Calhoun caught up with the threatening and mysterious mentalist at the rear exit of the building, just before Rajelis could step out in the alley and disappear. Already, Grady hoped, Tom had notified the police and they were en route to question the tall, fleshless young man. Calhoun was unsure of either of their rights but felt certain he didn't have to tolerate such things on his own television program. As Rajelis's lank form appeared in the open doorway, car lights fleetingly illumined the bleak alley, and the vehicle's tires squealed as it shot backward, in reverse, to collect the mentalist.

"Why—answer me that?" Calhoun demanded. He put out a rather meaty hand to catch the other man's arm and momentarily detain him. The forearm felt soft, bony. "Why the hell are you doing this?"

To his surprise, Rajelis did not leave, but turned from the door with an unmistakable gasp. One long hand fluttered to his head in the way people try to ward off brilliant light. "Prophesy is my profession, Mr. Calhoun."

"You know what I mean, pal," Grady snapped. "Answer me just one question, okay? Will you do that?" A pause. "What have I ever *done* to you?"

Rajelis pursed thin lips and raised his coat collar against the slowly, sparsely descending March snow, then slipped his sunglasses into place. A yard or so away, the car door opened—it was an expensive vehicle, probably a Cadillac, maybe a car provided for him while he was in town—but Calhoun could not make out the silent driver's features. "You have done nothing," said Rajelis, softly, "to me."

Then he darted into the back seat with as much nimble haste as Grady had ever seen. It's almost, he thought, *as if Rajelis is the one who's frightened, and not me.*

2

Saturday, March 19.

It had long been Grady's way, on the morning after a show, to sleep late. Or to *try* to. Grown-up response to a time when he'd been one of five little half-orphaned, poverty-touched Calhouns, and Mom had insisted they all pitch in to make up for their late father's absence. Nobody slept late in that household!

And even after Jean Calhoun had thrown Grady out—an unfair description, since Jean didn't have a violent bone in her body—he'd found himself a decent apartment and made himself remain abed, dealing with his despair over losing Jean in a state of relative comfort.

Sometimes, too, the popular and harmless-looking Grady had his mind taken off his unwanted divorce by awakening to find women younger and fresher than Jean lying beside him. Of late, twice, he'd come to consciousness and his first sight had been the naked Bud Rocker. Longing for another woman and feeling blue were impossible with such a sight.

This particular pre-spring morning, Calhoun didn't have his former wife on his mind at all, but he also wasn't finding it easy to keep his eyelids shut. Only part of his problem was the raw sunlight burning through his drawn curtains, unerringly finding and fixing itself on his twitching lids. The terrible things threatened by that crackpot fool, Rajelis, had twice awakened him during the night; now the surges of outrage and anxiety he was experiencing were just impossible to overcome. Grady had no memory of ever seeing the cruel youth before; why had the mentalist singled *him* out for such pointless and malicious attention?

Not that there was anything to worry about. Not much, anyway.

Merely four charming children ranging in age from fifteen to three, Calhoun's beloved "quartet of quintessential cuties" who, if they *did* come to suffer mightily now, probably meant that Calhoun would die for them at his own hand. Jean had claimed a lot of really nasty things about him, but, even in divorce proceedings, she had never thought to question Grady's almost heart-breaking adoration of the "ferocious foursome" he'd fathered. Even she knew he was a good father; half the city did, since he mentioned them on *Confab* every chance he had.

What made falling back asleep a virtual impossibility today was that when his pal, Homicide Lieutenant Wayne Sojourner, had shown up at the station late last night, he'd come to tell Grady that the mind reader hadn't precisely threatened anyone by name and so Calhoun probably didn't have a viable charge to pin on

Calvin Rajelis.

"I've got *four* of 'em, dammit, Wayne," Grady's shouted, "and they have *names,* baby—*names*: Tim, Cathy, David and Petey! Petey, as in Peter Edward Rose Calhoun-the-baseball-player Petey!"

Tom, Grady's director, had calmed him down and he'd apologized to his black police friend. Profusely. They had liked each other since Wayne had appeared on *Confab* 16 months before and the stocky Sojourner had fended off every question Calhoun threw at him, managing to make the police department glow with pride instead of looking dull with tarnish, the way Grady had planned. Each man had known the other was doing his job extremely well, and professionals often came to admire professionals.

None of which did anything for Grady's worry and his state of nerves this Saturday morning. *I mean what I've said, that the Rajelis creep is almost undoubtedly a phony looking for more headlines,* Calhoun thought; *it's the 'almost undoubtedly' that scares me shitless.*

Which, as a matter of fact, he was when he gave up and got up for the day minutes later. Constipation at points of anxiety had been Grady's *bete noir* for years. "*Bete goddamn noir,*" he grumbled loudly as he gave that up, too, and threw on some clothes.

That was when he finally remembered that he'd asked Tom Simincola and writer Gill Riffey to meet him at Channel 61 at one o'clock, ostensibly to begin planning next Friday's program. Riffey, who worked two evenings a week at Grimelda's as a trumpet player in a combo, doubled—or tripled—as the show's researcher, and Calhoun had loved the man's silken horn playing so much that he'd hired him for *Confab* the minute he had discovered Gill also had a background in TV. The two men—Tom, his director, and Riffey—were probably Calhoun's closest friends.

And he knew damned well he hadn't fooled them when he'd said he wanted a meet for the next program.

They knew he wanted their company, and their help.

But what surprised him when he hurried into the blue-green room at five 'til one was the fact that program manager Andy Sutor was there too. Patiently waiting.

"What bringeth thou here today, Goodly Sir Employer?" Calhoun inquired. "Knoweth not it is Saturday?"

Andy pressed back his shoe-polished hair. Even when he was being nice he seemed a near parody of pomposity. "A compulsion to play Royal Canadian Mounties—or a Scotland Yard inspector, perhaps." A minute shrug of impeccable shoulders. "You know. Riding to the rescue just in time."

Despite himself, Grady was touched. "I appreciate it. Andrew."

Tom laughing at the conference table but still managing to look ten feet tall, couldn't resist one of his ever-so-politely put jibes. "You're king of the 61 ratings, Grady. We can't afford to lose you." His kind, careful smile removed the sting.

As Grady was slipping into his chair, Gill Riffey's gaze drew his attention. It was a gaze of grave concern, the sort Calhoun had never seen on the trumpeter's face before.

"I watched the show at Grimelda's," he began, "and it didn't look to me that Grady's the target as much as his family. And maybe Bud Rocker."

Grady studied the writer's somber expression before replying. Whether it was accidental or not, Gill's dapper mustache and somewhat extreme choice of wardrobe always reminded him of Doc Severinson, the *Tonight Show* bandleader. Sometimes Gill Riffey used a jazz musician's *patois* so earnestly that it appeared forced, and Calhoun had longed for some time to tell Gill he was talented enough on a trumpet that he didn't need to adopt other people's mannerisms.

"You're absolutely right," he told Gill, nodding. "But the question seems to me to be whether or not Rajelis is a dangerous psychotic or just a phony mind reader with poor taste in the way he goes after his headlines."

Andy Sutor cleared his throat to draw their attention. "I think," he began in his artificially tentative, discreetly officious style, "it's apparent from our collective presence today that we opt for the former." A faint shrug. "Not that I'd care to say so on camera and get sued by a madman."

"Have you checked with Jean to make sure the kids are okay?" asked Tom, suddenly. Leaning toward Grady, he was so tall that, though seated, it amounted to a concerned lunge. "Now that I think about it, what of your brother—and your mom? She's back east, right?"

Calhoun nodded, sighed, allowed his gaze to drift around the familiar room. Sutor had made sure everything in it was blue green; the four easy chairs for *Confab* guests, those drawn up to the conference table, the inexpensive drapes, even the folding chairs stacked against a distant wall like checkmarks in a fan's box score. Now Grady felt distinctly blue green himself. Simincola had touched a nerve.

"Mom is 70," Calhoun said softly. He glanced at his favorite Omni pen and became aware for the first time that he'd been nervously turning it end for end for end. "And crumpling at the edges like some old taffeta dress." He had believed Mom needed to be in a home for at least a year now, but she wouldn't hear of it.

But Mom couldn't even tune in *Confab* in upstate New York, where she was alone. Quite alone. An attack on her would be savagely unfair, faintly ridiculous. "I'm seeing my family tomorrow," Grady continued. "Taking the kids on Sunday, in accord with modern times' favorite cliche." Reddening, he slapped one arm against his forehead. "But I sure as hell should have *called* them to be sure everything was okay." Calhoun got clumsily to his feet. "You guys pardon me while I go do exactly that?"

All the others nodded and Grady, passing the lanky Tom, was headed for the door and then his own office.

"You didn't say whether you had contacted your brother, Timmy," Tom Simincola called to the departing Calhoun.

"Gosh, I didn't, did I?" Grady snapped. "Fuck you, Simincola, you old pry."

But then he paused at the blue-green room door to glance back at his friend—who was pretending to be hurt—and winked.

Tom knew how Grady felt about Timmy Calhoun, and Grady rather wished he'd never told him.

"Yes. I heard the show." Jean, when Calhoun had phoned her. The way she snipped off the ends of words like a dummy gardener snipping off the heads of flowers and thereby devaluating them was standard Jean Margaret Calhoun, and Grady knew he didn't need to ask if his ex-wife was well.

"It's called *watching* the show with TV, Jeanno," Grady retorted. " 'Hearing' it is for radio. Got it?" They'd gone through this 500 times before, but it was ritual, it was one of the unmisunderstood routines that had kept them going together—a means of letting off steam by kidding on the square.

"Who needs to watch you?" Jean demanded. But the satisfying putdown was victimized by her exhausted, old-before-her-time inflections. He wondered when she'd begun sounding so weary, but it had happened in such ancient, intimate times that even their dinosaur love hadn't engraved the date in their flinty hearts. "I saw lots of you while we were married, Grady; plenty. And I memorized each and every expression.

"Jean—"

"You have 17 of them, Calhoun. Did you know that? Exactly 17 facial expressions, and you run through your entire repertoire in just under four minutes. *Every* four minutes."

"Dammit, Jean—"

"You could run the hundred fucking yard dash in the Olympics on that kisser of yours, Grady. But your mouth would beat it out, and your ambition would be the first to break the tape!"

"Look," he sighed, "I didn't call you this afternoon for badinage, baby. Right? I called you for *goodinage*. Okay?"

A pause. He detected the sound of a Viceroy being lit, one of the "Filter Kings" Jean got down daily as if the Surgeon General meant to raid her house—their old house—and confiscate all her smokes. She'd even hidden them, Calhoun remembered. Living with Jean got to being like sharing the house with a pusher.

"Goodinage, huh?" she said. "That was funny the first time, Grady." Her voice sounded still more feeble in his left ear. "I really laughed, back then."

He didn't know how to go on. There was a time he had worried about her health because Jean became so lifeless, seemed so used up. Now he felt sure she was simply saving sleek cylinders of her life the way she did her precious Viceroys, storing up every iota she could of her stamina. To become the hardiest and most domineering old bitch of all time. "I only called to be sure you and the gang were okay."

"We're all ginger-peachy out here in Televisionland, Calhoun." Her reply was quick, and he knew she'd known he would call. Why had he loved her so long? Why did he, in a way, even now? Jean coughed, so violently that part of it might have been genuine. "Well, Petey has been complaining today—the way he does whenever he'd about to get one of those colds of his."

"Any fever?" His feelings for her, hers for him, were instantly lost sight of. "Jean, *did* you take his temperature?"

"Of course," she replied, and Grady could see her nodding. To win as many points from life as she could, Jean's nods were always vehement, decisive to the point of arousing doubt. "It was 99, but you know Petey." The abrupt laugh startled, annoyed Calhoun. "Remember when Tim was Petey's age, we told him we were going to take his temperature, and Tim wanted to know when we'd return it to him?"

"Yes," Grady said coldly. "I *do* know Petey—and I know he's not our healthiest child. Or as healthy as he looks. Will you take it again now, Jean—will you please? I'll wait."

"It was only two hours ago that I took it the first time," she said, more exasperated than tired for a change. That heartened Calhoun. "And Petey's taking a nap now."

"Wake him up," Grady told her firmly. "Just enough to get the thermometer in his mouth or under one arm."

"That expression," Jean said, "the one you're wearing now? It's number 17, one of the last ones you created for that rubbery, phony face of yours. I don't think Tim and Cathy ever saw it, actually; David was probably the first. God knows, *I* never saw it aimed in *my* direction."

"Dammit, Jean, I need to know how Petey is before we hang up!" Grady looked to his office door when he realized he'd nearly shouted. He took his feet off his desk, carefully put them on the floor, and sat up, inhaling. "I'm supposed to take all four of them tomorrow, Jeanno, and I need to know if Petey's apt to be going along."

"All right," Jean said. Her voice was wearier than ever as it faded away until he heard the phone clump against the telephone desk, half imagining he heard her footsteps, tromping off toward Petey's room. *The innocents,* Rajelis's autocratic tones sounded once more in Calhoun's memory, *shall suffer for you.* Surely the man hadn't meant to harm a three-year-old! And besides, if Petey was coming down with the sniffles, what could Calvin Rajelis have to do with that?

"Ninety-nine-point-two," Jean said, speaking rather loudly as she clapped the phone to her ear, and Grady was so happy she was back after eye-witnessing the fact that Petey remained alive that he had to ask her to repeat the thermometer reading. "Ninety-nine-point-two, almost," she said somewhat querulously. "But children's temps tend to rise as the day wears on."

Homey maternal wisdom, Calhoun thought sourly. "Thanks for checking," he said aloud. And surprised himself by meaning it. Sweat dropped onto his desk blotter, forming a nipple, and he couldn't think where it had come from for a moment. "Jean, please, will you—"

"Will I notify you if it rises," she finished for him, sighing plaintively. "Yes, I will. What time shall I tell the children to expect Mr. Television tomorrow?"

He told her, ignoring the fresh wild shot, then hung up and returned to the blue-green room with the discomfiting feeling of stepping from a past that had gone bad to a future that could easily turn out to be worse.

Various procedures for locating the

threatening mentalist and dealing with
him awaited Grady when, apologetically,
he took his seat again among his business
associates, with organization-minded
Andy Sutor reading them off from a list
they'd made, one by one.

But nothing sounded reasonable and
Grady was nearly relieved when the topic
shifted to that of next week's show.
Gill Riffey, friend/trumpet player/writer,
reminded them all of the subject that had
already been selected weeks before—each
of *Confab*'s main themes was laid out weeks
in advance, in order to line up the
guests—and reminded Grady, in particular, of the people who'd be on camera
with him. The theme was "Why Don't Local
Book Pages Review Books?" and the point
was that the two local newspapers
generally reprinted book reviews from
leading critics on either coast. When they
didn't, Riffey's research showed, they
usually reviewed nothing but historical
reflections on the state's not especially
distinguished accomplishments or nature
treatises by professor types published—
mainly for the library system—by the
state's university and college presses.

"It's not exactly the most spellbinding
theme we've ever picked for ol' *Confab*,"
Andy Sutor droned. Then he held up his
palms, smiled. "Not that I want to put
the knock on you people or anything
else at 61, now. Last month's ratings were
downright soul-satisfying!"

"To be honest," Calhoun murmured,

yawning, stretching, and hungering for a rerun of his aborted Saturday morning of scheduled sleep, "I'm just as happy it isn't a red-hot controversial topic—after the furor Rajelis generated last night!"

"Our Andy will probably want the SOB back on the show as soon as humanly possible, assuming the creep is human," Tom remarked, peering at the program manager over thick glasses that had worked their way down his long nose. "Once we get the ratings for that program!"

Grady clearly saw the crimson rise in Sutor's aristocratic features and wished his friend Tom would think a fraction of a moment before saying whatever occurred to him. In local TV, sometimes even more than in network or cable television, programming had a way of swiftly ballooning only to be unfathomably punctured and sent reeling. Andrew Charles Sutor mightn't be the hard-nosed and heavier-handed boss Calhoun had imagined when they first met.

But Andy's own advancement in a fiendishly competitive industry depended upon the ratings system, and Grady Calhoun sensed that the young PM would, in a squeeze, put Channel 61's interests ahead of anything or anyone.

Timmy's message was on his answering machine when Grady got back to his apartment that evening.

For a full minute, Grady tried to think

of an excuse not to call his brother back, one that would fly, could be convincingly repeated the next time Timmy physically cornered him and asked why Calhoun had ignored him. *What of your brother?* Tom had asked in his customary pushy-polite fashion.

What of my brother, indeed? Calhoun mused, working his Omni pen between his restless fingers. What of nepotism tried and always let down? What of red faces when he, himself, had wound up on the carpet because of sweet, loving, alcoholic Timothy Calhoun and that nether-region side of nose-thumbing, profane, who-gives-a-damn, patience-stealing drunkenness that no one believed about Timmy until they experienced it?

What of time-devoured yesterdays filled with adulation for the big brother who'd preceded Grady into the cold, adult world, presenting every opportunity to little Grady on a platter and steering him around almost all the pitfalls from drugs to get rich quick schemes to broads on the make and—

Maybe you never repaid yesterday's big bro because, like the loved but dead, yesterday was never available for thanks and all that remained of Christmas-and-double-dating big brothers was the obligation to follow them into the mortuary, and the hole in the ground, and oblivion.

Maybe he's not drinking yet, thought Grady, waiting for the phone at the other end to be picked up.

"Thish is the resadence of Timothy Calhoun you have reached," said Timmy's voice, and it was obvious after one uttered word that big bro was pretending to be an answering machine. "Mr. Calhoun, who'sh the star of upstaging, a black-and-whi' Philco television screen, and a Chee-Eee radio thass a gift from his lit-tul brother, is *almost* out now. Leave y'message at the sound of the beep."

He's jealous of my goddam answering machine, Grady thought with dismay and frustration. *And he's gonna fart or something!*

Instead, however, Timmy made a sound midway between a Bronx cheer and a belch, the latter less due to Timmy's gifts of humor than to what he'd already had to drink that evening.

Grady suddenly had an idea. "I was returning your call, Timmo," he said grinning and feeling the grin widen; "sorry to have missed you but I'll get back atcha in a few days, and—"

"Ho'dit! Whoa, Grade-A—hold *on* a minute! I *knew* it was you, little bro." The amiable-sounding voice that was a virtual alcoholic duplicate for Calhoun's own took its best shot at sobriety. "How're you?" Desperate pause. "You there, bro?"

One last second, Grady considered hanging up, then succumbed. "I'm here, big brother." It occurred to him that Timmy probably had seen last night's program and needed to share his brotherly wrath. "I haven't got a lot of time right this sec so make it fast, okay?"

"They fired me, Grade-A." The statement was couched in Churchillian tones, a March of Time pronouncement on the sorry condition of humankind. "*Would* you believe it? One lit-tul day off and all m'contributions have been forgotten, like that." Grady listened for the snap of Timmy's thumb and index but didn't hear it. "Many long months of ded-i-ca-ted service, and *whop*. The p'verbial ax."

"You did nothing to deserve it, right, Timmy?" Grady said in his cheeriest *Confab* accusational inflections. "Wasn't your fault?"

No reply for a long moment, followed by two or three additional long moments. "Can't take it much longer, little brother. Cannot. You've got it all, Grade-A—fame, fortune, fans—but n'mind that."

"Thank God," Grady said in mock gratitude.

"Never—mind—that," Timmy said loudly. "M'almost 40, bro, little bro. Turnin' 40, and not many places left t'hire a guy who drinks." Pause. "I drink, Grade-A, y'know that?"

"There's been this vicious rumor," Grady offered. "Look, Tim—"

"Tim's my nephew," Timmy said stoutly, as if he expected a demurrer. "My nephew; my namesake." A snorting sound, emotive and not narcotic. "How's my lit-tul nephew, Tim, the namesake?"

"He's fine, Timmy's fine." What did he

want? Why had he *called*? "I'm getting the cue for the end of another show, big brother. You have any closing comments for that vast viewing audience out there?"

Timmy got the idea instantly. "Can I say 'fuck' on television?" he asked brightly.

"No, no; you can't say 'fuck' on television. Anything else?"

The strong impression of concerted intellectual labors going on was conveyed, along with the lingering prior suggestion of a man wrestling with a problem too mammoth, and too recently renewed, for him to handle.

"Wanta say I *love* you, little bro," Timmy said finally. "Can you say 'love' on television?"

"Y'know, Timmy," Grady said quietly, "I haven't the foggiest notion."

"Okay; s'all right. Perfectly okay." Some clatter, the noises of a man attempting to rise with an impediment in his lap, seemed to wreck the older man's poise. What he said was laced with emotion. "Need help, Grade-A—y'hear? I need help."

Grady sighed, but covered the phone mouthpiece in the hope of concealing it. "What do you want me to *do*?" His patience was waning. There wasn't a thing malicious about Timmy when he was in charge of his faculties; once, however, he'd been in the studio audience for a *Confab* program and had informed the world that *that* man, the "wond'ful star of this wond'ful show," was his very own brother. It was so hard to forget such things. Now, Grady expected Timmy to ask him—as he'd done before—to find a job for him at 61. Which he had; twice before. That was no longer possible, conceivable; Andy Sutor had already fired Timmy twice. Suddenly and devoutly, Grady wished he hadn't returned his big brother's phone call.

"Didn't say *you* could help." Timmy began crying. "There's nothing you can do. But still, little bro, I do need help." Wistfulness, the first Grady'd heard in Timmy's sound-alike voice. "I am suffering, y'see? Suffering real *bad*, bro. Grady, my bro."

Almost, Grady said merely that he knew Timmy was and how sorry he was about it.

Then the possible, darker meaning of his brother's admission sank in. And, miles apart, two men named Calhoun stared at their phones and knew they were really trying to make out the defining outline of the unknown.

3

Sunday, March 20.

Driving up to the two-story, ten-year-old house fashionably far north of the city, Grady thought suddenly that divorce was the illegitimate father of *deja vu*. At a glance, everything about the tree-lined neighborhood was as familiar to him as his own lake-blue eyes or persistent gift of gab, and he'd made it a point to know the names of most of his neighbors, while he'd lived here with Jean and fathered their children. But enough people had moved out, since the divorce Calhoun hadn't wanted, that an offputting element of the improbable or fantastic set his nerves on edge every Sunday when he came for the kids. Additionally, Jean had painted their house since the split-up, and that created just enough personal, additional change to remind Grady that he was an outsider, an interloper now.

Jean brushed his lips with the exact touch of an artist who doubted the wisdom of adding another stroke to the canvas. Then she called for the kids—"Your father's here, gang"—and Calhoun felt even more separated from reality than he had on his drive through the neighborhood. As a rule, the children were dressed in their finest and waiting for him in the front room; frequently, either ten-year-old Cathy or Petey, the youngest at three, was peeking through the picture window in anticipation of Daddy's arrival.

Then there was Jean, whose sardonic volubility over the telephone yesterday had led Grady to expect her to be in an abusively garrulous mood. He'd hoped for, needed that. So long as she warded off the temptation to converse with him, even

Grady knew he had no chance of winning her back. And now, while they waited at the front door of the familiar steps for the kids to dash down them, Jean was more taciturn than ever.

Studying his former wife under partly lowered lids made it all worse. Taller than news anchor Bud Rocker, nearly as tall as Grady himself, Jean had been exclamation-mark straight, but burdens and disappointments were starting to bow her shoulders until, cemetery silent and distant as death, she seemed to be posing some question that was only beginning to take shape in her heart. Not that she wasn't lovely, still, to him. Jean's medium-length brown hair never had looked a solid mass to Grady, and he'd liked the way he could make out each fine hair springing straight out from her scalp. He could now, but a lightness he knew was gray had started to gleam here and there like fool's gold. Her habit of standing with arms crossed beneath her small breasts, once insouciant, now looked exhausted. In the sweet moment her lips were upon his they'd been dry like old toast. It was as if she might be changing into a different kind of beauty, meant for another man, a different life.

To Calhoun's mixed joy and concern, Cathy and David, who was seven, appeared at the top of the stairway with little Petey riding their crossed arms, working on an artificial laugh. One glimpse informed the Irishman that the three-year-old's cold had grabbed hold; moisture glistened in each of Petey's nostrils and his forehead seemed translucent beneath the cap of yellow hair. Where he'd gotten that hair Grady didn't know; moments when he couldn't believe his good luck in winning Jean for his wife he'd wondered if Petey were his, and automatically forgiven Jean.

Where's Tim? he wondered abruptly.

"Since our Peter in*sists* on going with us," said fastidious Cathy, insufferably maternal at ten and as much Petey's *bete noir* as constipation was their father's, "David and I will make *sure* he doesn't overdo." She and the black-haired Jean lookalike, David, sort of bounced the sweaty, giggling Petey into Calhoun's arms. He smelled sour, and Grady's heart went out to him. "But it's *my* idea, Daddy."

"I'd have bet the homestead on that, kitkat," he said, craning his neck over Petey to kiss Cathy's and David's moist mouths in turn. *You can judge if a dog's sick by feeling his nose,* Calhoun mused; *with people, it's their lips,* and made a mental note for Gill Riffey to research the theory. "Where's Tim?"

"Here."

That recently acquired baritone came from behind Calhoun, and from 15-year-old Tim, who'd been given his Uncle Timmy's Christian name when Jean and Grady had held hope for and regularly loved Timmy.

It occurred to Grady that his oldest child had been alone in the darkened dining room and he looked slightly abashed, as if he'd been watching his parents kiss.

"Big kid," Grady said, freeing his right hand to pump Tim's. Although Tim had never said so, he assumed that the teen-ager no longer wished to be kissed. "Got an appetite?"

"Sort of."

"Your turn to pick where we enjoy a spendid Sunday repast."

Tim's earnest face raised to Grady's. "The kids really like fast-food places." Looking at that face, for Calhoun, was more like looking into a combination time machine and mirror than he preferred, because his face was all he had given Tim. "I guess that's okay."

Grady sighed. "It's your choice today, big kid," he said shortly. "Pay no heed to the gallery." Why couldn't Tim have had Jean's face and some of his interests, his talents? "Your call."

Under pressure, Tim reddened. It was as if neon lights had been switched on beneath each of his numerous pimples. "All right, I choose Denny's."

The groans from the other three kids, even though Petey's was both after-thought and mimicry, substituted for Calhoun's silent one. He should have known what Tim's choice would be—a vividly painted family restaurant chain with greater variety than that of most fast-food places, but not so much more spiffy that Tim's sister and brothers would feel left out. Grady had yearned for a Sunday meal with courses and mute, preternaturally eager waiters.

"You wanta come along?" he asked Jean at the door. "It probably doesn't break any laws when an ex-wife goes somewhere with her ex-husband and their brood."

"I appreciate the goodinage," Jean replied, a careful yard and a half away from Grady, "but every time you ask me to accompany you it seems so much like too little, too late. Puts me in a foul mood."

"Well, they might have fowl at Denny's," Calhoun joked, then stopped. Already, the fearsome foursome were rattling around in the car like jellybeans in a jar. And he knew what she meant, inescapably: the last time he'd taken Jean or the kids out to eat—prior to the divorce—was before Petey's birth, maybe before David's. He said hopelessly, "It was a thought."

"Don't buy Petey a lot of crap. His temp's almost up to 100." Her arms were akimbo, elbows like sword points. "And please get them back before five."

Grady adjusted a Pacers cap he'd donned for the kids' amusement. "Oh, I will," he said with an effort at jauntiness. "I have a date at six."

The instant he said it, he regretted it.

"Another one with 'Blossom'?" Jean asked. It was only faintly more than a statement. "I wish I could honestly say how happy I am that you're starting to find happiness again."

"Who said that's what I'm finding?" Calhoun demanded, and pulled the front door to.

But driving to the nearest Denny's, on Pendleton Pike, Grady found it hard to concentrate on what Tim was telling him about a new book he was reading. Where Calhoun was loquacious and had always been drawn to TV and the performing arts, his oldest son was somehow a throwback to times when books served as the pipeline to what was fresh, exciting, hot conversational fodder. Grady supposed he should be happier than he was that Tim got good grades and stayed out of trouble, but talking with him was like discussing things with Grady's own father. In a way, he thought, Tim embarrassed him, showed up his own intellectual weaknesses; and besides, Jean was on his mind again and Petey, squeezed between them on the front seat, seemed even more adorable in his brave, wan condition than he usually did.

Parking in the lot behind Denny's, Calhoun was almost startled when the other children, Cathy and David, hopped out onto the winter-gray pavement. He hadn't spoken to them since picking up the "cutie quartet" and had virtually forgotten that the middle girl and boy were along for the ride.

What the hell is the matter with me? he

wondered as he held the door for all of them but Tim, who insisted upon being last in line. *A man doesn't divorce his family—just his wife!*

Once they'd ordered—Calhoun made sure Petey got all the crap he wanted—he tried to make amends by addressing most of his remarks to David and Cathy. How was school; was everything okay with their teachers; were they making new friends. And with the utterance of every forced show of interest, the seven-year-old and the ten-year-old became increasingly preoccupied, clearly bored.

What did they *want* from him?

And what had Jean been telling them about him? Was she dredging up the past the way only women could do, or, worse, manufacturing Grady Calhoun character faults to paint him in a worsening light?

His nerves were so much on edge that by the time the accident occurred, Grady was a mute masculine mountain of incoherent, spastic appeals for affection, and the shock of what happened stayed with him for weeks.

Young Tim had ordered coffee and then beckoned for a refill, doing so with a nonchalance and quiet pride that Calhoun had found amusing. For an instant the teenager's show of gathering maturity reminded Grady of himself and his own first taste of coffee, back east. He'd been thinking that it was right and proper for Tim to say things to him in new-baritone asides, as if seeking a *mano a mano* relationship, and how satisfying it was that Tim, at least, seemed to be able to relax around him.

Then David, who so resembled his mother, momentarily neglected by Grady, had stretched out his arm in front of fair-skinned Cathy—God alone knew what the seven-year-old was trying to do, or get—and Tim's hot coffee was splashing all over Cathy's pale arm.

Shrieks of torment and shock brought all activity in the family restaurant to a halt. Grady was aware that little Petey had begun to cry and whisper his sister's name as if praying. David Calhoun was pressed against the booth's backrest, horrified by what he'd accidentally done and awaiting punishment. Hand clasped round the other wrist, and the pale skin swiftly turned scarlet. Grady groped fumblingly across the bolted table to his only daughter, uncertain what he was to do, knocking over his Country Scramble meal and hearing the words of the mentalist, Rajelis, as if he were among them, shouting his implacable warning into Grady's ear: *The innocents will suffer . . . the innocents will suffer . . . the in—*

Quite without show, Tim scooped ice from all their water glasses and held it gently to his little sister's scalded arm, just as quietly assuring the waitress who'd come running that "Sis will live."

Then, as the child stopped screaming, stopped crying entirely and began to appear chagrined by her outburst, Tim's gaze met his father's.

"No harm, no foul," he said calmly, smiling. Then his young, crinkly blue eyes filled with deep concern. "Hey, Dad, accidents happen. Listen—are you okay?"

4

Sunday Afternoon and Night.

Ernie didn't even seem to see the enormous beast charging down upon him or, perhaps, at age two, Ernie lacked not only an understanding of threatened sudden death but of fear itself.

She had wanted him not to know fear, too, God forgive her, and Ernie's awful, untimely death was going to be her fault, too—her most grievous and unforgiveable sin—if the house-sized monstrosity only yards from her little boy gobbled him up. *Your fault, your fault,* the Greek chorus chanted in minor tones that sent her shredding nerves in an unraveling path toward the brink of insanity; *your most grievous and unforgiv-a-ble SIIIIIINNN.*

How could the voices just *stand* there while she was frozen in stuff like quicksand, incapable of dashing out to the street and saving little Ernie-all-that's-left-of-my-marriage-precious Ernie? She didn't know why she was stuck, unable to throw herself between the beast and simply grinning little Ern, she didn't know why her whole life's bottled-up resolve and determination refused to *hurtle* her to the little guy's salvation. *Your sin, your fault, your ONE MORE TIME UNNNNNFORGIVABLE SIIIIIINNN.*

She had a glimpse, a moment's keen, calm, white vision of acute clarity, when she could just make out the smiling man who'd unleashed the monster, the snarling beast—a man like all men, at the single glance afforded her, except for the gaping, hungry, deep-set eyes and the impossibly wide and all-encompassing mouth. It was locked in something so like a mad but pleasant frozen smile that she nearly forgot Ernie's peril, Ernie's demise; and now that appeared definite, fore-ordained, as if her child and she had lived their short shared lives together in dimly aware knowledge that this time, this time of little Ernie's hideous death, was over the horizon, over the hill, over the short periods of calm joy that mother and son had known together, over the rainbow—

Your sin; Yourrrr guilt, the chorus chanted—and she recognized the voices as her own, entirely *hers—over the horizon! Over the hill. Over the periods of contentment!* sang the chorus called Death that dwelled within her and her fears.

Mist spun and swirled as the great beast reached Ernie and she waited for her little boy's scream of terror or terrible pain—she waited, incapable of movement, to hear the cracking bones and Ern's last squeal of bloodied pain. Frozen, waiting, she listened to the chorus sing of death. . . .

Listening to Bud's voice rise from a gutteral growl of cheerleading pleasure to a mid-level wail of incipient fulfillment, Grady grinned with sweaty anticipation and accelerated his motions. She needed to rise to it the way a building was constructed, from the basement up, floor by floor. He saw the way her head was crammed back into the pillows, how her wide mouth had become a pleading grimace, the shining skin of her whole mocha-colored little body as his lovemaking worked with hers until the thrill fanned out to her reaching arms and clutching fingers, her strongly thrusting legs and her braced, splay-toed feet. Beneath him, her dark nipples were like stars about to blink out, or explode, and the vision made Grady feel universally, cosmically puissant. Where they were joined was a wet tangle like a primogenital pool from which all human life had sprung; and the musk of her, him, them, seemed that instant the headiest costly perfume from another galaxy's supremely mystical planet.

He let go, searingly, undammingly, his lower body outthrust and fleetingly fixed as if time had ceased to be told, as if an instant had arrived when all things good had been made—or made possible—

And Bud's phone beside the bed was jangling, bringing her wide-set eyes open in clouded torment and preempting the beginning of her own sweet release with prime-time reality. "Shit, shit, shit," Bud groaned, her narrow hips collapsing to the mattress; "*oh*, shit, shit, shit, *shit*!"

"Ignore the phone." Thinking it was not too late, Calhoun resumed his pumping and soon sensed that he, too, was not finished. The daylight awareness suffusing Bud Rocker's face gave her the revivifying and wise look of the pert Bud Rocker reading the evening news—the weekend anchor was at work at Channel 61 this evening—and Grady's unvoiced fantasy of doing it with Bud while she reported stories from Washington or the Middle East might almost have come true.

But, "Get off of me, you big turkey," Bud ordered him, and he rolled away and sat on the edge of her bed, staring out the partly drawn curtains at waning daylight. The *misery*, Rajelis had said—*in the light*.

They'd never left Bud's house after he arrived at six, full of the need to report daughter Cathy's coffee-scalding. Happily, she'd suffered only first-degree burns and would not be scarred. But Jean's ice-grim attitude when he'd explained what happened and all the kids made it clear that the accident hadn't been his doing had filled up a few momentarily emptied chambers of guilt.

And worse, reminded him of what might still happen to any or all of his loved ones, if Calvin Rajelis's predictions reached fruition.

By the time Bud had hung up, he had quickly showered and redressed, except for his Indiana Pacers cap. That he'd left in the back seat of the car. Wordlessly, he handed the naked Bud one of the two cocktails he'd made and then leaned back against a spare pillow. "What's up? Sutor got a special assignment?"

Shivering, Bud slithered beneath the covers, looking very young, indeed, with just her tousled head and bronze shoulders showing. Daytime murmured of spring, but by evening it was still chilly, and winter seemed adamant about retaining its domain. "Susan," she said simply. He felt cold toes on one ankle. "She had a nightmare."

"Your sister spoiled *that* because of a goddamn *nightmare*?" Grady couldn't believe it. Yet, on second thought, a thought based upon knowing Bud's sister, Susan Swagerty, fairly well, believing it wasn't the most difficult thing he'd ever had to do. "I'm glad you're a little less conscientious about things than she is."

"I'm not!" Bud exclaimed, and punched his arm. Her wide mouth pursed in the most transitory of pouts. "But Susan is ridiculously conscientious about her child."

Calhoun chuckled. "Old Ernie. Except for my Petey, Ern probably *is* the cutest little guy around." He lit them each one of Bud's Viceroys—when he smoked he much preferred unfiltered cigarettes, claiming that one might as well have a recognizable flavor if he or she was going to use them anyway—and caught the newsperson's eye. "The nightmare was about Ernie, wasn't it?"

"It was." Bud nodded. Her blanket descended two inches, and Calhoun immediately wished it would either go to the rest of the way down or that Bud would replace it. "Something about a gigantic animal about to eat poor Ernie. And some weird guy with a mouth three feet wide, or something." She accepted the cigarette, mumbled how she despised looking like a living cliche.

"Why was Susan sleeping, anyway, at this time of the day?" Grady asked. Then he grinned. "Had she been in bed for reasons . . . *sin*-ilar . . . to our own?"

Bud shook her head harder than seemed necessary. "Sis hasn't had so much as a date since Darrel Swagerty hit the bricks." She glanced away, clearly disturbed. "Susan's even more religious than I am, you know. She's a sweet girl."

Frowning, Grady rolled over to her. "You're just as sweet as overprotective Susan." He coaxed the blanket down from Bud's breasts, kissed each of them on what he called "the safe part." Most of Bud's *Evening News* viewers would have been surprised by their newslady's ample figure, since Bud had never wanted to depend on it in any way.

"Don't start something you can't

finish, Calhoun," she snarled.

"Who says I can't finish it?" Grady demanded.

Then the phone rang again. And this time, almost atop Bud, Grady answered it.

"I'm sorry to b-be such a nuisance," Susan Swagerty's voice apologized. In the background Grady heard an odd rumbling sound, like thunder but not really like thunder. "Did Amanda tell you about my . . . dream?" Susan was one of the last persons to call Bud by her original name. He said that she had. "Grady, it was more than a nightmare. It was, well—like a *vision.*"

Despite himself, Calhoun's sympathy —and his curiosity—put in an unscheduled walk-on appearance. "In what way, Suze?"

A brief silence. "I c-can't explain, Grady, I'm sorry. Except . . . for how *real* it was." She paused, and Calhoun wanted to tell her that visions weren't supposed to seem like the height of reality. "I don't need to speak with Amanda again but I . . . well, I wanted her—and you—to know what's happening. To *hear* it. All right?"

"What do you mean?" Suddenly Calhoun felt keenly apprehensive. "What do you want me to hear?"

"*Listen.*" Then, apparently, Susan was extending her arm and the telephone at arm's length. Toward a window, probably.

It sounded as if every dog in Susan Swagerty's neighborhood was barking.

Except for the few who were howling. It was probably an hour or more before it got really dark, but two or three pet dogs, Calhoun realized, were howling like the harbingers of death.

"Maybe there's a female dog around there," he said into the mouthpiece; "you know, in heat."

Susan didn't even argue with him. Clearly, she wished Bud had answered her ring, but didn't want to ask to speak again with her sister. "Tell . . . Bud," Susan said, pulling herself together, "about the dogs. Or don't. But Grady?"

"What is it?"

"*Do* tell her I'm terribly afraid for little Ernie." She was on the verge of tears, but fighting it. "Because—I think my dream was . . . a warning."

He did, over an hour later, when discussion of Susan's nightmare wound down and it occurred to Grady Calhoun for the first time—chillingly, with a feeling of confronting forces he could never understand and had never wished to confront— that he couldn't gauge the *scope* of Rajelis's tasteless, terrible prophecy: "Perhaps the creep didn't mean my family, alone, or maybe he didn't mean my family at all." Calhoun had followed Bud Rocker downstairs to the kitchen, where the two of them were cooking a makeshift dinner. "He spoke of the people around me, of people I cared about. Not that I'm absolutely wild about your sister."

Bud pushed the button on her microwave and spun to face him, shorter than ever in bathrobe and bare feet, but not a whit less ready to beard the lions in their dens. "*I am*," she said angrily. But Grady thought he detected tears deep in her well-placed eyes. "I *am* wild about Susan. For God's sake, Calhoun, don't you follow what I'm saying to you?"

He hadn't, but it came to him then, and his heart sank. "You *are* close to me," he said, staring at her.

"And if anything happened to my sister, Calhoun, I think I'd just die, my life would just about be over."

"Her suffering," Grady said, "would be yours—"

"And my suffering would become one of those deep sorrows that Rajelis claimed would eventually drive you to . . . to taking your life," Bud said. When he reached for her she whipped away, pulled plates and saucers from her cabinets and began to set the table in the adjoining dining room. "You would grieve because of my grief, wouldn't you, Calhoun?" she called. He stared fleetingly at the swinging door that had closed behind her and nodded sadly. "I mean, I know we're both ambitious as hell—but you do care something about me, right?"

He didn't answer. What the two of them had figured out suddenly seemed to be uncannily accurate, a perceptive insight into the mind of a madman. Rajelis mightn't even know about Jean, or the children. If he was capable either of black magic or simple homicide, the targets he chose might very well be Calhoun's business associates, his girl friend, and—

The swinging door swung wide, banged shut again, and Bud was back in the kitchen. "You'd better tell me that long, pregnant pause of silence was your idea of a joke, Grady Calhoun," she told him, fists on her hips, "or I may *help* that looney-tunes mentalist out in his campaign to knock you off! Suicide isn't the only way you can go!"

He'd gone to the midwest after his little brother's departure from the east because Grady had promised him a job and their mother had been Timmy's temporary choice of scapegoat. Actually, he was returning Mom to that role at the time and would nominate her for a third designation before gradually getting it through his alcoholic head that somebody else was responsible for making him a drunk.

He had never figured out just whom that individual was, but distance from the two brothers' mother had mellowed Timmy enough to let the old lady off the hook. At times, while he was, like most drunks, too self-protectively shrewd to say so aloud, he'd been pretty sure Grady was at fault. Or Grady's happy marriage, which elicited a number of crocodile tears from the older brother when it came apart. Or Grady fathering children, or advancing in his work, or finding a fine apartment even after he'd lost that *mansion* to the bitch Jean, or . . . well, precisely how Grady had made Timmy start drinking and continue to do so varied over the years.

But those buck-passing faults of Timothy Calhoun, along with his alcoholic disease, habit, preference, or weakness, were essentially the sum total of the man's negative qualities. No one had noticed, including Timmy, but the jobs Grady had found for him were incredibly different, and those Timmy had acquired on his own were equally diverse. He was so unstintingly and unobservedly versatile that he'd walked into yet a different sort of business over a Sunday luncheon and exited with both an application to fill out at his leisure and quite justified expectations of being hired.

He had the application plus the new company's literature in his jacket pocket when, just before nightfall Sunday evening, he went out for a constitutional. Timmy thought of the almost sober strolls he took on the eve of major job interviews in that term, even, as tonight, believed that he might begin to exercise himself back into fighting trim. After having a few laughs with good ol' Grade-A the other night—Jesus, it'd been fun pretending to be on *Confab* and screwing it up for his brother by swearing!—Timmy had halfway expected his little bro to drop by for a visit. Both of them had enjoyed that conversation, even Grade-A; Timmy was ready to swear to it. After he got the new position tomorrow, showed little bro just what *big* bro was capable of doing, there'd be lots of good times together, Timmy knew that. "No doubt about it," he said aloud, swinging around the corner and heading north, rather more unsteadily than at the beginning of his constitutional. The late-winter sun was bleeding all over the sky, he noted, turning it into a used Kotex. Timmy chuckled at the image, righted a tendency to veer toward the curb, and wished—for an uncountable number—he hadn't drunk the two beers before heading out. At the time it had seemed an ideal concession, since Timmy had allowed his booze and brews alike to run out on Saturday without stocking up for Sunday. There was nothing left to drink in his rundown apartment, and real men should be able to handle a couple of cans, and there'd be pre-cious little after he got the new position tomorrow.

"Pre-cious lit-tul," Timmy said aloud, and froze on the sidewalk.

Was that ol' Grade-A himself across the street, waving his arm? It certainly *looked* like little bro's shape, the sort of fancy duds he wore; but it was difficult to be sure with that Kotex sky seeping all over the street.

But why, Timmy wondered, trying to trot ahead and get a clear glimpse of the waving man's features, would Grade-A be over here on the street *behind* the apartment building?

"Timmy!" The man with Grady Calhoun's build ran forward a few steps, stopped with the fading sunlight brilliant upon his face. There was no way to see his features, but who else could it be but Grade-A? "Over here, Timmy—*quick*! There's something important I have to tell you about Tim."

About Tim—Timmy's nephew! Unhesitatingly, wobbly now from his unaccustomed jog, Timmy shouted a greeting and hurried out into the street, glad to see that his brother was actually seeking him out, but concerned about his nephew. "Be there in a minute, little bro!" he called.

The two-ton truck making the green light at the corner struck Timmy at the waist, threw him forward, and rolled over him—primarily, the entire left side of Timothy Calhoun's body. The literature from Max Levin Imports was jarred from Timmy's jacket pocket and fluttered in the truck's wake.

Instantly, before the shaken driver could stop, collect himself, and run back, the waving man was kneeling before Timmy, who clutched life by the fingertips of his soul and knew, immediately, that he'd never seen the waving stranger before.

But he knew he would have remembered the man if he *had* seen him previously. There were the strangely staring, unblinking eyes that scanned Timmy with an expression that sought confirmation of his imminent demise. There was the mammoth, grinning mouth—a mouth like the rear end of a garbage truck with teeth that seemed cast from tin cans and old Tonka toys. There was the impression Timmy had that the man wasn't going to speak or call for help, or even acknowledge with pride the terrible deception that, a moment later, made Timothy Calhoun perish.

Half a block away, the burly driver of the two-ton was jogging toward the scene of the "accident," the death. It was possible, in the vivid flash of dwindling daylight, to get a clear fix on the bystander stooped by the pedestrian; it was suddenly clear to the driver that the pedestrian wasn't moving a muscle. And, more clearly, that he himself didn't have a dollar's worth of insurance.

Before he stopped and ran pell mell back to his vehicle, the burly man saw the bystander retrieve some papers from the street, look at them incuriously, and drop them back into the street. He also saw the bystander stroll away in the opposite direction even as he cranked up his two-ton and got the hell out of there.

5

Thursday, March 24.

Because Timothy Calhoun had died as the result of an apparent hit-and-run accident, his funeral was put off by the autopsy and police inquiry. That gave Grady time to notify their mother as gently as humanly possible, and for her to fly in from upstate New York.

At Bud's thoughtful prompting, he'd volunteered to go get her. Just as he'd expected, Mom cooly rejected the idea, and he tried to get the old woman to find some close companion who would accompany her. Mom had flown very little.

"All my friends have long since gone, Grady," she told him in the same tone with which she'd indicated that Timmy's death was no surprise. A lack of shock was seemingly Mom's way of telling herself that there was no reason for a massive upheaval of emotion. She'd always adjusted amazingly well. "The ranks are thinning, Grady. Myrtle Reilly died last fall, did you hear about that?"

Mom had, he knew, known Myrtle most of her life—but she was scarcely the same thing as an elder son! It seemed to him there were many aged like Mom, who detested great change so much while being able to convince themselves they'd anticipated bad news that the two factors compounded a sort of anesthesia against

sentiment. Still, Grady ached for his
mother. Ethel Margaret Calhoun had lived
her long life pretending to be quite invul-
nerable, shock-proof and supremely well-
adjusted, thereby casting an image that
actually *did* appear to hold trouble at
bay—largely because it kept most other
people away. Viewed from one angle, it
was enviable camouflage, it projected
strength, even—by a circuitous route—
conviction about one's religious faith.

But it also made it virtually impossible
to be *close* to such a woman, and vice
versa. Mom's ranks had always been thin;
any defections by death reduced them to
near nothingness. What happened,
Calhoun wondered, when such persons
really had to have assistance? He'd fretted
more, yearly, over the possibility that his
mother would have a heart attack, which
she might survive if only someone else
was there to help. Or did Nature really
oblige them by simply mowing them down
before they were forced to consider a
retirement or nursing home?

In person, at the Winter Mortuary,
where Timothy's remains were on display,
the aging mother maintained her mask of
aplomb save for a minuscule tightening of
her powdery lips and a slight sagging
against Grady's side. What she could not
know but probably wouldn't have cared
about anyway was how dejected Grady felt
when he saw the extent of Mom's decline.
The hungry earth itself was sucking her
down, and in, inches at a time; weight loss

had turned her never meaty arms to a
liquid that flowed toward the replenishing
soil. Stooped, Mom's downward gaze
awaited the eventual descent uncomplain-
ingly. All Grady's contemplations meant
to prod Mom into a cozy place where she'd
be cared for, fed a balanced diet and be
surrounded by others in the event of a fall
or crippling illness, became focused and
sure as he led his leaning mother toward a
bolstering easy chair. Asking her to
abandon her home and fly here, move in
with him, he understood was a waste of
both their times—and Mom wasn't in a
position for such extravagant loss.

    Yet for the life of him, Grady couldn't
find a way to broach the subject and,
forcing it while her firstborn lay pastily
painted and motionless in a box at her
back, seemed malign, bizarre, and narrow.

    It was nearly an hour until the
services began. The coffin-and-catafal-
que-commanded room that Calhoun had
believed would remain three-fourths
empty was steadily filling with callers.
They entered as inconspicuously as they
could, traces of what might be the city's
last winter snow dusting their heads,
looking like football fans whose team had
just lost. Timmy, it seemed, had actually
had friends, and none of them gave a
speedy impression of being alcoholic. Two
ex-employers of the older Calhoun brother
introduced themselves; a majestic-
looking middle-aged man named Levin
arrived to tell Grady that he would have

hired Timmy "for top pay," had he survived another 18 hours. "He had something, that Tim," Levin mourned.

Bud would not be present, at least for the services themselves. She'd come yesterday, Wednesday, before Jean and the kids. Then Grady had striven to dissuade his former wife from bringing either David or Petey, the youngsters, because of his settled conviction that they didn't belong in such a depressing place. Not that anybody, he added to Jean, did.

Now she had insisted on bringing all four of the children, saying to Calhoun that the sooner young people were exposed to "life's realities, the better." He kept to himself his further view that the longer kids could wait before meeting more kinds of reality, the happier they'd be. At least, little Petey's cold seemed to have dried up, or almost so; that made Rajelis' assumed role as an illness-bringer mercifully less convincing.

But it was Grady's firstborn who grieved the most for Timmy, whether because his uncle had shared his name or for subtler reasons Grady could not specify. He had almost to force Tim away from the waxen corpse and, when Tim spotted his seldom seen grandmother, looking at him as if she wasn't sure of his identity, Tim's tears flowed copiously. *He'll get precious little comfort from Mom,* Grady thought, and was astonished when his mother's minimal hug and sole pat on the back seemed to soothe his son. *At that age,* he thought, learning, *being family is enough.*

"They are very nonverbal at 15," Jean whispered. A cautious nod encompassed the room. "This is all quite necessary. Tim and the other children are, well, entitled to this."

"Like folks are entitled to broken hearts, right? Or the heartbreak of psoriasis?" He edged away.

Tom Simincola, Calhoun's writer/ trumpeter pal Gill Riffey, and the two cameramen came in looking like wraiths, looking strange, different, to the Irishman. Taking their awkward hands, he recalled other acquaintances in funeral homes seeming similarly different. Maybe it had to do with the fact that most people didn't think about the democratic curse called Dying except when they were trapped into attending funerals. "Andy's minding the store," Tom said softly, close to and towering above Grady. "He'd be here today except for his firm commitment to making Andy Sutor rich and powerful."

"Andy said he sent flowers," Gill whispered, and craned his neck. "Where d'you think they put the cheap vases with the single roses?"

Calhoun kept from laughing aloud with enormous difficulty. He had always inclined to breaking up at solemn occasions.

After the nondenominational service —it was Timmy's request, another chance

to chide his scapegoat Mom, who'd reared
her sons as Catholics—Grady bid a private
farewell to Timmy, whose body was to be
cremated. Mom, to Grady's considerable
relief, had announced she wanted the urn
with her elder son's ashes "at home, where
Timothy belongs." The cleansing, slate-
wiping tears that Grady had expected and
needed at his final instant with Timmy
refused to come. Even earnest prayer did
nothing to elicit images of good times
shared together as boys. *For an ambitious
guy,* he reflected, *it always boils down to
moving ahead to a new combat zone.* You
didn't so much put things in the past as
lose all sight of them, virtually everything
but the times of breakthrough and
triumph. That second, he didn't care
much for himself.

Lt. Wayne Sojourner of Homicide was
waiting patiently at the bottom of the
steep mortuary steps, wind-bitten but
coatless, a grave and dark icon who sym-
bolized things Grady no longer recalled.
He remained taller when Grady still had
two steps to go before reaching the sidewalk and offering his hand to the
detective.

"You know I'm really sorry, am I
right?" Sojourner gentled his automatic
and powerful handclasp. "So let's get on
with what I have for you—and what I
don't."

Grady wondered, as he had before,
about the genes that gave such a tall,
powerfully constructed man such a

chirping, high-pitched voice. "Shoot."

"There isn't much." Sojourner flipped open a pocket-sized notebook, angling it so that the parsimonious sunlight had a chance. "We're reasonably certain it wasn't a homicide, but we haven't completely ruled it out. Considering that Timmy had had a pretty successful job interview and that he was sober, we're ruling out suicide." Single sharp glance at Calhoun. "Thought you and your momma would like to know that. She's Catholic, right?"

Calhoun grunted. "He was sober?"

Sojourner shrugged. "A few beers, just before he went out for his evening stroll. That's it." Wayne screwed his earnest, homely face into a thoughtful, restrained grimace. "No leads on the mother who ran him down and then booked, Grady. Now, don't get excited, but we found some prints on the literature of Max Levin Imports, and I'm looking into that. But just because he was your bro. I'm not sure what the fuck it would prove if we *can* put a name to the prints—assuming any are there but Timmy's."

"Wayne, you're beating around the bush. A fact. Aren't you prepared even yet to find Rajelis and bring him back here for questioning?" He'd put on his best affable inquisitor expression, but thought he knew what Wayne's reply would be.

Sojourner surprised him a bit. "I thought we should check out the prints, see if they *can* be pinned to the bastard.

Shit, Grady, it's one hell of a long shot that the bastard was back in town. But I thought he was spooky on your show—and sincere as the Klan." Clumsily, he clapped Calhoun's shoulder. "If his fingertips happen to turn up on that business literature, it could be a new ball game."

"Thanks for trying," Calhoun said, so hoarsely he didn't think Wayne Sojourner heard him.

The policeman was staring up the steps at the mortuary, as if expecting the fires of cremation to billow out Auswichian puffs of smoke. Or were they more like papal announcements at the Vatican, with the new choices made? He snapped his notebook shut and returned it to his pocket. "Calhoun, dammit, I don't have a scrap of evidence for bringing that sumbitch back to town."

Grady nodded, sighed. The mortuary doors were closed and no one was in sight. Business as usual: there'd be a short wait until somebody else died. "Do what you can, all right, Wayne?" he growled, sounding husky. The tears were ready now to come, and Grady was already shuffling toward his car. Bud was perched inside on the passenger's seat, waiting there to listen or to help. Over one shoulder, Calhoun called, "Now the people I care about *have* begun suffering, don't you see that, Wayne: Where's it going to end?"

But he *knew* where, if Rajelis had his way. It was meant to end in suicide. His.

When Rajelis phoned the first thing that passed through Grady's mind was the stark realization that the mentalist somehow knew his whereabouts, suggesting he'd remained in town—

And he also knew Bud Rocker's phone number.

That was far more frightening.

For a moment Calhoun wondered if they had simply been followed. They'd dined simply on scrambled eggs and toast after driving Mom to the airport—Ethel Margaret Calhoun wouldn't even consider staying over; she seemed driven to flee her younger son's adopted city before he could broach the retirement home issue, and she had been shocked to hear that he might one day remarry—and then there had been the quiet conversation most grieving individuals require, sooner or later. When Grady had finally shed tears they'd been anguished, embittered, intimate. Neither he nor Bud had so much as mentioned Rajelis or his cruel predictions because to do so would have been an intrusion upon the past, an obscenity against the present and the hopes they shared.

Considering Calhoun's sorrow, Rajelis might have begun following them at any point, and now he was on the phone, cool and unflustered when Grady shouted, asked how the man dared to bother decent people at such a moment.

"I merely felt that I should call and express my condolences, Mr. Calhoun, since I . . . heard . . . about your brother's passing.''

"Where are you, Rajelis? I gather you're back in town."

"Oh come, sir,' the mentalist said in his remembered reedy accents, "let's be somewhat sensible about this. My travels are such that I scarcely notice my whereabouts until time to attend my own performance." The voice at the other end inhaled, changed the subject. "Despite your worthless brother's demise, I imagine you found it heartening when your youngest child's illness proved to be a . . . *passing* one."

Rajelis's meaning was clear as cracking ice. "If you try to kill another member of my family," Calhoun shouted, on his feet and bent in outrage over Bud's telephone, "I'll find you, I'll *slaughter* you!"

"Please, please," Rajelis said quickly, "do not fear that all those for whom you care are going to die." An odd, hooting laugh that somehow brought the mentalist's face to mind clearly, the dark glasses devoid of personality, expression, emotion. For a moment the face seemed meaningful, a clue. Then it slipped away because of Calvin Rajelis's patronizing inflections. "Surely, sir, even you are not so shallow and superficial that you are unaware of the fact that there are *numerous* ways for a human being to become unhappy. Miserable; engulfed in excruciating, even soul-twisting sorrow.

Enjoy the variety of my fascinating demonstrations if nothing more, Mr. Calhoun!''

"I think you read about my brother's death in the papers, or caught the news on a Channel 61 newcast!'' The idea leaped to Grady's mind unbidden, and he felt abruptly relieved, hopeful. "You're capitalizing on it, aren't you, Cal? The way a dozen terrorist groups claim the 'credit' for the assassinations of another group entirely!''

"Don't you dare me, Calhoun." For the first time since Grady's life had been changed by meeting the mentalist, Rajelis sounded irritated, almost angry. "What's happening to your loved ones *can* be accelerated. . . .''

"Bullshit, man," Grady fired back, nearly out of control. He knew Bud was only two feet away, gesturing with her hands to calm him, but he didn't care. Maybe what he'd come up with was right, and the son of a bitch had done nothing at all! "Wherever you are, Rajelis, you couldn't kill a roach with a tommygun!''

"It's *marvelous* the way you're encouraging me, Mr. Calhoun! So . . . let's find out!'' He sounded joyful now; the ire was gone, and suddenly it was like discussing the efficacy of electrocutions with an executioner. "*Select* someone, Calhoun —whomever you please! Choose the next victim for me and I will be delighted to learn, with you, how long it will take the dying roach to perish!''

Grady fell silent, speechless.

"Will it be that brazen, seductive, overambitious little lover who's trying to bring you to your senses this moment, or your former wife, perhaps? Select, Mr. Calhoun—*do challenge me!*"

He didn't have magical powers, Grady struggled to convince himself; *that* comment, his most recent tactic, was based on simple psychology. But clearly, Grady had gone too far in daring Rajelis, much too far. The bastard was only psychotic, but it made no sense to "accelerate" his murderous plans.

"Why?" Grady asked. "Why do you want to do these terrible things?" He clutched the receiver with both hands, his heart beating wildly, sickeningly. "At least tell me what you're doing this for! Will you do that much, Rajelis—tell me why?"

For a moment the prolonged silence made Grady believe the mentalist had hung up. But finally, in a hate-filled whisper, Calvin Rajelis gave Calhoun his answer:

"Seera," he said. And repeated it lovingly, sinisterly, stretching out the two syllables until they seemed to vibrate through the telephone cord and receiver into Grady's soul. "It's all for *Seera.*"

Then the phone was dead.

6

Friday. March 25.

He was not himself now, he sensed that much and wondered, occasionally, about it. When he wondered it did not advance to the state of curiosity, nor did he make that first effort, these days, to obtain any clues to his condition. Not that he was singularly stupid—no more than he had ever been, anyway.

It was that he had somehow altered.

And since, in the procedure of alteration, he had been given special abilities —powers, maybe—that arranged for him to make human beings uniquely miserable, to place them in agony or even in death, it really seemed best to him not to force the issue. It was satisfactory this way. And being . . . modified . . . drastically, or even losing the capacity both for curiosity and his own personal autonomy, once quite dear to Billy Salvo, were infinitely better than the blackness. The charry, lightless, perpetual night.

Anything would have been better. That much Billy remembered, nodding ponderously; that much he still knew.

He sat awkwardly in a worn easy chair in one of his three rented rooms in that part of the city that had once been its finest neighborhood. He neither knew that nor the name of this city in which he'd been—for want of a more clarifying expression—reborn. Reborn whole; restored to adult manhood with a face and form that were fundamentally what he'd always known: He was extremely ugly, again; muscular; outwardly normal. Normal, so long as one could accept the discomfiting fact that the Mansons and DeSalvos and Geins and Bundys did not *look* abnormal. Maybe, at the crucial instants, to their victims. At those terrible, final moments.

And upon those occasions, when Billy'd been told to go do harm to other beings, he'd also known—in ways he couldn't comprehend (and that he didn't particularly want to understand)—the discreet form he should take when he appeared to the pre-chosen victims. But how he changed, what went on inside of him that made the modifications happen, Billy didn't know either. Or care. He merely did that which he knew, suddenly, in his thoughts, in a dazzling, undefendable flash of idleness-to-deed. Some way or other Billy Salvo simply *knew* those he was intended to attack, where they'd be located, and precisely how to implement the newest particular infliction of evil.

That was enough, for Billy; now. If it hadn't been that would have been all right, too, since he was incapable, these days, of questioning anything whatever. Once, he sensed, he had been able to feel curious about things and challenged damned near everything. No longer, and it was just fine, too, no sweat, no problem, this life was good and fulfilling in its limited form. Part of the limitation was that very little about this old city where he'd been reborn looked familiar, even when he was obliged to roam and to rove all over it. He thought, dimly, that the city had been changed too.

Which did not matter in the slightest.

Among the relatively few things he knew about himself were these: He did not have to eat, and almost never did; but he could dine if that was necessary. He had no need for elimination of wastes because whatever he did eat or drink was promptly burned up in his body in a fashion that Billy neither comprehended nor wondered about.

He also had a hunch that he would eventually meet a man or woman who held the secrets to his reborn condition—all of them—but he didn't actually look forward to the encounter or believe that any explantions would necessarily be offered to him. In this, there was a very distant, faintly nagging feeling of subjugation, but that, too, was quite acceptable to Billy.

Because it was all much, much better than the frightening blackness, the perpetual night, that he had known. That he could no longer think about because of the mad terror that engulfed him, form-lessly, without dimension or void, when he did.

Yet the changes in Billy Salvo were rather more extensive than he perceived, primarily because, without curiosity, he also lacked anything remotely like imagination. He had no one who was a friend, even a companion. He had no family, no daily job, and no duties, aside from the periodic ones of adminstering abject misery, torment, and death; no hobbies, no pastimes, no radio and no TV.

He knew nothing about that anyway, so he didn't miss them.

The only human creature he'd met to whom he had not given anguish, or worse, was the landlady person who had rented his rooms to him—rooms to which he'd been directed, somehow; he had never wondered how, or from whom the directions came—and he had no feelings whatever about the landlady person. He never gave her any money, an article he certainly did recall with occasional stirrings of mild interest, but knew that somebody else was sending her money to house him. Which was good, since he had no money whatsoever and, half the time or better, forgot that such an article existed.

But he wasn't mad in the usual sense of the word, or even exactly an idiot. Billy had enormous blanks in his circum-scribed mentality; gaps, more of them than there were others that had been filled in.

Now it was the middle of the night, but Billy never slept, either. This, despite the fact that he often felt quite tired, depleted, exhausted. Fortunately, when he had harmed or stolen the life from others, his sense of physical well-being was immediately restored—like lightning. Much of what kept Billy Salvo going *was* "like lightning," indeed. With Billy, the anti-creator, his violence was devoid of judgment and justice, usually of passion; it amounted to his own version of art for art's sake.

Reclining wearily in his old easy chair, Billy experienced—for a minute flash of time—an interior, private glimmer of something quite like a psychopathic daydream. Ages ago he had found that he was schizophrenic and possessed homicidal tendencies. The terms had stuck in his mind. Without bothering him. No doctor and no hospital, after all, had held him for long. He remembered that, knew he'd been far too clever for them. It had felt so *special*, then, he had taken the data they provided him about himself and accepted it as high praise, as the professional verification of his own almost unique, godlike individuality.

But now the knowing of his psychiatric condition of the almost forgotten past jarred him perilously, disturbed Billy in a manner that matched up the remembrance of his special kind of insanity with his present absence of all salvational cunning and freedom, and Billy sensed that the white darkness was again coming, for him—

And felt with daggerish, gibbering horror that, with his eyes wide open, unable to stop it, that damned white darkness was sucking him under a hot, glaring blanket until elongated shadows of palest hue tore further holes in his delicately reconstituted existence like painful shafts of cold steel, until . . .

Until two stark, vertical lines making the number *11* materalized in Billy's mind's eye and stood there, shivering, compelling his gaze, his whole attention, his whole loss of selfhood.

Then came the images of a globular Something, and they promptly detonated into a shower of blinding redness. He pressed helplessly back against his chair, unable to make the terrifying crimson vision vanish or, behind its blood-test smear, the white and upright magical *11*. Which then became shining spicula, each spike like a shard of colorless sunlight fleeing into the distance and trailing Billy in its wake until he wanted to lunge forward physically to see what waited for him there; truths, facts—explanations! Each spike was as crammed with throbbing, liberating data as the newest microchip—

But he perceived vaguely that he had no notion what a microchip was, or a computer, and floundered in the ignorance of rising doubt. Pain came in waves, too, boiled into his functioning physical eyes and carved hungrily behind the balls of his popping eyes, but that was all right, okay, since Billy'd always secretly *liked* pain even if he was only receiving it.

Gggoddd, Billy thought or possibly said when the kaleidoscope of fresh color/

pain blasted into his mind. Red/white; white/red; red/white—more than even Billy enjoyed, too much to handle.

Then nothingness. Momentary total and depersonalizing, meaningless nothingness, lacking even a curtain of black or the carving curse of crimson. Relief, of a sort; a canceling-out that debased and destroyed, but not, once more, not permanently.

He sat up and knew he would have much to do, very soon. A great deal. His head had not gone through a clearing process; it was, simply, cleared. Only the exhaustion remained, apart from the few things he always knew, these days, and all those things he never remembered. And he attempted to close his red-rimmed eyes, despite the fact that he could not sleep.

But another scrap of information he hadn't sought about himself came into his mind.

He couldn't close his eyelids either. They wouldn't close.

But that was all right. He could still hurt people. He was still permitted to do that. Distantly, he even recalled that he'd learned about his unclosing eyes the other day.

But he'd forgotten it.

7

Sunday, March 27. Nearly Noon.

Back inside the old two-story house, everything the same and yet everything somehow strange after the passing of his
brother, Grady felt almost unreasonably
grateful when he found little Petey himself
again.

"It's as if he had never been sick at
all," Grady told Jean, averting his face to
keep his ex-wife from seeing the glad tears
standing in his eyes. "Isn't that amazing?"

"Not particularly." Jean, forcing their
winter coats on David, and Cathy, in turn,
had scarcely looked at him since he
arrived.

There'd been a nearly infinitesimal
drop in temperature over the past 24
hours, but this was Jean's way, over-
dressing the kids. Grady got Petey's bright
red, hooded coat out of the front closet
with a clanging of coat hangers. "Well, I
think it's amazing. Surprising, anyway."
What the hell was wrong with Jean today?
She didn't use to be quite so moody.

"Kids are like that." She added a scarf
around Cathy's neck, and Grady wondered
if the kid would be able to go on breathing.
Jean glanced briefly his way. "I don't
think he even remembers being ill."

Grady had worked the cloth coat onto
his youngest son's suddenly limpid

arms—little ones' limbs turned to cold spaghetti any time you had to dress them—and now he hoisted the boy above his head. There was a shower of appreciative giggles. "That right, buddy? You don't 'member having the old sniffles?"

"Uh-huh," the three-year-old said, rosy cheeked and happy to be going somewhere with Daddy. He meant no.

Lowering Petey, Grady saw the other younger children waiting impatiently by the front door. The oldest sibling was missing. "Where's Tim?"

Jean, pale and distant, was already turning on the television in the living room. She didn't appear to have heard him.

"Isn't Tim going with us today?" he called.

Her eyes, when she turned her face to him, were unusually bright. Then a veil seemed to fall over them. "He said to tell you he couldn't go this afternoon."

"Why?" Grady demanded. "I mean, why not?"

But she was turning up an IU basketball game the network was covering and clearly, as she sank into a chair and fixed her gaze on the screen, eager to watch it. Which also surprised Grady, since she'd never liked Bobby Knight, the Hoosiers' coach; considered him "gauche." She snapped, "Why don't you ask Tim if he's here when you get back?"

I will, Grady promised himself as he went with the other children to the car and pretended to listen to what they were saying. *You better believe I will!*

Cathy, the ten-year-old, exercised her option for picking a place to eat by selecting the nearest Wendy's. David groaned aloud because he was already a McDonald's freak, and Grady wondered when they'd be old enough to prefer a complete meal. Tim was his hope in that department; the fact that the teenager already liked Denny's seemed to suggest some kind of gradual incline in taste. Maybe this was another topic for Gill Riffey to look into.

But why in hell *wasn't* Tim with them this afternoon? Digging into a wide bowl of chili and then wadding up more small crackers to give the dish body, Calhoun felt a shiver of fatherly apprehension. He'd done enough programs about the hazards of growing up in modern America to know that any 15-year-old boy—even his own—could apparently go sour overnight. When he and Jean were still married, when Grady'd believed they led a charmed life and were marching as a family unit into a golden sunset, he'd also genuinely believed that his children were immune to the peer pressures and group temptations that preyed upon them like something entirely tangible, and purposive.

They were no longer an unbroken unit now, however, and regardless of how Jean tried, in her rather overprotective way, she couldn't replace a day-to-day father image. Not at a time when a kid like Tim really needed one. What in Christ's name *was* Tim's problem now? His appetite entirely gone, Calhoun stared surreptitiously at Petey with a rising concern for the little guy's almost fatherless future, and found his coffee tasteless. The specter of drugs—of middle-aged bastards in raincoats lurking on the fringes of the playground, peddling kinds of chemistry that definitely did not promote better living—surged into imagination. Even as he remembered the old Tom Lehrer cautionary lines about "The Old Dope Peddler spreading powered happiness," Calhoun reminded himself that the guy on the playground these days could just as easily be a substitute quarterback or a cuddly little cheerleader with bronzed bare legs.

"Oh, shi-it!" David cried, and barfed.

Grady jumped away from the table and most of it missed his pants.

"Da-ad, I'm *sorry*," the seven-year-old bleated, looking white-faced and terrified. Cathy, customarily maternal, had hidden her face in mortification, and Petey was filling in for big sister, throwing yellow napkin after yellow napkin into the part of the mess that had hit the table, and making it worse.

"Well, don't *sit* in it!" Grady snapped, raising Petey out of the way and reaching in for David. "And stop looking so scared—please! People'll think I beat you when you get sick!"

By the time he'd done what he could to make David socially presentable again, and managed to share a laugh or two with the boy, Grady led him back out of the men's room and found Cathy the color of split-pea soup. She'd taken off the scarf Jean had knotted around her neck and Petey was staring at her with the fascination of a spectator at the onslaught of the black plague.

"I don't feel so very good either, Dad-deeee," she moaned.

Grady nodded, believing her. Cathy only stretched out the second syllable of his paternal name when she was ill or wnated something, and all Cathy wanted now, obviously, was to be at home.

"I'd arranged to take you to a Pacer practice," Calhoun said somberly, picking his daughter up and carrying her toward the door. They'd already paid after choosing their food from the cafeteria line. "Coach Ramsey didn't mind. But I think we'd better postpone it for another time."

"I'm *fine,*" David argued, in Calhoun's wake. Indeed, he looked that way now when Grady glanced back at him.

"Well, your sister's not." He paused while little Petey used all his strength to get the door open. Cold wind whipped at them and Cathy, who seemed to be enjoying the special treatment, hugged Grady's neck. "Methinks there is a bug going around."

"He already got me," Petey protested, tugging the car door open and looking extremely earnest. "So can we go,

Daddy?"

But that was breaking one of his cardinal rules—no one-on-one outings except on birthdays—and, by the time he'd driven them home, Calhoun's argument for fair play had daunted Petey and David into silence. Not agreement; just grumbling silence.

"Dad! Hullo."

Tim was hanging up his coat in the front closet when Calhoun and the other kids entered the house. Instantly, without a shadow of doubt, Calhoun recognized the flicker of guilt sliding across his teenaged son's unlined face. Obviously, Tim had not expected them to be back at the house so early.

"Cathy," Grady said gently, "David, I want you to go right up to bed and rest for a few hours. Petey, go get your mother." He took his daughter's warm-lipped kiss, then the ten-year-old's afterthought peck on the cheek, and waited until the three of them were on their way. He turned then to Tim. "What's up? Where were you?"

"Out," Tim said quickly, and blinked. "Had something to do."

"That," Grady said drily, "was fairly obvious. What I want to know is—" He broke off as Jean joined them by the front door. "Don't get all upset, but David whoopsed and I wouldn't be surprised if Cathy does before the afternoon's history."

"*They're* sick now?" Jean said, glancing toward the stairs and then down at Petey. Petey nodded with great solemnity. "It must be something that's going around."

"The bug already bit *me*," Petey announced proudly in case she had forgotten. "*I'm* all well now."

Grady grinned and stooped to add a hug to the little one's growing collection. When he did he heard the front door at his back close, ever so quietly.

Tim had left. The closet door was ajar and Tim's coat still moved faintly on its hanger.

"Damn it!" Calhoun exploded, and started for the front door.

"Let him go," Jean called; "for now. I need to tell you something, anyway."

"I knew something was on your mind," Grady said. Shaking his head, he stepped away from the door and took Jean by the elbows. "Something's up with Tim. Did you find pot or coke in his room?"

"It's not that." She pulled away, leaned against the wall with an unreadable expression on her face. "I'd have called you, asked you to come over or something, if it had been drugs." She shook her head, looked angry and confused simultaneously. "Grady, I can't even be absolutely certain anything *is* wrong."

He felt himself losing his temper. "Well, what the fuck does that mean, Jeannie? Obviously, something's wrong; he scarcely said two words to me, and then he . . . he sneaked out the front door as if he had something to hide."

"Maybe he does," Jean whispered.

"Can you give me a clue?" Calhoun demanded. "Will you *tell* me, for heaven's sake, what happened that made *you* suspicious? Could you possibly tell me what Tim's done, or said, or—"

"I think he may be," Jean said, and added one other word that was mumbled so badly it was unintelligible.

"What?" Grady asked, his arms on either side of her and his palms bracing himself on the wall. He stared down into her face in an effort to get it, next time. "What was that?"

Jean began to cry. "His friends," she said haltingly. "Well, *one* friend in particular. A new one." She gradually shifted the focus of her vision to her ex-husband's intent face. "They've been thick as thieves lately. And I think . . ."

"*Finish it,*" Calhoun said softly with enormous intensity.

"I think Tim's new friend is homosexual."

Talked out of confronting his eldest child with the suspicion, Calhoun broke his Sunday-night date with Bud, popped open a beer, and sprawled out on his bed to think. Across from him, fading daylight slipped tenuously through the drawn curtains and the chill in the air was more reminiscent of the winter they'd believed they'd passed than embryonic spring.

He'd imagined a lot of awful problems

that might develop because he no longer lived with the kids—hell, give Jean the benefit of the doubt, he mightn't have been able to hold them at bay if he'd been around regularly—but not once had it occurred to Calhoun that any of his children could be gay.

He hadn't even had a chance, or taken the time, to evaluate and appraise his own feelings about that life-style—if that was really what it was—and it seemed to him then, as the day began to die, that his oldest boy might as well have become a deep-sea diver, Communist, or a member of the Jovian High Council for all he was prepared to deal with it. Bad enough Tim had been such a bookworm all his life, he had to go and find an even worse way to isolate himself from his own father!

Not, Calhoun reminded himself with a measure of relief, that he or Jean had the slightest proof that her suspicions were well founded. If it came down to that, all she had to go on was the sudden, over-night fascination Tim appeared to feel for a boy he hadn't even known a full week before. And, of course, Jean's repugnance —was it only some odd sort of maternal jealousy?—for the other, the strange boy.

Grady dragged deeply on his Lite and dribbled a little on his shirt. He was becoming a slob lately, with all that was happening—*to people I care for*, he thought, despising the recollection. His own mother had believed you could give power to the very people you didn't want

to give it to, by overstressing their bad
influence on your life. Grady made himself
turn on his side, away from the faint and
rather troubling illumination from the
bedroom windows, and made an effort to
think deeply. This was something he could
not remember doing for a long time;
thinking deeply. *If ever,* the words razored
into his mind, and he frowned. But wasn't
there some truth to it? However embarras-
sing (even privately), however self-
belittling the confession was, didn't he,
didn't everybody Grady knew, spend most
of their mortal lives—particularly as
adults—doing everything in their power to
avoid deeply questioning, self-probing,
honest analytical *thought*?

   "You're full of it, Calhoun," he rasped
aloud to himself. But it wouldn't wash, he
didn't buy it. Regardless of how skilled,
how competent or brilliant the average,
modern American got in doing his job,
didn't he do just what was necessary to
keep abreast of its daily demands and
then, when quitting time came, go home
to turn off and drop out until morning?
Wasn't that what the weekend was
about—having two days and three nights
to shut down and run like a goddam madman away from all responsibility,
obligation to reach decisions, need to
think?

   Horse crap! Wasn't almost everything
that wasn't constructed for use in work—
except for some of the books ol' Tim read
and maybe a little dose of TV and a flick or

two—geared toward *sparing* modern society a moment of exploratory thought? Geared to *rush* them all past the crucial points of living when nothing except deeply reflective thinking — contemplation; understanding; adjustment and planning; seeking *truth*—would prevent the onslaught of more of the personal disasters that were tearing this society apart?

But I'm turning it into society's *problem, making it* society's *fault,* the Irishman realized, irritated with himself. *When it's all mine. Who am I to fucking judge whether other men—other* people—*use their brains from time to time, or not?*

Because he hadn't, Calhoun knew, not really. Not for a long time.

It also ran in the family. Poor, sick, drunk old Timmy, his own brother, had addled his wits with booze. But was it any worse than befuddling your brain with the kind of ambition that made you simply *pretend* to care enough about your own family, the kids you yourself fathered? Because, Grady knew then, he should—if he was any kind of a father at all—know for a fact—a *fact!*—that Tim Calhoun couldn't conceivably be an addict or a thief or a fairy! Parents who were on *top* of things couldn't be surprised by astonishing, out-of-the-blue ideas like Jean had laid on him!

But it wasn't Jean's fault, he thought, and shook his head in stubborn, vastly belated fidelity.

It was Rajelis' fault. All of it, all this goddamned nightmare—Cavin Rajelis' fault. He focused on that, hard, and strove for a solid half a minute to buy it. And ultimately decided that, in a way—on one series of related levels—he was correct. Calhoun finished his Lite in a gulp. Rajelis had somehow created an intellectual or emotional climate in which he and his family were suddenly susceptible to misfortunes they'd managed to sidestep before. That much of it—*maybe more?* he wondered before slapping the thought aside—belonged on the crazy sonofabitch's doorstep.

—Surely not any homosexual tendencies on his son Tim's part. A boy either had leanings that way, or he didn't.

For a while Grady tried to figure a means of getting in touch with the bastard, threatening or buying him off somehow. But it was Sunday night, things were shut down, there was no way to get info easily about Rajelis' current stop on his performing tour. *Soon,* Calhoun thought, *soon I'll find him, and I'll make him stop this, get out of my mind and the thoughts of my loved ones, or I'll—*

"Kill myself?" Grady Calhoun asked himself, aloud. Because that would do it. That was what the bastard really wanted, those were really the terms of his pledge to stop.

Except that, regardless of how many things were going wrong in Grady Calhoun's life, despite all the misery and the sickness, there wasn't enough *proof* to justify so much as a hundred-dollar bribe, let alone taking his own life!

Light through the closest curtain centered on the place just above Calhoun's nose, between the eyes, and drummed persistently into his pineal gland until the minimal glare began to disorient, to make Calhoun blink; and he sat up, realizing—

Realizing that he was still the best damned listener in the talk show business, and Calvin Rajelis hadn't just predicted his family would be placed in torment for Calhoun's sins, real or imagined.

Rajelis had said it would all be done . . . *by light.*

Timmy, poor wasted ol' Timmy, had *died* just as the sun was dying for the day. "When there was still plenty of light to see how to get it done," Calhoun muttered, aloud. This sonofabitch didn't *think* the way the other bad guys had thought, he didn't act out his vengeance, his plans, at night—

He went after his victims—however the hell he did it—*at dusk,* and *at dawn!*

What that implied, how it could be of use to him, Grady had no immediate idea. Settling back against his propped-up pillows, he ransacked his memory for what he'd heard—learned—from other guests on his program. Because the bottom line for television's Grady Calhouns was that they learned diddly from books or anything *except* the intelligence shared by other people, verbally.

And he seemed to recall hearing that most human beings were born between midnight and six A.M., the peak at somewhere around four o'clock in the morning; that people were inclined to die, as a rule—*was* there a rule?—when the sun was rising, or when the sun was going down.

Quite specifically, Timmy Calhoun hadn't died during the day—not precisely then—but at twilight. The "light between the two," by definition, meaning . . . the light between day and night, night and day.

Excited, Grady jumped from bed and ransacked the place for a dictionary. Books weren't exactly what he owned the most of, but he finally unearthed a cheap Funk and Wagnall's standard desk dictionary Jean had given him once in Tim's or Cathy's name, and looked the familiar word up.

Calhoun verified his definition and came upon something else, information that might or might not help him to draw closer to an understanding of his psychic foe: "The period during which this light is prevalent," it read; and again, "A condition following the waning of past glory." But whose past glory? That "Seera" whom Rajelis had mentioned over the telephone?

Was it possible that the goddam weirdo had this all tied up with something . . . atmospheric? meteorological? Could the time of day, or of season, somehow have something to do with the way Rajelis was turning Grady's family into the walking wounded—and some who would walk no more?

Calhoun sank down in a chair with the seldom used second volume of the dictionary clutched in his hands and a thirst for knowledge filling his spirit for the first time.

Out of the blue, the word or name *Seera* sounded familiar.

She saw the man walking the dog on the leash the instant she and Ernie went out on the front porch. Tomorrow—Monday morning—was trash pickup day, and the two-year-old wasn't much help, but Susan Swagerty was alone in the world and believed herself fortunate that Ernie wanted to help. The man and the dog were half a block away when mother and son carried the trash out to the curb, each of them shivering and laughing because of how hastily they worked; but by the time Susan was back at the front door of the house, both the neighbor and his pet were nearly abreast of the Swagerty property.

I don't like his looks, the young mother thought, tearing her gaze away, looking to Ernie, who hadn't started back from the curb. He'd found a string that had come loose from the trash can dangling to the street and was clumsily, conscientiously replacing it in the can.

"Come on, baby," Susan called. Something about the neighbor man's wide
smile as he turned his large head to stare
fixedly at her seemed hungry; *starved.*
"Let that go and come to Mama."

"Jutta mint," Ernie called back, fierce
in his determination to please his mother.
But the string had stuck to his stubby
fingers and, while he'd manuevered it
above the rim of the galavanized can, he
couldn't shake the string loose.

Crazy twilight, Susan thought,
starting to fret. Night was rushing toward
them like someone with a mammoth
blanket, eager to enfold them. But by
some trick the scant illuminations that
remained had pooled out like something
carelessly spilled and formed a loose foot-
light around Ernie, the strange man, and
his dog.

Achingly, that moment, Susan
yearned to run with all the speed she
could summon out to the curb to her small
child, grab him into her arms, and race
back to the house. But she folded her arms
across her breast and, shivering, throttled
the impulse. It was difficult enough for a
young divorced mother and her normally
boisterous little boy to be accepted in a
neighborhood these days without behaving like some fool neurotic. "Ernie," Susan
whispered, her tone more intent.

He replied, too, but she didn't hear
what he said. Her nervous gaze had
strayed back to the man and the dog on
the leash—but it *didn't look like a dog.* It

looked like—

He released the creature from the lead, then, just as effortlessly as could be, and Susan realized that the animal had not been straining at its leash because it was untrained—

But because it was trained. To attack. To attack Ernie.

Susan saw it almost with little Ernie's eyes, from his vantage point. Saw the thing that was not *quite* a dog rush soundlessly and loomingly forward and saw how it got bigger and bigger the way it would seem to a tiny little person. Saw how it ate up the pavement in almost no time at all, that it was nothing *remotely* like a dog but a four-legged nightmare, and then saw it rear above Ernie at the apex of its powerful thrust and bear him tumbling down to the cement, half in the street and half on the curb, little legs and feet flailing out and striking the trash cans, sending one flying in a terrible clanging-and-rolling sprawl that spewed bits of garbage like bits of flesh in a geyser over little Ernie's head.

The squeals might have come from an animal—from the beast—but they were surely Ernie's because the nightmare thing was as silent as death, as efficient as a killing machine. By the time Susan reached them she sensed the neighbor man's presence yards away, as noiseless as his creature, frozen in place and staring at the tableau. From the trash can Susan wrested the leg from a card table that had broken that week and she *punched* at the beast with it, instinctively *hacked* at its head and meaty shoulders instead of wasting time in wild swings. She wasn't strong anyway, and she had somehow known by the time she reached Ernie that she could not hope to knock the beast unconscious, only to make it back off. And Ernie went on squealing, screaming outright sometimes, and other timeless moments saying "No-No-No-No" at the top of his terrified voice; and Susan went on hitting, punching, her arms becoming heavier and pained until she'd *hit-hit-hit* ninety or a hundred times at the mauling four-legged nightmare, and she realized that it was almost *dark* . . .

And the neighbor man who'd released the horror upon her small child had turned to run, was already in the distance like a dwindling vehicle, running as fast as his legs would take him—*without his creature.*

And the beast itself was nowhere in sight—impossible, that's impossible and insane and *cannot be*—

But Bud Rocker's sister Susan's two-year-old boy Ernie *was* still there, a dog's leash curled like a dead snake in the gutter beside his red-splotched body crumpled at her feet, unmoving.

She dropped the bloody table leg she'd used on her only child and the phantom silence of new night splintered before her outcry.

8

Monday. March 28. 4:08 A.M.

Grady Calhoun got to go to two of the four places he hated most in the world even before it was dawn: Methodist Hospital, with Bud, to act as surrogates for Susan Swagerty in waiting to see if little Ernie would make it; and the jail, to take Bud's anguished sister the news.

Spring seemed an empty promise at four o'clock in what was laughingly called "the morning," and they'd had to park across the street in an all-night lot. "If you want to add on my brother Timmy's funeral, and the mortuary," Grady told Bud as they were hurrying over to the night-shrouded jail, "nothing's left but a summons to some courtroom to make my ecstasy complete!"

"At least Ernie looks as if he'll live," Bud said breathlessly, ducking under Grady's braced arm while he held the door wide for her. She was still unnaturally pale, and Calhoun knew it was more because of horror over what had happened then due to the late winter chill. "Whatever can have possessed her?"

He held her hand as they approached an expressionless, exhausted-looking officer behind the information desk. "We'll ask," Grady told Bud, privately wondering if it was possible that Susan had literally been possessed.

Despite the circumstances, the sisters fled into each other's arms after the red tape was snipped and Susan was permitted to see them with a male guard posted at the door to the room. Almost immediately, however, Susan broke the embrace and whispered one word like the wail of distant wind: "Ernie . . . ?"

"Multiple contusions," Bud said forthrightly, almost in her *Evening News* voice. But she reached out to grasp Susan's hand. "Definitely a concussion. But he'll pull through—and there's no need for surgery at this point."

Calhoun, too uncomfortable to sit at the pocked, wooden table with the sisters, locked his hands behind his back and beneath his topcoat and frowned. The doctor in emergency at Methodist had been even more candid, knowing that Bud was not the mother—and knowing who had actually inflicted the blows. "Touch and go," he'd announced, "whether the boy's suffered any permanent brain damage." Grady studied Bud's sister closely for the first time; it wasn't enough, now, to regard Susan as simply overprotective or neurotic. The apparent fact was that he was contemplating the face of a mother who'd tried—for no reason whatever—to beat her infant son to death.

But he found it impossible to recognize the similarities of face and form between the two women, and the palpable horror in Susan Swagerty's flushed face, and ignore the possibility that this was—in ways he could not conceivably understand—Calvin Rajelis' work.

Before Susan had told them much of her story Wayne Sojourner was noisily barging into the room. Calhoun had phoned his friend from the hospital, begged him to investigate and to meet them in the women's wing of the jail. Grady couldn't have been less surprised to see the big man enter, or much more relieved. This was going to be hard for Bud.

"I've read the statement you gave the arresting officer," Sojourner told Susan without preamble. "We need to talk about that." Without ceremony, he lowered his bulk into a chair opposite the mother. "Unless you've planned all along to opt for temporary insanity."

"Easy, Wayne," Grady said softly. Now he did sit, trying to meet the Homicide lieutenant's gaze with his own, and failing. Sojourner's dark eyes were boring intimidatingly into Susan's. "I didn't get you out of bed at this hour to—"

"All I told you on the phone," Sojourner growled without breaking eye contact, "was that I'd try to get your friend's sister O-R'd, and to find the facts in the matter."

"Lieutenant," Bud put in, regaining a measure of her peremptory professional confidence, "exactly what is my sister charged with?"

"Child abuse," he said quickly, "but

it's merely a temporary charge. To hold her. That's why I think I can get her out of here in a few hours." This time he did look at Calhoun, then to Bud and back again. "Unless I believe this woman simply started trying to beat her baby to death in the street."

Unsaid was Sojourner's obvious intention to do nothing for Susan Swagerty if that kind of brutality was what he felt to be the truth.

"I h-hit him," Susan said in a tight voice that made Calhoun's back teeth ache; "I hit Ernie over, and over, and over. But he's all I h-have. What I told the other officer is true." Her voice broke, and she began to cry. Grady couldn't recall ever seeing a woman with such red eyes. "I can't *help* it if it sounds so ridiculous."

"Tell us, honey," Bud said, gently. She squeezed her sister's hand. "Tell us just what happened."

She did, haltingly, and Wayne Sojourner allowed her to say it all without interrupting. Occasionally, he scribbled in a notebook, shook his big head or nodded. Calhoun, who'd probably heard more lies and more improbable stories than the rest of them—even Sojourner—found himself believing what Susan said.

And when she told them how she'd looked up to see the "strange man" running away, covering enormous amounts of distance at each stride, and looked down to see that the beast had disappeared "and I r-realized I'd been striking my Ernie," he knew it was true and felt chills along his spine like dead fingers clutching it.

Sojourner grunted, snapped his notebook shut. "Same basic story," he admitted; "doesn't sound rehearsed though." He paused, let himself think out loud, and Grady knew he seldom permitted himself the luxury. Maybe Wayne was suggesting a line of defense. "It's not impossible, at twilight, that the dog got away while you were distracted by your neighbor running away."

"Oh, no," Susan answered promptly. "I'd have heard it—it was immense. And—it wasn't a dog."

"They did read you your rights, didn't they?" Sojourner muttered. But Grady could see he was impressed by Susan's naive candor, even while it destroyed the out Wayne had given her. The policeman wriggled his bulk into a more comfortable position and Calhoun saw for the first time how tired the man was. "If it wasn't a dog, Mrs. Swagerty—what *was* it?"

"A thing," Susan replied. "Something . . . monstrous." She shuddered, looked away. "I don't know what it was."

"Great," Bud Rocker said, and sighed. She'd covered too many trials as a newsperson not to know how hopeless this testimony would prove to be. How costly.

"The man." Calhoun and Sojourner said it simultaneously. Calhoun nodded to his friend to continue. "His face; his appearance." A tiny tick of a pause. "Was

he in his twenties; tall and thin; white? Did
he wear dark glasses?"

"Did you hear him speak?" Calhoun
added before Susan could reply. Boyish
and eager, he leaned across the table to
her. "Did he have a high, reedy sort of
voice?"

"Grady," Sojourner growled warn-
ingly.

"I didn't hear his voice," Susan said,
shaking her head, "but that doesn't sound
like his description." Helplessly, she
glanced at Bud, her look-alike wide eyes
begging for understanding. "It was all . . .
so . . . strange. Unreal, in a way; but I
thought it was the twilight." She tried
hard to remember. "I recall a huge mouth,
very wide. He—smiled. A lot. I believe he
went on smiling even after the . . . monstrosity . . . attacked my little boy."

Calhoun slumped back in his chair,
more disappointed than he'd imagined he
would be. Rajelis, apparently, wasn't
involved after all.

"One thing," Susan said in a small,
feathery voice. Looking straight at Wayne
Sojourner, she seemed to have grasped
the proportions of her problem for the first
time. "One piece of . . . well, evidence. I
guess."

"I think I know what it is," Wayne
murmured, nodding. "They took it along
with your purse and other things at the
desk."

"Yes, they did," Susan agreed. Her
anxious gaze took them all in. "You know I

don't own a dog, Buddy." She looked straight at Sojourner. "That terrible man left the leash behind."

"I didn't think you'd take that nutcase seriously."

Calhoun frowned back at his black friend, replaced his coffee cup in its saucer. "I don't like threats, pal. Especially not threats against everybody I care anything about."

"I didn't say we wouldn't locate him," Sojourner said. "You knew I'd try to trace him for you. But what you're suggesting— first, in your brother's case and now, in the Swagerty's woman's—well, it's pretty farfetched, man."

They'd gone to an all-night place in downtown Indianapolis to drink coffee and try to wake up. At last, the temperature was definitely rising and taking off the chill and, through the streaky windows of the out-of-the-way little restaurant, anemic filaments of light were struggling to produce another morning. It did not immediately occur to Calhoun that, if he was correct about Rajelis working his arcane magic only at dusk and dawn, those he loved might once again be under psychic attack. That very instant.

"It'd help," Sojourner continued, "if you had some kind of clue to explain the mind-reader's desire to *get* you. Sure; crazy's crazy, and even making threats like that on television is weird as crap. It doesn't begin to explain why he's after your honky ass or how the fuck—pardon, *Ms.* Rocker—he could be behind anything that's happened."

"Every now and then," Grady began, "I think I'm on the verge of making some kind of connection. Between Rajelis and me. But I'm positive I never met him before the night he appeared on my program."

"Find him," Bud said. The men turned to look curiously at her. "Find the bastard and ask him. *Make* him tell you."

Sojourner almost laughed. "I can't make that sumbitch tell me anything. Not 'til he breaks the law."

"Do you have to wait until someone else I love is murdered?" Calhoun demanded.

"Someone *else*?" Wayne repeated, eyes narrowing. "Is *murdered*?"

"Don't you see that Rajelis is fulfilling his threats, Wayne?" Calhoun pressed his slight advantage. "People close to me are being struck down—"

"You told me you didn't even *like* Susan Swagerty!" Sojourner exclaimed. He glanced at Bud, regretting the remark. "I'm sorry, but it's true."

"But he cares about *me*!" Bud retorted. "If there's any truth whatsoever to what Grady believes, Lieutenant, Rajelis is doing one hell of a lot more than even meets the eye. He's *testing* Calhoun, can't you see that? And *making* him care about people—more, anyway, than he has before. If anything happens to my sister, I'll be devastated—and so will Grady! I'm beginning to think that crazy bastard really does understand psychology, or even reads minds! And another thing."

Sojourner's black eyes blinked. He throttled an involuntary yawn. "And what would that be, *Ms.* Rocker?"

"If he can read minds—remember what my sister told you because I think she'd pass a polygraph test—maybe he can put things *in* them too!"

9

Still Monday. 6:59 A.M.

The dreams fell away from Tim with the discomfiting feeling of sheets being stripped down, and, even after the boy had reached a level of early wakefulness, it took awhile to realize that somebody was staring at him.

When he did—when he had realized that it was eyes on him, as incuriously assessing him as the unblinking eyes of a cat, even an insect—Tim Calhoun sat up with the sheets clutched demurely to his hairless chin.

"You," he said, identifying the un-announced visitor immediately, despite the fact that his upstairs bedroom was still steeped in shadow and only an aureole of light shone around his window shades. "What are you doing here so early in the morning?"

The visitor watched as the 14-year-old boy belatedly turned his head to squint at an alarm clock, pregnant with unsated and unreleased commotion on a bedside table. For an instant the visitor might have seemed paralyzed, or ataxic, so outwardly uncomprehending and loosely quiescent did he hold his own boyish body.

But Tim was accustomed to the queer behavior and posture of his new friend and was glad to chalk the boy's peculiarities up to his own presumably unsociable disposition—heretofore unsociable, since both youngsters seemed to sense that they had finally formed a close peer relationship.

"I'm glad you're here," Tim tried a second time, "but how'd you get in without waking Mom or the other kids?"

Still the second boy remained silent, even expressionless. Which was basically okay with Tim since he, himself, lacked the gift for gab of men such as his father. The new relationship he'd managed to make with his visitor was predicted more on mutual loneliness, or happenstance propinquity, than anything else anyway— apart from the impression young Tim sometimes had that his friend was exceptionally deep and held in his rather big head a wealth of untold secrets. He was special to Tim, that was all; he'd begun tagging after Tim a couple of days ago on the walk home from school. And he'd laughed an odd, nostril-twitching laugh when Tim had tried a joke.

But now the unexpected presence of somebody staring at him in his bedroom when it was scarcely dawn, without apparent intention of explaining why he'd come, was starting to get on Tim's nerves.

Which was when the visitor smiled that absolutely amazing open, ingenuous smile of his that seemed to begin as a straw-sized pucker and fan out until it was almost capable of eating the whole frigging house! It seemed . . . generous . . . to Tim Calhoun, that grin. Full of secrets as ever, but on the verge of revealing them. "*Lonely,*" the other boy said in that flat tone of voice that matched his customary absence of facial expression for giving away nothing. He did not appear to see anything incongruous about smiling while he was admitting that he was unhappy. "Felt *lonely.*"

"Yeah, well, okay," Tim said. He returned the smile but felt puzzled. "Except, how can you feel lonely if you're in bed sleeping?"

The visitor, who might have been a year or so older than Tim, went on smirking from ear to ear, went on sort of slumping on the edge of Tim's bed with no sign that his limbs had ever moved before or ever would again. He had these enormous basketball player hands that he dangled between his legs, not even clasped, and he went on looking incuriously at Tim. "Wasn't in bed," Billy said tonelessly. "Never . . . sleep."

"Never?" Tim laughed. At last, he dropped the bedsheets and scratched the center of his hairless, naked chest, and yawned. He had to take a whiz like mad but all he had on were his Jockey shorts and Billy'd awakened him from some kind of really hot dream. "Why not, Billy? You have insomnia or something, man?"

Billy stared back blankly, but something happened to his face, maybe his forehead, and it was as if he were running the term through memory cells that didn't access efficiently. He bobbed his big head finally, though, almost happily. "I think, yes," he agreed with the word. "In-*som*-nia."

"Right," Tim said. Which still didn't explain how Billy'd gotten into the house. But Tim thought he might let that one pass, anyway. There was no harm to what his new friend had done; it was just kind of strange. But Tim had known plenty of times when he might have behaved bizzarely if it would have made him feel a lot less different from his parents; particularly Dad. And now that he thought about it, neither of his folks would ever understand why he thought Billy was all right; fun in a way, and a good guy. He looked awkward when he walked, which was the way Tim imagined he looked himself, but Billy could run like somebody on the track team. He didn't appear to have a bunch of confidence, either, but there were funny little times when he gave Tim the impression that he was both strong as an ox and might be handy to have around if Hog Baker or Rosey Cross decided to make a move on him again. And Billy obviously hadn't gotten up his nerve yet, either, to ask a girl for a date.

All of which was why Tim had avoided introducing Billy to either Dad or Mom. What the shit, you didn't select your friends for how swift they were mentally or just because they always did the same things the same way everybody else did!

"I wanta take a piss and a fast shower," he told Billy, reluctantly putting both legs the edge of the bed. But Billy didn't budge and his big, immobile leg was touching Tim's. "You wanta wait downstairs for me?"

The wheels, again, were chugging around slowly in the other boy's brain, Tim could tell that. He thought for a minute he could damn near see them work if the sunlight was just right. Except he didn't remember ever quite seeing Billy in anything but shadows, sort of, just like this. "A shower," he said slowly, "that's like a bath. Right?"

"Right." Tim just succeeded in keeping himself from grinning.

"Can I take a fast shower?" Billy inquired.

"No, man," Tim replied, frowning. He stood up, paused a moment to look down at his friend in confusion and mild annoyance. "You can take a shower at your place.''

Billy's big hand reached out, the fingers cluching, viselike, on Tim's wrist. The enormous mouth was hanging open, but it wasn't curled up at the corners. ''I want to . . . take . . . a shower,'' Billy said flatly, expressionless as always but obviously in a sudden, dark mood of the kind Tim had not witnessed before. The fingers tightened and the pain was shocking; intense. But then the grip relaxed and the corners of the mouth turned up as comprehension dawned. ''I can take one—at my place?'' Billy asked.

''What do I care?'' Tim snapped, pulling his wrist away and trying not to let the other youth see the tears of pain in his eyes. ''What the hell is the matter with you, Billy?''

For an instant there was no answer.

Then Billy raised his head, settled his unquestioning, hollow gaze on Tim's smarting eyes. ''Lonely,'' he said simply. He reached for Tim's hand and held it briefly, almost tenderly. There was no warmth to it, although it wasn't exactly cold. But there was no further pain administered, either, and what Billy'd said served as an apology. ''I'm . . . *alone*, Tim. And so lonely.''

Tim sighed. Then he slapped the other boy on the shoulder and turned toward the hallway and the short walk at the door, glanced back and saw Billy staring down at those large hands dangling motionless between his bony knees. ''You can wait here 'til I'm through. Then we can walk to school together."

And it occurred to Tim during his stroll to the bathroom that he couldn't recall ever seeing Billy in school or, actually, anywhere except to and from school. And now, of course, here in his own house. Hell, he didn't even know ol' Billy's last name!

Stripping off his soiled shorts and stepping into the tub, Tim thought he heard footsteps coming from his bedroom but wasn't certain. It might have been Mom or even Cathy, who often got up early to do a bunch of girl things before leaving for the day. Just for a second, when the overhead water hit his face and before it turned warm, Tim wondered how good an idea it was to leave his new pal alone with everyone else, for all he knew, still asleep. *Unguarded*, the word occurred to Tim.

But that was crap and so was the rest of it. Most little kids never remembered to ask their friends' names until they were 12 or 13 years old, because they didn't know there was more than one Alan or Bobby or Laura or Mary in the world unless they had a bro or sister by the same name.

When he padded barefoot back down the hall to his room, one of Mom's big guest towels wrapped around him because he'd forgotten to take fresh shorts with him to the bath, Tim was surprised to find no one at all waiting for him. The room was empty.

He was more surprised, and puzzled, when he checked downstairs to discover how Billy had gotten in and all the doors and windows were locked, and Mom had even remembered, last night, to switch on the burglar alarm.

Billy Whatever was neater and even cooler then Tim had known.

He was weirder too. . . .

He'd visited the recently finished Aquarium, Baltimore's impressive pride and joy, yesterday afternoon; late. Like any tourist, in a manner of speaking. To test himself. He did it only in part because he remained a young man and sometimes liked to let himself go in a particularly playful, exuberant fashion. The nightclub where he'd be appearing had provided him with a car and he'd decided to drive it down to the Inner Harbor mainly to find out if—despite Billy's ongoing exist-ence—he could regenerate his old skills. Those of a rare, psychic command that once had been in a constant, evolving state of improvement. Those which repre-sented his second, basic obligation to Mother. She had, after all, consecrated him mind, body and soul to the Forces, and Rajelis felt that he owed it to her living memory not to neglect the former.

At first, though, when Salvo had successfully been made manifest and that one reliable ally Calvin Rajelis would ever know—with beloved Mother gone for years—had come forth to do his bidding, he'd

been dismayed by a feeling of queer deple-
tion. Even when he had confronted Calhoun, that materialistic idiot, Rajelis had
sensed himself unequal even to those
fairly simple occult maneuvers he had
mastered many months before Seera's
strange suicide. And he'd wondered for a
while if the Forces of Suffering themselves
were sapped and enervated by the
acceptances of mortals who strove to
establish oneness with them. But of
course, there was a difference.

William Salvo had not voluntarily,
courageously, sought them, as Rajelis
had. Billy—that which was peculiarly and
specifically the William Salvo of that
incarnation—had been seized involuntarily by the Forces, in common with all the
ignorant and gutless fools who believed
they might perform deeds of evil without
paying *homage* to They who made such
luxuries possible. Not sought, and
accepted, like Mother; as he had been.

Still, Calvin had never been warned
that the connection between Billy's
incarnation and his own would render him
an adept little better than Seera herself
had been before her ultimate capitulation.
Rediscovering his special abilities, as a
vital complement to the knowledge
Mother had drilled into him, was more
than a matter of vanity.

Salvo had to be controlled and, when
Calhoun finally broke and, in taking his
own life, sent his spirit into the hands of
the Forces, Salvo would have to be

returned.

At the Aquarium, on a fairly typical March day in Baltimore—with the temperature seemingly grayed and swallowed by uneasy winds invisibly stirring well out on the Patatsco—attendance was down, and Rajelis was left largely to his own devices. He'd begun jogging back down a flight of stairs believing he had seen everything there was to see when, straight ahead of him, he saw the silent parade of sharks. It was an intentionally shocking surprise planned, obviously, for all Aquarium callers.

He'd never seen anything like them before, except in movies—several species of shark in a mammoth, curving tank arranged in such a way that they swept around a turn and, for one awesome instant, appeared to swim directly toward the visitor.

Rajelis was in love, immediately. There was something mystifyingly and sensually absorbing about the scene to him—no, more than *one* "something." There was the noiseless, timeless, sunless and enviable environment provided for the sleek creatures. The marrow-freezing menace of how they seemed virtually to materialize—and at just under eye level —then swim effortlessly past without leaving a ripple of water. It was as if they were encased in a mobile of clear plastic, and *it* turned. Their absence of sound and fuss was like the subversion, without warning and wholly unexplained, of a massive cancerous growth. But above all, it was simply the sharks themselves; the earnest, unchanging, implacable sharks: They were perfection. Rajelis broke out in sweat; there were just he and the dun and off-white and silver torpedos that ceaselessly circled, circled. His slim shoulders were bunched in order to put his long face with the unreflectable dark glasses nearer to them. His mind raced. All they really were, were eating machines. But their greed and their singlemindedness had made them one of the longest-living creatures—

And they appeared, most species, almost exactly the way they had looked well before man straightened his spine and shed his tail! Almost since time's dawning, sharks and roaches—as indestructible in their mass as . . . But Rajelis found no metaphor. His fascination now became total, his heart skipped a beat. He knew and adoringly responded to nature as he never had before. He even removed his dark glasses to study their approach unimpeded by anything except the protective glass itself; he pressed his perspiring palms against it like a boy gaping into a candy store window or a peeping Tom watching every private movement of a woman undressing. He was bound not to miss a moment. Transported, Rajelis imagined for one boyish second that he would never be able to tear himself away from a sight of such sublime perfection; and, when they appeared to recognize him, as they circled and returned to see him, again and again, to notice his admiring stance, he stared back into their utterly flat, unhuman eyes as if they might be the last monsters to have withheld their sweet, baneful secrets from him.

And he whispered hoarsely, involuntarily, "I love you." It was the first time he'd ever uttered the words. But unreciprocating, forever circling, the smug, sleek devils went again on their merry-go-round ride and Rajelis saw with rising envy that their evil was entire. It omitted malice, substituted routine and apathy for revenge, and hatred. They were purer. They were also, in many major respects, more humanlike.

Which meant they were just as willful, and knew nothing of They from whom the gift of evil flowed, and he tried at once to summon his powers of childhood, tried harder, then succeeded—succeeded in turning the sharks, first one and then two, three, many more; he used his resurgent, Seera-taught skills to make the sharks turn in the water in a frenzy of consternation never known before by their kind—turned them in direction and against nature, knowing what must occur.

Moments later, Rajelis had fled from the exhibit. It was not because he even remotely feared those men who ran, shouting, to save the sharks before they had torn all their number to savage scraps, but because he had suffered an orgasm. Because he'd never had one before, he believed for moments of elegant horror that he was hemmorhaging and washing his manhood away.

Then this morning, at dawn, he remembered the extraordinary experience with nearly as much febrile vivacity as he had enjoyed the actual moments. Only the photograph of quite a plain young woman with bangs distracted him from another climactic moment. Whether it was true, as he had read, that expended passion wasted the reserves of one's morale and blunted the shining focus of hatred—which he thought was surely true—he had frightened himself badly and was not quite ready for another involvement with such uncharted personal terror. But now that he knew he was again able to function as a magician, Calvin drew from his trunk the crystal ball that he carried with him everywhere and, regarding the young woman in the picture through slitted eyes, fondled the ball in both his restless, slender hands.

Rajelis did not expect an image to appear in it. What it was to him, most of the time, was a means of centering upon Seera. It was something of hers she had believed in and therefore something that was more closely a part of her than the bloody locks of her hair that he'd finally discarded many years after her suicide.

But when the image of the ordinary-looking girl with bangs swam into shape in the crystaline surface, Rajelis recognized it instantly as both an omen and a promise. The promise was the one Mother had made to be with him, always, when he needed her, to keep him centered upon his quintessential purpose; the omen was a restated prophesy that suffused his mind with her crooning voice: "What separates us from ordinary people is that we know Night is coming—the soul's Night; the Night of All Death. And our task—"

He chanted the rest with her, aloud, forgetting entirely his whereabouts in the old row house: "Our task is to teach the others dread. Not to warn them, but to make them feel dread just as some of the ordinary people have felt a promise. Dread of the Forces of Suffering." He opened his eyes and gasped.

Around his mother's beloved face, liquids geysered, ran, seemed to suggest the silently swimming sharks. Parts of his mind understood he had summoned her reflection, no more—an image Seera had left in the crystal ball by sweet virtue of those uncounted times when she had peered this deeply and deeper into its depths—magically summoned her stern, instructive features. But the sharks, whose presence with Mother's image Calvin could not explain, were now one shark, wide of mouth, big-bellied yet graceful, beauteous; and Calvin's new sexual excitement was nearly more than he could bear. Leaning over the ball and hugging it hungrily against his lower stomach, he wept but held back; he strove to focus upon Billy Salvo, his mindless, incomplete, dependable William who was tormenting the fool Calhoun even that instant through his eldest child. And the thought of the smaller children he meant to kill personally, before Calhoun's eyes, pushing the bully over the brink; and the fervor of his desire—the interwoven complexity of it—was almost overwhelming.

Then he glanced down at himself and at the crystal ball and saw the future for a fraction of one instant, a slice of time-to-be he had not ordained: another, older female face, distantly familiar, the eyes boring up at him in piercing accusation. Outrage! She'd *replaced Mother* in the crystal ball! Seera and the lubricious, regal shark had been replaced by *another* woman!

Rajelis hurled the glass globe back into the trunk and scrambled to his feet. Even before the sound of shattering could reach him he was ripping open the door of the rented row house front closet and lurching out, lividly, into the unfurnished room.

All his passions had fled save for that obligatory one that he reserved for those closest to Grady Calhoun and, ultimately, Grady Calhoun himself.

But his out-of-balance inner eye retained the image of the sharks and, a few miles away on the Inner Harbor, an unbreakable aquarium tank crashed to pieces and the great fish within it were expelled into the terrified faces of the high-school children who had come to see them.

BOOK II

"(Day) lendeth light To see *all things* . . ."

—*Edmund Spenser*

10

Friday. April 1.

Calhoun began the last day of his work week by awakening from a nightmare in the psychic nick of time, so tense that he knew damned well he was constipated again even before he'd found his way to the bathroom.

This was scheduled to be one busy day—capped by his *Confab* program that night—and Grady loathed above everything beginning his Fridays as an anal repressive. At some point during every *Confab* show's phone-in segment, some turkey was bound to call and, one way or the other, intimate that Grady Calhoun was full of shit. This simply infuriated him because he knew, deep down inside—*very* deep—that they were right.

By now, Grady'd tried every remedy known to man short of surgery to conquer his long-standing miseries, neither with success nor conspicuous relief. Much of the problem he could trace to the way that Mom had been one of those mothers— they were a legion—who regarded the regularity of little boy bowel movements as a test of theological faith; a religious obligation. She'd marked-out his "duty" plainly: he was to "grunt" every morning before breakfast (which he detested, but which served as a sort of grace period). When he had become a self-convicted

140

failure and it was time to leave for school, Mom had promptly dosed him with Milk of Magnesia.

But that wasn't the end of it. Since she'd striven to conceal the chalky stuff in a variety of juices—to make drinking it relatively palatable—Grady'd grown up hating fruit too. Worse, infinitely worse, his mother had taught him as well the meaning of terror: whenever Calhoun had not "gone" by the time she picked him up at school in the afternoon, his mother had made him lie on carefully arranged news-papers while she loomed behind him, hot water bottle raised high like Liberty's lamp. Enema time.

Last night, anticipating just such a sin of omission as he was confronted with this morning, Calhoun had swallowed two heaping tablespoons of bran, washing them down as quickly as he could with nose-wrinkling gulps of that liquid that he detested more than all the others: prune juice. Grady recalled a distant time when his deceased father had chuckled about the nemesis of a cartoon detective named Dick Tracy and a villain called Pruneface. Grady had avoided Pruneface's appear-ances as the plague; no criminal, he'd believed, could be more frightening than *that*.

Now, tugging up his trousers and staring disconsolately into a toilet bowl that definitely lacked bulk, he wished he'd gone ahead and taken a laxative the night before—any of the eight or nine varieties of pills and liquids crowding his medicine cabinet to overflowing. Citrate of magnesia would probably have been most speedily efficacious but, if you swallowed too much, you ended up feeling that your large intestine, left lung, and adam's apple would be leaving next. On his citrate days, Calhoun had little left for his really tough *Confab* guests.

He'd always been one of the talk show hosts who prided himself on "doing his homework," on really boning-up for "in-depth" conversation with his guests. That meant doing what he called "reading" the book or other literature supplied to him ahead of time by the guests' advance men.

Since Grady hated to read, he'd laboriously conceived a method for deducing and highlighting the major points of any book: With pencil and notepad at the ready, hunched studiously over his dining room table, Calhoun skimmed the publication and watched for anything in italics, or anything ending in an exclamation mark. He would pause to read this emphasized material, lips moving while he sounded out the words, then attempt to frame a cogent question— sometimes a challenging one, preferably emotion laden or bearing satirical overtones—which he jotted down on the notepad. The rest of his prep-time was spent in literally studying every word that the publisher had said about the guest anywhere and everywhere on the dust jacket or covers of the book. If the guy, or gal, had some kind of public record—a sports personality, for example—Grady would phone Gill Riffey and ask him to round up some statistics.

His system had enabled Grady Calhoun to boast, more than a single time, that he was "the best read talk show host this side of Cavett."

When the show was over, he'd either save the book for Tim, his son, or give it away to the library—a thoughtful gesture that seemed to enhance both his reputation as a nice guy, and a philanthropist.

It also kept him from cluttering up his built-in bookshelves with books, and left plenty of space for the television set and VCR that really belonged there.

By eleven o'clock, Calhoun had grinned and quipped his way through an interview with one of the community-serving local magazines and taped several promos for next Friday's show—mentally thanking Jim Gerard, a former, long-time local talk show host for having taught him how to do each five- or ten-second promo in a single take. Not that Gerard knew Calhoun had been his pupil; it was a case in TV, nationally or locally, of all your work being right up on the screen for instant cannibalization, and Grady was no more guilty of "learning" from his predecessors than anybody else in the thriving business.

He approached his own office at a quarter to twelve, outwardly a blithe and relaxed spirit who wrung the hands of a couple of sponsors who'd stopped by and paused to kiss the prettier of the two receptionists. None of them minded, Calhoun felt, when he bussed them or patted their adorable fannies; they were surely professional enough to understand that the man in front of the cameras had a right to crank himself up any way he could before air time. Everybody at an outlet benefited if the star did well.

Or so Calhoun had always believed until he was stopped by Andy Sutor, the program manager, before he could get into his office and check out the fan mail. In a way, it was his own fault that he ran into a downer because he made the mistake of asking the darkly handsome Sutor how things were.

"Things," said Sutor, sonorously, "are not good, sirrah. Not good at all." A perfect brow raised. "One might almost say that they are odiferous—in short, that they stink."

"Surely you jest, oh-great-white-poobah-of-the-ratings-watch," Grady replied in kind. But his heart sank. The last thing he needed on a day when he couldn't crap was news that his numbers were down.

"Here." Andy handed him the cup of coffee he'd just poured for himself. "I daren't drink this with my belly roiling the way it is already today. The numbers, Calhoun, the numbers." He rolled his large brown eyes, and if it hadn't been for the fact that his custom-tailored suit made him look eminently successful, Calhoun might have imagined him indigent. "A shocking, positively *shock*ing decline in the overalls."

A twitch began in one of Grady's eyes. "How do you account for it?" The question was salient; it was Andy's job, precisely, to account for any slippage of the local numbers.

Sutor sighed. "Primarily, it's the six o'clock news." His thumb turned downward, and jabbed. "Plummeting, Grade-A." Andy's expression became ruminative. "Who knows? Perhaps the feminist trend is leveling off."

"Feminist trend?" Grady asked, afraid that he knew the answer to his next question. "What does women's lib have to do with it?"

"Maybe nothing. Maybe everything." A shrug. "It was never what anyone could call *natural* for the gentler sex to man the anchor; contradiction in terms, correcto?"

Grandy sipped his coffee, began to worry about Bud Rocker. "I don't know about *that.* Women—"

"Are born to do weekend weather," Sutor finished, emphatically bobbing his head. "And if they're real foxes, maybe they're qualified to do it every day."

"I hope," Calhoun began slowly, "you aren't going to do anything . . . um . . . impetuous." He rested the coffee cup on the nearest water cooler and saw the dregs in it slosh. "It wouldn't be your style, Andrew—correcto?"

Andy gave him a disarming business smile and a clap on the shoulder. "Absolutely not! But I might try a change in the lady anchor herself. Up in Noblesville, there's a truly cute little chick named Grace Sweet. Been doing a controversial late-late show called *Grace Under Pressure*."

A late-late show? A controversial *talk* show? Calhoun paled. "Ah, Andrew . . . the *Confab* numbers. Holding up?"

Sutor put out his impeccably tailored arms to bring Calhoun close and kissed his cheek. "You, sirrah, are our bright spot! The numbers have never been better, Grady! Even that program you fretted about, after your brother died—solid ratings! Without you and *Confab*, old friend, our Carsonogenic condition would be spelled the old way!"

Calhoun watched him bustle away, thinking ruefully: *Without me—thanks to that fucking mentalist—our overalls would be soaring!*

"There are *other* ways to have sex."

"And most of them are either acrobatic or immoral," Judith said, not even turning her head to glance down at Tom, her husband.

"You didn't seem to think so," he called as she hurried into the bathroom, "before we got married."

"Just what is that supposed to mean?" she asked. He might have believed they were finally going to talk it out, but Judith had closed the door and the director was pretty sure he'd heard her lock it. "That I trapped you into marriage?"

"No," he said, sighing, talking more to himself than to his very pregnant wife, "but it's turned into a trap somehow."

"What was that crack?"

Simincola stood, hoping that would encourage his erection to diminish. These days, with the baby's arrival practically imminent, his penis seemed to be on 24-hour alert.

But he was clinging to the fact that he wanted this child at least as much as Judith did, and he knew, whenever he could make his passion subside and approach the situation in his usual kind, wryly witty way, why Judith refused to take any chances at all: This was definitely their last try at having a baby. Doctor Barber'd made it quite clear that all Judith's failed pregnancies had taken a heavy toll, and, at her age, she had no business trying again.

When she came out of the bathroom the tip of her small nose red from crying—always in that private, no-fuss way she had—Tom was standing behind the door. He wrapped his impossibly long arms around her—God, why had she ever decided to marry a lug who looked ten-feet tall when she was no bigger than a minute!—and gently hugged her.

"Hey!" he said into her ear. "I love you."

"Same here," she said softly. It wasn't a lot, but she didn't struggle to get away.

"Sorry I seem so persistent, Jude," he told her, huskily. "Somehow ol' Norbert lacks the spirit of romance."

Judith reached behind her to pat Norbert, very briefly. She twisted in his arms to kiss his chin, the best she could manage when they were standing. "That's just about all ol' Norbert lacks, Tom—if that means anything to you. It's not your fault. It's just nature."

Tom Simincola wished with every fiber of his long body that she'd put her hand back on Norbert and, at the same time, that she'd move to an arm's length away from him. "I know," he groaned. "It's nature's fault all the way."

"Ernie's feeling much better," Bud said as she slid into the booth with Calhoun and Wayne Sojourner. "But Susan." She shook her head. "I wonder if she'll ever forgive herself."

"I can understand that," the lieutenant remarked drily.

"You wouldn't," Grady snapped, "if you could imagine even for ten minutes that Susan told you the truth. That she thought she was protecting Ernie from some sort of half-dog, half-monster."

"Kiss me."

Grady turned his head and found Bud's uptilted to his, lips slightly parted. "Right here in front of God and all these people in Grimelda's?"

"I don't know if I can cope with this," Wayne said, smiling; but Bud nodded and Grady obliged. "You white folks sure are exhibitionists."

"You black folks," Grady retorted, "have forgotten how to have any fun."

Sojourner's squeaky voice chortled. It sounded like a small puppy yapping. "Wish you'd all get your stories about us straight. Are we oversexed or not?"

Bud, who had enough black blood to have qualified her for membership in the race when the Klan was at its grotesque peak, winked at Wayne and patted his cheek. "You and I know," she said with an impish glance at Calhoun, "that being oversexed is an impossibility."

Grady grinned at her but privately thought how wan Bud appeared. Any doubt he had about the effect of her sister's tragedy on Bud had long since fled. What Sojourner apparently couldn't buy was the quantity of guilt Calhoun himself was experiencing. He'd considered warning her about the idiotic ideas Andy Sutor was mulling over but thought better of it. Bud couldn't take much more right now.

So he told her and Wayne about Jean and his ex-wife's fear that Tim might be a homosexual in the making.

"Jean wouldn't recognize a gay person if he announced it to her!" Bud flared. "But if Tim is gay—not that I believe it for a moment—it's not the end of the world. You do know that, don't you,

Calhoun?"

"Lord," Sojourner sighed, shaking his head, "they're off and running again!"

"No, Wayne," Grady said quietly, slowly, pursing his lips and looking very serious. "We're not going to fight over this. Bud simply doesn't understand that a father has certain *expectations* from his son." He swiveled his head to look at Bud from beneath raised brows. "Most of us dads, somehow, never have the good sense to lay aside money for our boys to attend beauty school. That's all." He shrugged. "Pure shortsightedness on our part."

"Gays can do anything straights do!" Bud exclaimed.

"Right," Calhoun agreed, nodding. "It's *how* they do it that bothers me a bit. In pro basketball, for example, most fans might find it a little funny when the players started calling time-out for broken fingernails." Then he laughed ruefully and, before she could respond, covered her mouth with his. "I don't think Tim's ready for marceled hair anyway. This is Rajelis' work too."

"That's really reaching for it, Calhoun," Sojourner muttered. He shook his head and returned his attention to a huge cheeseburger.

"Maybe," Grady said. "But the timing is right. The time of day, that is." And he explained to them what he'd remembered about Calvin Rajelis's exact threat, about suffering being inflicted upon Calhoun's loved ones by light, not darkness.

"I just remembered," Bud said, looking shocked. "The night of that show—when the psychic was your special guest? On the evening news, I reported a solar eclipse!"

"On March eighteenth?" Calhoun asked. "An eclipse?"

"Hell, you know what it means astronomically," Wayne put in, hastily swallowing a big bite of his sandwich. "Even school kids know that."

Grady's gaze narrowed as he studied Bud's animated face. "I think what she really means, Wayne," he murmured, "is *astrologically*. Ms. Realism-of-the-Year wonders what was happening that night from an *astrological* standpoint!"

'You're missing the point!" Bud snapped, angry. She pushed back a salad she'd only been toying with. "What I believe has nothing to do with it. But Calvin Rajelis is a weirdo, right? Isn't it possible to surmise he might put a lot of stock in the stars and all that crap?"

"You're right!" Calhoun exclaimed, looking flushed.

"And there was an astrologer on that *Confab* show with you and the minister, and the tiny numerologist and Rajelis, remember?" Bud was just as excited as Grady now. "I think you ought to contact her, Calhoun. See what she can tell you about it."

"I don't even remember her name," he replied. "But I can sure as hell pull the

tape and find out!" He looked at Wayne
Sojourner and sounded nearly apologetic
when he spoke. "I guess this is pretty
ridiculous from your standpoint, big
fella."

"Not," Sojourner said thoughtfully,
"not quite as ridiculous as it seemed to me
before."

"You've checked something out,
haven't you, Wayne?" Bud demanded.
"You've *found* something!"

The officer raised his wide, pale
palms. "Nothing for the six o'clock news,
Ms. Rocker. Something."

"Well, tell us, man!" Grady insisted.

Sojourner finished his glass of ice
water first. Then he planted his hands on
the edge of the table and leaned forward
toward his friends, lowering his voice. "My
men found some prints on those papers—
that company literature—your brother
had in his possession when the truck ran
over him. Two sets of prints in addition to
his own. One set belonged to Max Levin,
and Levin turned out to be the man who
interviewed Timmy for a job."

"Who do the other prints belong to?"
Calhoun asked at once.

Wayne shrugged. "We don't know," he
answered, and the others groaned. "So
far, the trace hasn't turned up anything.
I'm not saying your brother was murdered;
I'm not ready to go that far, Calhoun. But
I'm a thorough son of a bitch." He tapped
his empty water glass with a shiny big
nail. "And we do know where Rajelis is

now."

"Wonderful!" Bud said, her widely spaced eyes widening. "Where?"

"He's in Baltimore for a performance." Again he lofted a large hand to stay their questions. "I'm hoping to get the cooperation of the local authorities in detaining him, just long enough to ask a few questions for us." Wayne smiled cunningly. "Maybe get them to supply a little subtle pressure; nothing strong-arm, of course."

"I wish you'd haul the bastard's ass back to Indy!" Calhoun exploded. His out-flung hand knocked a knife from the table and he didn't even see it fall. "There must be some legal way to manage that."

"There must not be," Sojourner said calmly. But Calhoun had never heard the policeman sound firmer, more decided. "I want no part of a legal system that permits our citizens to be 'hauled' all over the frigging country without sufficient evidence." Then Wayne's expression softened and he touched the sleeve of Calhoun's sports jacket. "But you didn't let me finish about the fingerprints."

"I'm sorry," Grady acknowledged, hopeful again. "You mean the ones you guys couldn't identify?"

"I do," Sojourner nodded. He paused, stood, carefully stretched his long frame in the controlled fashion of a big man who has learned that carelessness leads to breakage. "You see, we found another set of prints on that dog leash your sister kept, Ms. Rocker.''

"Go on," Bud and Grady said simultaneously.

"They match the prints on the literature Timmy Calhoun had in his possession when the truck hit him.''

11

Saturday. April 2.

April Fool's Day had passed surprisingly free of further unfunny jokes. As a matter of fact, Calhoun's show that night had been almost flawlessly produced and directed, his guest stars alternately informative and wittily profound—and Grady knew that he himself had rarely been in better form. Ten minutes after they were off the air, he'd even celebrated with a dump in the closest men's room that made him consider getting in touch with the Guinness people.

It's the damndest thing, he thought, souring on his drive home that night as other facts sunk in. *I'm the one who's under attack—unless I'm as neurotic as Bud doubtlessly still believes I am, secretly—but* nothing bad *happens to me!*

It was like reaching up from the *Titanic* to catch a ride in a whirlybird with room for one, and everybody you'd ever given a damn for was interrupting "Nearer, My God to Thee" to wave a brave farewell!

By the time Grady was under the sheets he was wide awake, deeply troubled, trying to get it through his head that anyone he'd ever so much as liked might be in terrible danger, and wondering who'd be the next.

He found out the next morning.

April Fool's Day seemed to have been celebrated later, back east. A doctor he'd never heard of dropped a bomb on Calhoun before he'd even climbed out of bed. "I fear she has . . . slipped . . . Mr. Calhoun. Slipped rather badly, and rather fast."

He didn't have to ask who. But he dealt with it the best he could and worked at brushing away the mental cobwebs. "What in Christ's name does that mean exactly, Doc?" Grady's best, at 7:30 in the morning, had never been anything to boast about. "It makes it sound as if Mom stepped in a tub of fucking bear grease!"

"Her mind, Mr. Calhoun." The doctor talking in his ear was a patient sort, apparently, and Grady knew at once that he despised the bastard. "Your mother has slipped—*mentally.*"

"But that sounds impossible, Doctor. Not that I'm calling anybody a liar," Grady added hastily. He twisted Cigarette One into his mouth and then saw his lighter, with his change, on a dresser beyond arm's reach. *Concentrate, Calhoun!*

Because he'd seen her just a short while ago, when she flew in for Timmy's funeral. And sure, she'd lost her eldest son unexpectedly—but Mom was made of sterner stuff. Stuff like pieces of flint, and granite, and old shell casings. Calhoun clutched the phone, hard, with both hands. "Who says she's slipped, Doc? There somebody out there trying to make a fast buck maybe?"

"Episodes, sir." The physician—what the hell had he said his name was?—was being incredibly earnest, and tolerant. Probably he handled a dozen old ladies coming apart every week, but this wasn't *any* old lady. "She's having—episodes."

"In my business, 'episodes' are shows that are part of a series, Doctor. Can you be a bit more explicit?"

"First of all, let me make it clear, Mr. Calhoun, that your mother is not exactly irrational. Or not frequently so."

She showed no signs of deterioration of any kind while she was in Indy, Calhoun thought, his mind churning furiously. *Zero slippage, episodes zilch.* "Doctor, you want to tell me what it is she's doing? I mean, Mom's always been a character, if it comes down to that. She's—"

"She is depressed, sir. Acutely depressed." The other man, who sounded like a goddam teenager to Grady, was getting more patient and tolerant by the moment. More patient, tolerant, *and* serious. "Mr. Calhoun, I'll put it to you frankly so you may grasp the significance of my call: I have never seen a woman who gave such an impression of . . . well, of terrible suffering."

Grady put the receiver out where he could look at it and didn't see it because he'd shut his eyes, instead.

It was the choice of terms that did it. "I am a psychiatrist, Mr. Calhoun." Great; swell, that was cool. A psychiatrist with acne and a hatred for independent old ladies. *Terrible suffering* . . . "I have tried to discover what, precisely, troubles your mother; to learn her symptoms."

"And what have you discovered, Doctor?" Grady inquired. He still hadn't opened his eyes and they felt wet to him.

"She seems to be . . . ah . . . imagining a stranger who is bothering her."

"Isn't that a possibility?" Calhoun snapped. "There are lowlife SOBs who like to hit on old ladies, aren't there?"

"There are. But your mother has been under exceedingly frequent and close observation, sir. And there has been no 'stranger' near her—particularly not of the sort she, ah, perceives."

"And what sort of stranger is that, Doctor?" Calhoun inquired.

"A peculiarly ordinary-looking man with a menacing manner," the doctor said promptly, "and an enormously wide mouth." Now Calhoun opened his eyes and they stared into the gloom of his early-morning waking nightmare. "Your mother believes he is the harbinger of death."

Bud came when Grady called for her.

She fixed breakfast for him; nothing remotely of the kind his mother had insisted he eat. There was no fruit juice in sight, Bud left his Milk of Magnesia and his hot water bottle where he'd put them, and Bud felt a measure of relief when he began to pop bites of his pork chop into his mouth. He'd longed for a farm-style breakfast for years; Bud had remembered.

But he went on talking around each bite. "It's my fault, you know." His eyes were very bright. "Because of some god-damned thing I did to that skinny psycho at *some* point in his life." He batted his eyes several times and they looked moist again with unshed tears. "Or because I haven't knocked myself off yet."

"I know how you feel," Bud said sympathetically, wondering how Calhoun could eat like that. And why he wasn't hog fat. She sipped a glass of orange juice and surreptitiously peeked at her watch. "But there's still no proof. And how can Rajelis possibly be in so many places at the same time?"

"How do I know?" Grady said, pouring catsup on his eggs and fried potatoes. "Maybe he has these huge, black wings; maybe he's a vampire! Hell, Buddy, I'm ready to believe just about anything."

Bud smiled. "That's nothing new."

"Whatever the mechanics are, see, I've become some kind of goddam *jinx*—isn't that obvious, even to somebody pragmatic like you?" He half-dropped a half-tossed his fork onto the plate. How could he be *eating* like this? Why hadn't he finished dressing before Bud got there? He felt like a fool in pajama shirt and jeans! "I don't recall ever seriously considering suicide before, but maybe it's time I began fucking thinking about it!"

"Grady . . . *don't*," she breathed. Anchorpeople kept up and Bud had read, more than one time, that people who spoke of killing themselves were more likely to attempt it than any other kind. Except for those who had already tried and failed. "Or I'll have to believe I made a mistake in even going as far as I have in agreeing with you. Look, Grade-A; it's impossible for you to judge how much of this is sheer coincidence; you're too *close*."

He froze, his gaze locked to hers; melded. He had seen something minimally askew about her when she arrived, something out of place—

Abruptly, he shot out his arm, snatched up her purse. One he knew she hated and regretted buying, because it looked capacious enough to put Tom Simincola and his pregnant wife up for the weekend. Without asking permission, he opened the purse, jabbed his meaty hand inside.

"What's this?" he asked softly, holding his find in the air.

"I believe," Bud replied, just as quietly and evenly, "it's a pistol."

"And you're just like Jean!" Calhoun roared. "You can't *stand* weapons!"

"Calhoun—"

"Don't 'Calhoun' me, lady!" he snapped, brandishing the pistol. "And don't tell me you haven't bought my story, lock, stock, and bogeyman!"

Bud grabbed it away from him, then her purse, and crammed the handgun into its recesses. Her coffee-colored skin looked flushed. She'd never seemed prettier to him. "I hate your bloody guts when you play grand inquisitor with me, Calhoun!" She paused, trying to control her emotions. "All right, maybe I do agree with a lot of what you fear. Maybe it's asking a lot of coincidence for so many people you love to begin coming unglued at one time."

"Unglued?" he howled. "Is that what you call Timmy dying—little Ernie having the crap beaten out of him by a woman who adores him? An old lady who could double for the Rock of Gibraltar in those insurance commercials who has her doctor ready to poke her away in the nearest funhouse?"

Calhoun leaped to his feet, turning his back on Bud because he was starting to cry again. "How many days, do you suppose are left of the 45 Calvin Rajelis 'gave' me?"

"Grady, please don't—"

"Do you think he'd get pissy if I just did it *now*? Before he decides to ruin all my kids"—Calhoun paused, turned back to her even though the tears were sliding down his cheeks now—"or you?"

"But that," Bud began soberly, confidently, "is why I have the weapon. I'll be on guard. And now we have reason to believe Rajelis has hired some kind of hit-man—right? A plain-looking person except for a very wide mouth, remember what the doctor said?" She arose and went to him, put her arms around his silly p-j-clad waist, and hugged, hard. "That's something to go on, Calhoun. We'll see him coming!"

Part of his torment, his frenzy, sub-sided and Grady shuddered against her.

But peering blankly over the top of her head, he asked in a whisper, "What earthly value is there in the days I have left—before the month and a half are gone—if all I can do is stand by and watch all of you suffer, or worse? And what in God's name is going to be 1-left to me after those 45 days pass . . . if all of you have passed too?"

12

Thursday. April 7.

Jean had been aware for quite some time that she had to get out of the house again. Occasionally, at least. With a man, if possible. In a way, if she stayed house-bound, it was dishonoring both the marriage that had died and the divorce that killed it. Because one of the con-tributing factors to her ultimate decision to divorce Grady had been the way he was content to spend all his leisure time at home, never wanting to go anywhere—

Aside from, of course, the long hours and frequent evenings he had spent at Grimelda's with Tom Simincola and his other cohorts.

She'd taken some flak and more than a few pointed stares or periods of silent criticism because she'd finally reached the decision to leave Grady Calhoun. And Jean understood the reasoning behind all that, even agreed to it; most of it, anyway. Never once had she seriously questioned Calhoun's loyalty to her; he was an unrecalcitrant looker, a butt-patter and sneak kisser of anything female and reasonably attractive, but he'd never given Jean reason to believe he was stepping out on her. And despite some hard times early in their marriage, along with the fact that financial security for a local TV personality's wife was only strong for the first few hours after he had signed a new contract, he'd always provided for her and the children.

But the truth of the matter was that, once Jean had made up her mind that they must part, she'd wondered why it had taken her so long to decide. And the only answer to that was simply that she'd had no communicably understandable reason for wanting out.

Except boredom. Some people, some *wives*, understood boredom as reason enough. More, Jean suspected, than were willing to admit it. A woman could, after all, be neglected in more ways than met the public's eye, and public personalities —whether they were celebrities with a capital C or those like fun-loving, lovable, always well-meaning Grady Calhoun— were champions of inadvertent neglect; *inconsiderate* neglect.

She had worked very hard at understanding Grady, so hard that it wasn't until she'd succeeded that she realized she'd never been understood by him— and, worse, that her understanding of Grady made her like him less.

Celebrities received so much attention and approbation, were so often greeted by total strangers wherever they went, and so able to use their renown to get the little things they wanted, that they lost sight of the fact that most people— most *wives*, especially those without careers—were going to be warmly greeted only by their loved ones. And a child's instinctive, casual affection was fine— wonderful—but it was nice if the celebrity mate, presumably adult, sometimes noticed you. There was also the fact that the adoring public never had to see the celebrity when he didn't shave or even bathe for days, because his last show hadn't gone well and he was sulking; when he chose to sleep 'til all hours and expected you to keep small children quiet as a tomb. Or when he snapped at you because you weren't the kind who could use sex as an instant ego-booster; weren't

as quick-witted or empathetic as he'd
trained himself to be, and couldn't read
his mind or, if you *could,* be gifted enough
as an amateur psychologist to speak the
exact, consoling words that he had written
in his own mind for you to utter.

In the end, seeking the divorce had
meant to Jean that she would have to be
the villain in the piece to everyone who
knew them and the wider public that did
not. That knowledge alone had kept her
silent, kept her putting up with a man
she'd always love but could no longer like,
or enjoy, for several tense and lonely
months.

When somebody finally asked her out
on a date then, it felt right—seemed vital,
even *essential*—and she gave little or no
thought to whether she even liked the
man who was interested in her. The fact
that he was, that she could spend much of
the morning and part of the afternoon
being *herself* instead of Grady's wife or
Timandcathyanddavidandpetey's Mom,
seemed sufficient.

But there was also the kind of date—a
brunch—that he proposed that appealed
to her. A nighttime date would have
seemed . . . imposing; rather more than
she wanted, as a return to the dating wars.
Dates at night—by dark—carried with
them certain inescapable connotations
for a mature, formerly married woman
who could no longer wave the flag of
virginity as a reason for resisting sexual
pressure. While the notion of sleeping with

another man than Grady Calhoun was one Jean didn't relish—and *why* she didn't was a nerve-jangling and bewildering multitude—it was actually less bothersome to imagine than the whole picture of sitting in a car trying to reason with the man, or, worse, fend him off. At this point in Jean's life, the sexual act itself was almost devoid of appeal; the notion of carrying on an intense debate with a virtual stranger over an issue that had always seemed ultimately intimate to Jean was tawdry, enormously agitating, and finally depressing.

They had met at the grocery a matter of days ago, and he'd told her he was a widower. There was something about the hesitant way he'd spoken, simultaneously shy and oddly practiced, and something about the way he appeared to have absolutely none of Calhoun's verbal cleverness, that had drawn her to him. True; before she left the house that Thursday morning she was unable even to remember his features and the moment when she had agreed to the date was peculiarly unclear; hazy. If Bill had displayed the slightest sign of being a smooth talker, Jean might have concluded that he'd virtually mesmerized her and she might have broken the date.

Instead, she chalked it up to her entirely natural nervousness and ran out to the car waiting at the curb with the alacrity of a teenager.

Within a block or two, her concern

about whether she looked nice—she'd taken simply *hours* to get ready for the date—had been replaced by concern for their safety. The man at the wheel drove with a dogged fixity upon the street that belied the way his car meandered down the yellow center stripe and once or twice veered perilously close to the curb and pedestrians. Worse, during brunch itself— by queer coincidence he'd selected Grimelda's, the same place Grady had always liked—Bill's minimal conversational skills sharply deteriorated. Picking at his food, he spent most of his time casting glances around the restaurant, rather as if he was expecting to see someone he knew. And, the instant she had finished eating and was trying again to make polite conversation, he was on his feet, throwing down a $50 bill and groping for her elbow, rushing her immediately out of the place. He didn't even wait for change, and, by the time they were driving back toward her house, Jean knew two things without question: She hadn't acquired another scrap of information about her first date in nearly two decades, and she didn't care if she never did, because she wouldn't be going out with him again.

No, make that three things, Jean thought when they'd almost miraculously drawn within a block of home. *The third is that I don't like him.*

There was a fourth, as well, but she strove to ignore it, to pretend that she hadn't really felt the thought take shape in her mind: that she found this man who was doggedly aiming his poor vehicle toward her place in such a herky-jerky fashion that she knew he'd eventually wreck the car's transmission the creepiest, most unattractive human being she'd ever met. It wasn't his features, really, although she had become truly conscious during their meal of his wide-spread, almost predatory mouth and atrociously sallow complexion; and it wasn't the way he seemed to strain to answer even her simplest remarks. She had thought him timid, even lonely, and while he might well be those things, they were entirely secondary to his overall personality.

He didn't have one.

That was silly, of course; she knew that even while she moved as far away from him in the front seat as she could get, dimly aware that she was getting almost hysterically eager to be behind locked doors. *Everyone* had a personality; it was part of being human, part of being alive. . . .

"Now," he said, and hit the brakes. The automobile stopped with a screech, throwing Jean off balance. She barely got her hands up in front of her face in time. What did he mean by "now"? The deeply felt, apparently unreasoning sense of hysteria brushed against her conscious mind like cobwebs in a dark cellar. But it was broad daylight *I have nothing to fear* and they'd stopped almost directly in front of her house *Why did I go out with this person?* and she would be inside in a matter of moments *It's still the noon hour and the sun makes it feel like spring's really here so why do I feel like we've parked in a cemetery at midnight?* and all she had to do was—

"Thank you," she said, her voice amazingly calm; cordial. *Just open the door now, very casually.* "I had a lovely time, Bill. You needn't get out." *You're not doing it right, the handle must press up, not down.* "I can manage." *It doesn't open—why doesn't it open?*

"Now," he said a second time and was upon her.

He neither kissed her nor touched her breasts. He was extremely, palpably clear about what he intended to do, and he did it. Part of her mind noticed other things, including the way he removed her skirt and panties without care but also without ripping them, as if he did everything mechanically, with the irresistible but joyless and unexcited predetermination of something programmed to do it. Although the man called Bill was violating her *will,* Jean knew distantly, almost unmistakable—and wondered if she'd gone crazy—that he wasn't solely relying upon *his* will. No time to think; suddenly she saw him free himself from his pants, saw through strangely strewn shadows a penis that was utterly flaccid—then saw something peculiarly and frighteningly unnatural when it snapped erect and immense without his touch or hers. It looked *bidden;* somehow it was *supposed* to do that. Worse, far worse, as horror was piled upon horror and the noontime nightmare played out like something preordained or predestined, Jean caught a clearer glimpse of the large male member right before he jammed it into her—and it looked in that bizarre flash of a moment as if it was—

Her head struck the sharp, opening apparatus of the car door as Bill hauled up her lower body, then crammed it in the rest of the way. She gasped first, managed to scream then; and he did nothing to prevent her so she stopped at once. *Sometimes they kill,* she thought, her ears ringing, her vagina throbbing. And, *He hasn't touched me, caressed me anywhere,* momentarily clinging to the fact as if it might save something of hers that mattered yet. *He entered me as if he'd been diagrammed or magnetized and yet he hasn't tried to kiss or feel me anywhere.*

He had made no noises, either, but she didn't realize that until he did. It happened at the moment of his release. His whole upper body bathed in sunlight, pasty-white, he threw back his head and twisted his massive, ugly mouth open. His flat, expressionless eyes were turned toward the blue-flesh skies beyond the vehicle as if he could look nowhere else that second. And, "The white darkness," he gasped, choking the words out—"so white, *so* dark . . ."

But he came then and Jean began to scream, over and over. Semen that scalded like dry ice seemed to penetrate all her vital organs and seep into the pores of her skin. Pitiless, he rammed his hard body against hers, harder and harder—not as though he wished to prolong his pleasure but as if pleasure had forever escaped him and he might get no other opportunity to seek it. Harder, though no more issued from him after the first terrible spurt—

And she felt him losing it and, at the instant he withdrew, he hit her for the first time. Exactly above one breast but below the line of her shoulder. She cried out and he hit her again, precisely on her bare, uplifted thigh. He hit her as she squirmed automatically away and dragged her legs down to feel frantically for the car door—just off the center of the spine and above the kidney area. All the blows were powerful, each brought pain that sickened; yet Jean knew with clarity that made it worse that he'd *held back*, that Bill was trying to hurt her greatly but trying not to kill her or even break bones—and knew that, in his mind, he *wanted* to do both. *It's all a message,* the thought rushed to her mind as if shouted into it by someone, something; *he's telling me something I'm to deliver.*

The door swung open with a rush. He shoved her with most of the strength heretofore restrained and she was half lifted up from the car seat, discarded with arms flailing into the afternoon streets. Excruciating pain seared one forearm, traveled to the shoulder and spread like wood flame. Minor bruises and cuts were made in one ankle when he tore the door shut, its metallic edge brutally slicing as it passed. She found herself lying on her back on the sidewalk, exposed from the waist down; she felt her panties and skirt flutter over her like secondary beasts finishing up as Bill belatedly forced them through the car window at her. She heard the engine fire up as an explosion occurring somewhere in another land, on TV; valorous, she drew back her aching legs and somehow rolled onto one side to stare after the car, blinking to get its license number.

Spastic, lurching like a lewd old man with his pants down, it rode away from Jean at an unhurried rate of speed—

But impossibly, it then became a black dot on the horizon, a horizon that was no longer her familiar street but a silver glare that was simultaneously as far as the eye could see and all around her. She blinked again, against blood dripping out of one eye—and the car, the man calling himself Bill, were no more.

Engulfed by a blaze of strange, consuming sunlight as if neither had existed.

13

Wednesday. April 13.

"But come ye baaack, When sum-mer's in the meh-ed-dow," Wayne sang; "Or when the vaaa-ley's hushed and white with snow . . ."

The homicide lieutenant's large hand fumbled to turn up the volume of his personal car's tape deck. It had to match his own rising bellow.

"—But I'll be here"—Bing Crosby and Wayne Sojourner's voices soared in mutual mock-Irish lyricism—"in summer or in sh-aa-dow"—his big, liquid eyes filled with sweet sentiment for a land he'd never known, a people of whom he'd never been a part—"oh, Danny boy, *oh!* Danny boy, I miss you so!"

And the plaintive old melody reprised a few woeful bars before subsiding, along with Crosby and Sojourner, into wistful silence.

Covertly, quickly, Wayne daubed at his eyes with his hanky, then switched the player off and, somewhat abashed, opened his car door and hauled his great body out of the Olds for another day's work.

God, how he missed Bing! It wasn't that he'd ever actually yearned to be an Irish tenor. But he'd always felt a kinship to Crosby that Wayne privately—very privately; even his wife and children only suspected it because he had never found the nerve to say so—seemed wholly remarkable to him. Both men hailed from the state of Washington originally. Both of them were born in the astrological sun sign Taurus. Both—

But he had forgotten the rest of the amazing similarities by the time he was prowling down the department hallway to his office, sweating profusely and realizing that either spring was finally here or he truly *did* need to lose weight, the way Wanda insisted. Well, Bing had gotten chunky in his middle years too. There was that picture he made as an alcoholic, with the white woman who became a princess; and Der Bingle had run around in his undershirt and shown definite signs of—

Work, Sojourner told himself firmly, stepping through the open door and closing the door quietly behind him; *I'd best begin thinking about work.* Crosby and good old pop music were gone and mostly forgotten by just about everybody, black or white, along with Satchmo and most of the Andrews Sisters and Duke, and now even the Count was gone and so would Sojourner be gone—from the police rolls—if he didn't get his mind on business!

"Andrews!" he snapped into the intercom, leaning darkly against his desk. He stopped, shuttering his eyes and shaking his enormous head. "I mean, Alberts—

sorry." What was he about to say in his customary, working-policeman peremptory manner? "Anything new on that fingerprint trace? The two sets that—"

Alberts interrupted him with an answer that caught Wayne off guard. It was an affirmative.

"Well, bring it in, man," Wayne ordered. "Let me see that report *now*!"

What was so rare about a morn in spring that started just right! Happily, rubbing his hands together, Sojourner waited for Sergeant Alberts with more of his old enthusiasm and excitement than he'd known in months—maybe years! 'Cause maybe now there'd be something definite to tell Calhoun, something encouraging at last; maybe he, Wayne Sojourner, *would* be able to do something to ease the nice guy's torment!

And, not quite incidentally, prove to Wayne all over again that he *was* a top-notch cop, not the product of some goddam quota system the way he knew some of the white uniforms and detectives secretly believed.

Then Alberts was bringing in the report with an absolutely unreadable expression on his boyish face, looking pale around the gills and all worked up at the same time. Sojourner scooped the report up from where the sergeant had dropped it on his desk and read it, fast.

He put it back down more slowly.

Right that instant Sojourner didn't know whether he had good news or bad for ol' Grade-A.

He couldn't even be sure he should tell him that the report was in.

When Gill Riffey played trumpet that way, Grady thought for the hundredth time, it was such a natural high that any guy who didn't have a tin ear should put down his glass or brush away his white line of coke and simply soar.

Well, ordinarily, Calhoun thought wryly, and reached for his glass. Tom, he noticed as he raised it, was wearing that goddam disapproving look of his again— the expression that read, like it was lit up in neon, "You really shouldn't drink like that." But your old lady didn't get trucked off to Seven Steeples—or wherever the hell that pimply faced shrink was sending her—and Grady rarely gave Simincola an excuse to give him that look. Besides, where in hell would Tom be today if he, Grady Calhoun, hadn't insisted to Andy Sutor that he use Tom's skills on the six o'clock news as well as *Confab?*

Of course—Besides, part II—where would Grady himself be if Tom hadn't telephoned him back east and told him of the opening for a talk show host in Indianapolis? Truth of the matter was, they were a team—the *Grady & Tom Show*—and had been for years. Calhoun signaled for another round and stuck his tongue out at Tom. Be nice if *he* remembered it worked both ways too!

"Play *Melancholy Baby,*" he called loudly to Gill, who'd finished a song and was fiddling with the instrument. He made himself sound tighter than he was because this was an old joke, based on the notion that middle-aged drunks *always* asked for *Melancholy Baby*.

Riffey grinned; Grady's request was also a coded request for *Autumn Leaves*, Calhoun's favorite standard. Looking dapper as Astaire, clad in clothing that would have made Doc Severinson's costuming pale by comparison, Gill began playing—and Grady thought again what a shame it was that rock 'n roll had come upon the scene and wiped out Gill Riffey's viable shot at the bigtime. Because music, not writing and doing research for a rinky-dink local TV outlet, was what Gill lived for; always had been, always would be.

Calhoun chugged half his midday cocktail and nodded to himself, still avoiding Tom Simincola's critical stare. Truth of the matter was, ol' Gill was a shitty goddam TV writer and wasn't much better at handling research—but he played one helluva sweet horn. No telling how far he'd have gone if the guitar hadn't replaced the trumpet on the public's preference list.

Or, Grady reflected, if Gill'd had the balls to get the fuck out of the midwest and toughed it out for a few years in Manhattan, or on the coast. Crap, lotsa places still used real bands and orchestras, even combos like Gill's. It was just that record companies no longer beat the sticks looking for pop and jazz musicians. Instead, they clustered outside junior

highs with the dopers and tried to sign
them up before the kids with any talent
signed long-term engagements with the
candy man.

*I wonder why Jean wouldn't let me
have the kids last Sunday,* Calhoun
wondered suddenly. But while it hadn't
occurred to him for an hour or two, it
wasn't the first time he had wondered
that—or why Jean had hung up on him
when he'd called. She'd sounded as if her
best friend had died or something, yet she
had refused to answer him when Grady
asked what was wrong.

For the first time it occurred to him
that one of the kids might be very ill—or
that Jean had caught Tim with that fairy
friend of his. Calhoun's heart sank; he
even pushed his glass away.

"What's comin' down?"

Grady glanced up. Gill had finished
Autumn Leaves and wandered over to their
table on a break. "Never heard *Melancholy
Baby* played more beau'fully," Grady said,
fetching a wan grin.

"You look like your pet monkey died,"
Gill said offhandedly, dropping into a
chair between Grady and Tom. It was an
old joke the three men had always
enjoyed. "An organ grinder can't cut it
without his chimp, champ."

"My monkey's just about the only
thing that *hasn't* died, or got sick as shit,"
Calhoun replied. He inhaled deeply,
striving for a clear head to tell his best
friends what he had to. "Gonna level with

you both: I don't wanta see either of your ugly mugs for a while. Except at the station."

Tom sat up straight and seemed to be taller than anybody else in Grimelda's. "Well, par-don *meee!*" he exclaimed.

Gill smoothed his pencil-thin mustache but kept a straight face. "There are two words that cover this situation nicely, pally." He held up his hand, the middle finger conspicuously pointing down. "If you can't hear this, I'll turn it up for you."

Grady chuckled and shook his head. "You both know all I know about that madman Rajelis. Gents, I've become a jinx—a pariah."

"A pariah?" Tom said quickly. "Well, go to the dentist!"

"I'm serious, Simincola!" Calhoun snapped. "Too many rotten things are happening to—well, people I care about—for coincidence. So keep your distance until it blows over."

"As the bishop said to the actress," Gill said quickly, smirking.

"You sound like a man with herpes," Tom commented, and the others smiled despite themselves. Another of their old jokes involved how long it had taken for Tom and Judith, his wife, to have a child. Tom's friends had purposefully started the rumor that he was impotent because he'd contracted herpes—from the organ grinder's monkey! Their minds worked in that sort of offbeat, connective style. "But it's not impossible that there's something to the looney's curse."

"You've contracted AIDS!" Gill exclaimed.

"No," Tom answered ruefully, "I've contracted Sutor's Looking for a Scapegoat Syndrome. Ratings are down, 'cept on *Confab*." Tom shrugged his long, slender shoulders. "Andy, to quote his unoriginal euphemism, is 'considering a change' on the *Evening News*. And since Grady, here, talked him into keeping Bud as the anchor, that probably means a change in director."

"He can't do that!" Calhoun protested vehemently. "That'd leave you just *Confab* at a time when you need all the money you can get for the baby on its way!"

"Tell me about it," Tom murmured.

"Well," Gill said promptly, "you're directing *two* shows now; and if Sutor bumps your ass from *one* of them, *that* means—"

"What are you so damned cheerful about?" Grady demanded, smiling. "Don't tell me the Calhoun Curse hasn't shat on your parade too!"

Gill tucked his handkerchief into and out of his trumpet bell in mock modesty, waggling his head from side to side. "Seems I just might become an overnight success 20 years late," he reported. "Rumor hath it that I'll be cutting a record gig in a few days. Up in the Windy City."

"That's fan-tas-ti-co!" Tom Simincola reached out a long arm on impulse to cuff the trumpeter's cheek gently. "All riiight!"

"Careful with the lip, Tomasino," Riffey cautioned, but his chocolate-fudge eyes melted and the grip was to cloak the fact that he was touched. "Horn blowers and male dancers must protect their chops!"

Grady tingled with new hope. "Maybe this thing is passing you over, Gill. And if I remember properly, you aren't even circumcised!" Winking, he produced a pen and clumsily made several calculations on a cocktail napkin. "One thing I'll thank Rajelis for, his curses are finite." He glanced up at them, slightly bleary-eyed. "There are 21 days to go 'til the whole thing's history. Just three weeks." Then scared and angry again, he wadded the napkin into a ball, put it in the closest ashtray, and set fire to it. "But I'm gonna contact that astrologer who was on the show with Rajelis."

"Freida Something," Tom said quickly. He'd always had a memory as long as his body. He snapped his fingers and his eyes brightened. "Freida Rehfeldt, that's it! And she lived south on 37, I remember—almost to Bloomington or the IU campus."

"That's not far from your cottage on that lake near Monroe, is it?" Gill Riffey asked Grady. "That summer 'mansion' your dear old grandad left you?"

Calhoun nodded. "Not far. If I had any sense, I'd gather up everyone I know and ship the whole lot of you down there.

Chances are, Rajelis doesn't know a thing about the place." He took a deep breath. "Look, Tom, I'll rap with Andy Sutor, all right? The thing is, you and Gill shouldn't allow yourselves to get into any kind of depression. That might make it easier for the bastard to reach you."

Gill smiled smugly. "Have no fear for me, king of the Hoosier airways. I'm gonna be an overnight success, remember?"

"I'd keep cool and stay loose like Grady says," a voice urged from above their heads.

"Wayne!" Calhoun greeted the police lieutenant, putting out a hand to tug Sojourner gently toward a vacant chair. But a glint in Sojourner's eye stayed his hand, left it inches from the big man's sleeve. "Aren't you staying?"

"Can't." Sojourner glanced at Grady's outstretched hand until it fell away. He looked, Grady saw abruptly, as if he had something he truly needed to say but was having second thoughts about saying it. "There's news, Calhoun. Some information. About the two sets of fingerprints that match."

Grady felt his heart skip a beat. But staring up at his official friend, he saw that the clouded expression was deepening. It turned Calhoun instantly cold sober. "Can you tell us?" he asked carefully, tentatively.

"S'probably a computer fuck-up somewhere," Wayne said. He rubbed the top of his head and glanced off toward the other, unknown patrons of Grimelda's as if he'd like to have been one of them. Gill had stood, his break over, but was lingering near the much larger man. Finally Sojourner sighed heavily. "See, Calhoun, I put a lot of pride in what police networking can do today, and this just doesn't make a goddam bit of sense!"

"Maybe you're just too close to it to figure it out, Wayne," Grady suggested. He realized then that Sojourner might just decide to turn and leave, and couldn't imagine what had made his vastly experienced friend so upset. "I gather that you've got an identification of the prints from Timmy's literature, and that dog leash Bud's sister was holding onto. Tell us: who do they belong to? What's the man's name?"

"That's the easy part," Sojourner snapped, and got it out. "William Salvo. A vicious sonofabitch, apparently; a cheap hood and sometime hitman."

"Now, that wasn't so hard," Calhoun purred. "Hell, Wayne, it even starts to add up."

"It might," Sojourner retorted—"if the bastard hadn't been *dead* for 33 *years.*"

He had driven almost automatically to Bud's, but his ambitions were ambivalent and even before the dark mood suffused him he'd turned off the lights and stayed in the car, shivering.

At one and the same time Grady

wanted to discuss Wayne Sojouner's amazing disclosure and knew that he was too tired and just inebriated enough not to make heads nor tails of it; in need of comforting, but unwilling to admit that the whole mess was getting him down even more; and sufficiently convinced that he was, himself, an ambulatory curse, and truly afraid to go near Bud. There was also the fact that he yearned for quick, passionate, consuming, and emotion-clearing intercourse, but Jean had never been able to understand that and there was no reason to believe Bud would.

Lighting one of his last Camels, Grady felt the light fire up around him in the darkness of the closed car and, though this was presumably one of the safe periods, he felt like a man giving the executioner a signal. In a way, it would probably have been kinder to shoot Bud than to make love to her. He'd had far less close contact with poor Timmy and with his mother, but look how the curse had ruined their lives. Calvin Rajelis—or Rajelis and whoever possessed a dead man's fingerprints—hadn't hesitated to strike out at them. The sonofabitch had known his feelings for them and the fact that he'd gotten at Grady through Bud's sister already made it clear that he knew Grady's feelings for the petite news-woman.

Maybe it was time to get in touch with Rajelis somehow and *demand* that he take action against Grady Calhoun—hit the madman, provoke him somehow into waving his fucking wand or whatever he used and—

The illumination from a streetlight, which Grady had only unconsciously acknowledged, was blacked out. A shadowy form loomed at the car window. Calhoun caught his breath and felt his fingers lock in fear on the steering wheel.

"Want some action, sailor?" Bud asked, opening the door and slipping inside, beside him.

"You scared the hell out of me," Grady said, turning to her in mild irritation.

Then he saw her pajamas pants protruding from under her topcoat; saw that the topcoat was unbuttoned; saw that the pajama top beneath it was also undone.

"Want to make hump-hump with virgin, sailor?" she asked him, smiling and moving closer. "Three dollar, cheap!"

He reached for her, knowing she'd seen his car lights or the glow of his cigarette from her window. In one small hand, he noticed for the first time, she held a steaming thermos of coffee.

"Y'know, Buddy," he said softly, "I don't think I've made out in a car since my fourth year of high school."

"Gee," she replied, letting him warm his hands on her, "and by then you only had two years to go!"

14

Monday. April 18.

For the second straight Sunday, Jean Calhoun had made up an excuse to give Grady—on the phone—for not allowing him to take the kids for an outing. This couldn't go on, she knew; even Calhoun had his limits, and the courts had understandably granted him visitation rights.

But so far Jean could not bear to face him after what had happened to her. However unreasonable it was, she felt dirty, sullied; as guilty as the man named Bill should have felt for raping her but undoubtedly didn't. And Jean knew perfectly well that, in the presence of a man who'd known her so well—who'd never mistreated her, might even still love her—she was bound to break down and tell him.

And this morning, when she awakened and began the routine chores that would send the children off to school for the start of a new week, she paid for it as she had last Monday; with misery. She felt simply abominable, and again she did not feel it proper even to inform her kids.

It wasn't just the recurring, intense pain that throbbed in her temples as if some powerful, malicious creature was using its great paws to crush her head like an eggshell. It wasn't even the sickening nausea she'd experienced immediately upon arising this morning, and a certain, almost hysterical fear that if she permitted herself to vomit it away, she might never stop.

It was the disorienting and terrifying feeling that she might be losing her mind.

Because now she felt guilty about *not* telling Grady. And after gritting her teeth to smile at the younger kids as they departed—knowing that she wasn't fooling Tim in believing for a moment that she was well, and yet relieved when he grudgingly left the house and took his own newly furtive ways with him—and after talking little Petey into going back to bed for another hour's sleep, Jean slowly faced the fact that she was being *made* to feel guilty.

For the first time she remembered what she'd sensed in that awful man's car: that the rape was nothing more than a sadistic message she was meant to convey. And even then, at that moment when she'd struck the pavement so painfully, she had known that the message was meant for her ex-husband.

Which makes no sense at all, Jean thought as she put the children's breakfast dishes down to soak in the sink. *We're divorced, for goodness' sake! Why would Grady care—*

But he would, that was the point. Jean squirted detergent out of a bottle, let an adjusted stream of hot water flow over the mess in the sink—

And realized that she hadn't considered, even once, reporting the rape to the police! Nor, now that the idea occurred to her at last, and the first flush of hunger for justice nearly made her forget her aching head and the sick feeling in her stomach, was she able to *hold* to the notion. The oddest feeling she'd ever suffered was sweeping over, and through her—the feeling that sections of her mind, the *control* of life's precious options that comprised a God-given right—and actual ideas themselves—were flowing down the drain in front of her along with the dirty water.

She clutched the edge of the sink with her hands, hard enough that she distantly heard a nail snap. Waves of pain the likes of which she had never experienced surfed through her brain's tissues and crashed against her frontal lobes. *I haven't even told the . . . the . . .* Common words jumped down the drain like skittering cockroaches, but she fought back, courageously, tried hard to focus on the right word or synonym. *—The authorities* —she thought, and day-to-day terms ran from her like mice fleeing a burning building. *I'll go call the—* And she felt pain that arced, took shortcuts, jabbed like hypodermics at her eyelids, alternating between left and right. *THE PO—* and Jean experienced a sensation like battering rams from the central cortex of her brain, beating outward, almost splitting the tissue of her individuality, her precious selfhood. *I MUST go PHONE—*

. . . *"Grady,"* she whispered, aloud. At

least, her lips formed the word, it was her lips. "Grady/must/know." And, *no one else,* her mind—what used to be her mind, anyway—whispered back, pretending it was someone else agreeing with her. *No one else must know but—*

"Graaa-dy." She spoke his familiar name lovingly, adoringly, and doing so soothed her so she pronounced the two syllables once again . . . *"GRA-*dee"— and felt surfeited by such cozy warmth that it coaxed the pain away like a traffic guard, *and* the sickness, and it told her with paternal reassurance that everything was going to be just wonderful *after* she had simply told—

"I will not." She said it aloud, loudly. She shoved herself spine-straight to stare defiantly out the window above the kitchen sink, past the Ivory Liquid and Comet cleanser at the very ordinary, early spring morning with the tentative sunlight warming the winter-browned backyard; at the old swing set they'd bought for Tim and each child in turn had used, and fallen from, requiring Band-Aids or maternal kisses or even, once, with David, a scary ride to St. Vincent's and stitches. She'd kept her cool every time, and maybe life had worn her down a smidge and part of her would never get over seeing Cathy put her frail arms through the upstairs window that time or how Grady'd driven on sidewalks when he had to while she held Cathy's "all-bleedy" arms aloft during *that* mad, terrifying ride

to the hospital, but she'd always stayed true to who and what she was and—"I WON'T TELL ANYBODY!"

. . . And a feeling of incredible hollowness started in her lower abdomen and scooped its way up, and around, and down.

But no more than that; an emptiness that made Jean feel she had achieved something virtually impossible that brought her to some unknowable state of arbitration . . . of high-court *consideration* of her case. Like winning a reprieve when everybody in the courtroom and on TV *knew* you were guilty as hell!

It was like a total hysterectomy of the spirit, but she turned then from the sink, quietly wiped her palms, vertically, on the apron Calhoun and Petey had given her for Christmas, and walked—unimpeded—into the adjacent dining room. Sitting down at the phone table, she didn't realize where her legs and feet had carried her until she spied one of her own hands traitorously groping for the telephone receiver . . .

Pulling it back was like ripping it free of jagged glass.

But she did.

And memories that she hadn't known she'd lost returned: the epilogue to her nightmare with the Bill-creature, when she had managed to crawl up to the bathroom afterward, torn off her clothes and bathed in the hottest water she'd ever endured, and found no traces of semen. The next morning, despite how unbearably sore she felt everywhere, she found no bruises of any nature on her face, neck, arms, or legs; whatever marks of the rape, the beating remained could be conveniently covered up with ordinary garments. And even though she'd felt bereft, heartsick, shamed, she'd decided not to tell Tim or Cathy or the others, and had forgotten all about it for long stretches of splintered time.

So time passed beside the phone table while Jean held her left arm in her lap, pinned there, concentrating mightily on nothing else but *keeping* the disloyal, hysterical thing prisoner. The sun climbed high in the sky—she watched it, dully, through the French doors—and then it was no longer morning nor yet noon. Now, though somewhat diminished, the nausea lingered. But the pain became gradually bearable and, knowing that she should feel a greater sense of victory, of triumph over all but impossible odds, Jean did not call her ex-husband, or anybody.

Tim came home for lunch right after the hands on the starburst clock she could see on the kitchen wall through the doorway stood straight up, and he looked awfully worried about something. It seemed, she sensed, to be her; but he asked nothing and she roused herself to fix him a sandwich of Vienna sausages—a Tim Calhoun favorite—and a small bowl of split pea soup. There was a lot of mutual staring between son and mother; then he announced that he'd be stopping to see his friend, Billy, after school, and Jean sensed that she wished he wouldn't but she said, All right.

She spent much of the afternoon watching two soap operas as if they were the most engrossing programs she had ever seen, no recollection left that she had been raped, or beaten.

"There are a lot of ways to approach this damned thing," Bud said, "if you can stay distanced from it."

"As the actress said to the bishop," Grady quipped lamely, trying to keep it light. It was a trip of around an hour from downtown Indy to Freida Rehfeldt's house, but every minute seemed precious to Calhoun now and he had to keep reminding himself not to gun the motor. "Like what? I confess that I'm out of my depths. This occult jazz makes me feel like I've taken a trip backward in time."

"Like this, for example," Bud replied, raising a clipboard. She hated to remove her gaze from the road with Calhoun driving in such a state, but she imagined he'd be better if his mind was occupied instead of his feelings. "I've done some research, however skeptical I may remain about some of the details. It seems that back in February of '98, a woman named Martha Place, from New York, chopped her husband to bits with an ax."

"That's cheerful," Grady nodded. "Make sure Jean doesn't read that article, okay?"

"She said she would have used black magic, but she was in a rush to finish the old boy off." Bud glanced at him from where she sat in the passenger seat. "My point is, one approach to take is focusing on Rajelis's revenge angle. Okay, the rest of our sweet Martha's little tale: Before the old witch became the first woman who ever died in the electric chair, Marty swore she'd avenge herself on everybody involved with the case."

Grady looked interested. "What happened?"

"By the first anniversary of Martha's execution, everyone connected to the case was dead."

"How'd they die?"

"The judge hanged himself," Bud replied, reading her notes and shuddering; "and four other men died under what was termed 'mysterious circumstances.' Grady, Martha Place *believed*—absolutely—she had the power to wreak revenge from beyond the grave. And they executed her at twilight . . ."

Above Calhoun's muskrat nose his blue eyes widened.

But he said nothing more until they'd located the astrologer's house. Outside Bloomington, where Indiana University was located, Freida Rehfeldt's home was on a long, curving road that led off the highway on the way to a summer resort called Inn of the Fourwinds. While most of the houses on the winding road had been either recently built or remodeled, Grady and Bud saw one or two farmhouses set deep in cornfields and passed an old one-pump service station that had been partly converted to a sort of modern general store.

The structure in which the astrologer lived surprised them. A ramshackle affair of indeterminate age, it gave the inaccurate impression of being supported by a single remaining wall and of being ready to topple under the slightest gust of wind.

"It looks haunted," Grady said, turning reluctantly into a gravel driveway.

"No," Bud said, shivering, "it looks as if it's going to be."

They crossed a creaking, wooden porch with exaggerated caution, not quite believing that it would crumble beneath them and plunge them into a cellar that was an anteroom to hell (as Calhoun whispered), and they jumped when the front door opened before they could knock on it.

Grady recognized the woman instantly, wondered why he hadn't remembered her, and then realized why: she wasn't remotely scary, old, or witch-like. In age, Freida lived in the middle of the unmarked terrain between middle years and elderliness, disposed to encourage the former by having plucked her brows and replaced them with a pair of inexpertly drawn brown lines. When she spoke it seemed a cue to some of the cats inside the dilapidated house to come pouring out; Bud attempted to count them, but a few were running as if their lives depended on it, while one or two paused in the center of the porch to turn their paws at impossible angles and clean them.

"I wondered when you'd decide to see me," Freida said. Smiling, she became a shade of the pretty woman she'd once been. "Come in, if you like cats."

"That's hard to say," Grady murmured, motioning to Bud to precede him inside. "I know Mrs. Katz, but I've never met her husband."

"You must overlook Mr. Calhoun's little jokes," Bud said to the older woman, pretending she didn't smell the same stench that was afflicting Calhoun's nostrils. Apparently Freida frequently worked so hard on her astrological charts that she wasn't aware of her pets' need to go outside.

"Everyone overlooks Mr. Calhoun's little jokes," Freida said, half giggling. She led the way to what might have been a front parlor, lifted stacks of old astrology magazines from a tattered couch, and gestured to them to sit.

"I begin to think you should have your own show, Mrs. Rehfeldt," Grady offered, and nearly sat on a sleeping kitten. It didn't budge and, when he was certain it hadn't died, he took it in his hands and lowered himself to the couch with gingerly caution.

"If that's a proposition, I'll take you up

on it," the astrologer said, plump hands pressed together. She didn't sit until her guests had. "Astrology is the oldest organized topic on the planet and it's had a bad press long enough."

Grady gestured to the stacks of old publications, almost as great in number as there were felines. Wherever he looked he saw cats on furniture and tucked between cushions, cats asleep in corners or giving him dirty looks and yawning from the top of crowded bookshelves. "From the look of it, Mrs. Rehfeldt, astrology's had a *lot* of press!"

"It's Miss Rehfeldt." She wore a faded muumuu that did nothing to restore her figure and folded the skirt around her knees as she sat, carefully, in a nearby chair. "Freida, to television personalities." Her eyes were vivid and seemingly intelligent beneath the imitation eyebrows. "There was a time when royalty, alone, was permitted astrological counseling. But I'm prattling." She leaned toward them. "You've come about that mentalist, Rajelis—and the solar eclipse, of course."

Bud gasped, audibly. "How could you know that?" she asked.

"Don't worry, I'm not a mind reader like that sinister young man!" Her laugh was merry, reassuringly normal. "But I don't appear in public much, being on your program was exciting to me, and I happen to be an *excellent* astrologer. After those threats Mr. Rajelis made to you I was certain you'd find yourself in dire trouble and need my services."

Calhoun frowned slightly. "I'm not sure I follow you, Freida."

"Isn't it obvious?" she asked. She spread her chunky hands and looked, wide-eyed, from Bud to Grady. "Rajelis timed his appearance on *Confab* with the new moon and solar eclipse. The effectiveness of that cruel curse of his depends entirely upon *astrology*."

15

Monday Afternoon.

"Tell us all about astrology," Grady said moments later.

"I wouldn't dream of it," Freida replied, laughing. "You'd both have to move in and stay for a minimum of six to eight months just to become conversant with the subject."

"Oh," Grady muttered.

"You weren't exaggerating, were you?" Bud asked, her mane of hair like an oversized halo. It wasn't exceptionally well-lit in the older woman's house, but Calhoun, to his surprise, felt relaxed and comfortable. It occurred to him that despite the fact that he really did well in putting his *Confab* guests at ease, and listened intently enough to what they said to make what passed for sparkling conversation on TV, he never really got to know any of them very well. TV was a mirror of real life, of contemporary customs, even in that sense, he saw; small talk was small.

"Not in the least." Freida picked up her nearest cat and stroked it in a practiced manner that still seemed to please the animal. "Scientists who almost unfailingly detest the very mention of astrology hate it when I remind them that their own idols—most of the founders of science for some three centuries—considered a man hopelessly ignorant if he knew nothing of the ancient art." When the cat wriggled to be released Freida opened her hands without stretching out her arms and the furry creature had its independence at once. "Astrology was taught in every university worthy of the name."

"I noticed you didn't just say 'eclipse,' but stressed *solar* eclipse," Grady put in. "Aside from, well, obvious astronomical distinctions—"

"Is there an astrological distinction?" Freida finished. "My, yes! In the early days of humankind, as you know, people worshiped the sun. That sounds pretty stupid these days, but if you live off the earth—if you don't have central heating—the sun can be a major consideration! It became a popular saying that the sun shines only on the righteous. But if the sun decided to hide his face—one way to describe a solar eclipse, right?—it meant one thing and one only."

"What was that?" Calhoun asked.

"Disaster was on its way," she answered simply. "Astrology refined such things, as the first organized subject—and one that was certainly *considered* a science for thousands of years."

"Thousands?" Bud inquired, raising a brow.

"Indeed! We're nearly 2,000 years into our present numbering system, or way of counting the passage of time. Three thousand years before that, the Babylonians practiced astrology. And taught that eclipses, in common with all things that happened in the heavens, only afflicted those people who were adversely affected by the particular zodiacal signs that were *involved*. A Gemini native such as yourself, Ms. Rocker—"

"How did you know when I was born?" Bud gasped.

"It's apparent to any good astrologer in a hundred ways," Freida declared. "A Geminian under the influence of a solar eclipse in Aquarius, say, or Leo, would certainly have no reason to expect anything dreadful to happen. She, or he, would anticipate *favorable* developments—if acquainted with astrology."

"I see," Bud said, adding honestly, "I think."

And what does this intriguing, offbeat woman see for May 2? wondered Calhoun, peering almost wistfully at Freida. That was when the Calvin Rajelis curse expired, when his 45 days were up—along with how many others, Calhoun could not, would not guess.

But he lacked the guts to ask such a question so baldly, so directly—What would *happen* to him May 2?—and knew it. "My loved ones," Grady said aloud, selecting words with care, "were . . . to suffer—by light. Not darkness. Particularly the times just before or just after night." He swallowed, hard, his glance briefly swerving to Bud. "And they have been suffering. The matter of *light* . . . ?"

Freida nodded. "There are data I do not have, data that would enable me to help you both considerably more. I'll get back to that. But we can get started today, at least." Shadows were growing across her littered parlor floor and several of her furry companions were yawning sleepily. Days were still short, this time of year; too short. "Let me say first that I believe your Mr. Rajelis is not an ordinary occultist. I think he is both cunning and very gifted. I also think he's mad. It doesn't take astrology to perceive that, does it, people?"

"It does not," Grady acknowledged. He was growing more impressed with Freida by the moment.

"The point is that not even a well-trained psychologist could know to what degree he's following his own principles of magick—I suspect certain special gifts, even arrangements of an evil design—or to what extent his obsession with driving you to . . . death . . . makes him go off on lunatic tangents." She arose from her chair and went straight to a shelf of books with a supple grace that was surprising. "It isn't a copout, people, to say that I've worked with many eccentric persons from time to time but rarely attempted to enter . . . combat . . . with a psychopath."

Freida's books looked at once quite old and frequently, heavily used. There was nothing of show to them. Some were crammed in, rising above the tops of those that gripped them in place—as if the astrologer had found what she sought in them, then replaced them avidly, anxious to get on with her work.

By the same token, though, Bud could see from where she sat that the other woman kept her books alphabetized by author. Now she withdrew one, leafed through it with casual, fond familiarity. Her eyes lit up. "I'll get to the subject of light momentarily, but let me first tell you how Calvin Rajelis's curse relates to voodoo." She hesitated while they registered surprise and, in Bud's case, a dawning comprehension. "There have been several scientific studies—anthropological—that show that vodun priests, called *houngans*, score statistically quite impressively in causing psychosomatic illnesses in others. Others whom they have cursed. However, the houngans' success ratio *drops* if they don't have the opportunity to inform their victims. Notice that Rajelis went to the trouble of coming to your city, of getting on your show. Unquestioningly, he has learned vodun, or voodoo, and needed for you to know what he meant to do."

"But there's a whopper of difference there," Grady remarked. "He hasn't done anything to me, directly."

"True." Freida nodded solemnly. "I only suggest that his idea was conceived as a variation of voodoo. And the mark of his knowledge—of psychology, among other less mundane matters—is that the curse is working despite the variation. Paracelsus said, 'No armour shields against magick, for it strikes at the inward spirit of man.' You see, he is using your *own* psychic bonds to attack the people you care for—somehow he is diverting them and, in the process, he may well be transforming them . . . from bonds of affection or love to laserlike, potentially lethal vibrations of immense harm."

"But how is that possible?" Bud inquired, moving up to the edge of the old couch. "Do you suggest some electromagnetic field, an actual physical property a person emits toward those he loves?"

Almost infinitesimally, Freida's shoulders moved in a shrug. "The greatest conceit of any people who call themselves 'modern' is their belief that they already possess all the facts. But Einstein demonstrated that great gravitational fields can literally *bend space;* warp it." Her eyes glittered. "And following the curves of warped space, *light* will bend around immense bodies. I cannot prove it, but I believe your Mr. Rajelis is utilizing some such principle—and, at the same time, I think he's engaged in altering time itself."

"When a psychic sees into the future," Bud began, "isn't he perhaps altering time in some way? And by saying that terrible things would happen to people close to Grady, wasn't he predicting it?"

"You," the astrologer said, shutting her book and reaching for another, "are a very bright young woman. Yes, of course, he was predicting what would happen. As for the rest of it, that's hard to say. Certain parapsychologists have suggested that the whole future is a sequence of probabilities. Rajelis may somehow acquire information about the *most probable* future—or, by worrying Mr. Calhoun on television to the point that he begins warning his loved ones, Rajelis may be *making* that most likely future occur."

"Why light," Grady asked, "instead of dark; night? Almost every horror novel or movie uses the nighttime for awful things to happen. Hell, we all grow up taught to fear darkness, and the 'witching hour,' right?"

"And you, sir," Freida Rehfeldt murmured, "are more intelligent than you permit yourself to be." She clucked her tongue almost maternally. "A standard attribute, I fear, for most so-called 'modern' young men. But you are right, Mr. Calhoun. We who are born as Christians are instructed to believe that light, itself, is associated with the Almighty exclusively. It's only a few hundred years since there were men of science—so to speak—who proposed that light was the stuff of which the universe was made. But think a moment, please! Think of what would happen if the Van Allen Belt no longer protected life on this planet from ultraviolet light, cosmic rays. Think of planets going nova, a brilliant burst of light. Think of laser beams, used for good and for ill." Freida closed her eyes. "Think of the flash of light before the mushroom cloud—that truly blinding light at which no one may stare, unprotected, without suffering blindness." She opened her eyes. "Think of the aftermath: radiation."

"Interesting," Calhoun said briefly. "Frightening too. But I don't see much help in all that."

"So impatient," Freida said, smiling to remove the sting. "Alas, people, I must progress at my own pace."

"We will pay you for your services," Bud said quickly.

Freida raised one brown, imitation brow. "And what shall my fee be if I succeed in saving the health, sanity, or the lives of all those the two of you treasure? Because you must not doubt, Ms. Rocker, that Calvin Rajelis will consider attacking you directly—when he is ready." She glanced affectionately toward Grady Calhoun. "If it's clear to me that you're very fond of one another, it is clear to Rajelis."

"I only meant—"

"You meant to be considerate, Ms. Rocker," Freida said with a definite bob of her head. "But let's not introduce the topic of money at this point. Your adversary is ruthless, and brilliant, and could not be bought off. If I'm to assist you, I owe it to you to be similarly—equally—scrupulous. As clean and clear as light which, interpreted as the color white, is traditionally associated with such purity."

"And it isn't always?" Grady asked.

"White can suggest a completely untrammeled, a manic mind." She began turning pages in the second book from her shelf, then paused, her eyes lighting up. "As to the matter of the mentalist's attacks at dawn and dusk, people respond to the rhythms of day and night. Most beings do." She blinked, turned her head in Grady's direction. "Are you aware that occultists have known for hundreds of years that each of us, to a high degree, is a *different person* depending on the time of the day?"

"I don't know how literally to take that," he replied carefully.

"I don't either," the astrologer said softly, "yet. Because I lack that data to which I referred."

Calhoun and Bud Rocker watched as she replaced her books and returned to her chair. She paused en route to scratch behind the ears of a small cat. "I'm not a magician, an occultist, nor a parapsychologist." She stopped, apparently changing her mind about sitting again. "I'm a professional astrologer—and I work from birth facts. Day and month of birth, place and hour if known."

"You want mine?" Grady asked eagerly. "No problem! I was born—"

"Mr. Calhoun, I erected your horoscope a week before I appeared on your program." She raised both hairless brows. "What is required is the birth information of the other involved party." Now she watched their brows rise in understanding. "Mr. Rajelis himself."

"Right; of course you do!" Calhoun exclaimed, and clapped his forehead. "Crap, I should have thought of that before we drove down here!"

"It shouldn't be too difficult to run down," Bud said, looking hopeful.

"I wouldn't think so," the astrologer agreed. "You must phone me with it as soon as you can get it." Now she moved toward the front door, clearly involved in the problem, but just as obviously aware that she could do no more without Rajelis's horoscope. "I want to determine why he selected a period of 45 days for his curse's maturation, which, at worst, is only a semisquare. Ninety days, which would represent a square or thwarting aspect, would—on the surface—have made more sense."

Grady and Bud stopped for Freida to open the door for them. Nodding, he saw that the woman was almost talking to herself; ruminating, trying already to deduce

Rajelis's most secret motives. He felt terribly relieved, more hopeful of making it through the nightmare than he had since the night of his *Confab* show and Calvin Rajelis's astounding threat.

But Bud said, "You have something else you need to learn from his horoscope." Her perceptive eyes had been scrutinizing Freida's rather plump features. "Don't you?"

"I do." The astrologer registered only mild surprise. She seemed younger than her years, fired by intellectual stimulation, or the urge to be of service. "My tentative notion is that a *second* person is tied up in this, or a secondary personality."

Calhoun was startled. "My God, that could be the case, Freida! And we didn't mention anything about it, so you—"

"On your way, people!" Freida patted their arms, ushered them out onto the creaking porch. Night was coming on and there was another distinct chill on the air. For an instant, the older woman remained framed in the doorway, her gaze skimming a number of faintly moving, lumpy shadows strewn around the front of her old house: Freida's cats, or part of them. "Call and give me that young and sinister madman's birth data as soon as you can, and maybe we can start corroborating some of my suspicions. You see, if I know just when he was born, I'll also know when *he* is vulnerable—and then the two of you can fight back!"

16

Tuesday. April 14, Dusk

Before he left the station for the day, somewhat earlier than usual because it had been a day of tough decision-making and he was bushed, Andy Sutor left something uncharacteristic on Tom Simincola's desk.

It was a note, not a formal memo. It was neither polysyllabic nor hip, nor even reeking of acronyms and cliche; it was short and sweet.

It wasn't a reprimand and it wasn't any kind of pink slip, because the director's *Evening News* assignment was . . . safe.

It told Tom he had faith in him, that the job itself was safe.

It was also the most fatally dangerous act of Andy Sutor's life. But he didn't know that or, without a doubt, he would never have written it.

Truth was, Andy wasn't worth much as a human being, but the part that *did* contain merit had surfaced Tuesday and he had decided his was a tightly run, highly capable ship and crew, and that whatever in hell was making the ratings plunge for every program but Calhoun's, it was nobody's fault. Or, if it were, not even somebody at the vaunted network level on either coast would've been able to pinpoint it, and Andy Sutor would be damned if he reached any rash decisions about firing either personnel or programs.

He didn't know that he was also damned if he didn't.

But he'd begun to think something was going wrong within a scant few minutes of getting back to the apartment. He hadn't the foggiest notion that his life and maybe his immortal soul were on the line, but, when the fires began, Andy was distinctly perturbed. Not because they were dangerous; at first.

Because nothing caused them. Nothing Sutor could see.

And when he did see what (or who) caused them, it was practically the last thing he ever saw.

The first fire began in the lapel of the handsome sports coat he hung up, as Andy unfailingly hung up his things, on a rack inside the front door. Since he'd quit smoking almost five years ago simply to avoid just this kind of accident, the program manager immediately flew off the handle. Instead of trying to put out the small but unmistakable flame in a fashion that might not have done grievous harm to the sports jacket, he literally ripped it off the rack—he heard the awful tearing sound in one sleeve even as he was rushing to his bathroom—and, tossing it into his tub, turned the shower on it. Full force. In the process, he splattered water on his shirt and both trousers legs and, swearing colorfully in German—one of four languages in which he knew swear words—he realized he'd have to change.

Andy Sutors do not run around water-stained, even in the privacy of their apartments.

He had wrestled off his shirt and unbuckled his pants when he saw the second burn begin in the cuff of one leg. Not a total idiot, and having learned something from his prior experience (if not a great deal), the customarily impeccable Sutor sat down on the john and, pressing dampened toilet paper against the miniature fire, tried to figure out what was happening.

The flame smouldered straight through the toilet tissue and burned his middle finger.

"Oh, Jesus!" he said loudly as it dawned on him that the fire in his trouser cuff was going quite nicely, now, and he should do something more effective to put it out.

All he could think of was adding it to his sports jacket, which, Andy perceived, was not blazing away but *was* sizzling and spreading as if hellbent on garment destruction. After he had impetuously thrown the pants on top of the coat, the two sets of flame melded into one and, had it not been for the shower he'd left running, the fire would have begun to burn the bathroom walls.

Unfortunately, Andy had automatically pushed up the small chrome handle, which ensured that bathwater would not run down the drain and the tub was beginning to fill up. Point of fact, if he permitted the shower to run another minute, the water was bound to start over-flowing onto his rather sensual and costly carpeting.

Horrified by the prospect, he stuck his arm into his unintended steambath to release the bathwater, and promptly set his T-shirt afire.

"What in hell is *happening*?" Sutor shouted, making it part scream, and literally tore the undershirt from his chest. It all happened so fast that he'd had no chance whatsoever of being burned, but after he'd added the T-shirt to the sports coat and slacks, he smelled something acrid and raced to the mirror over his medicine cabinet to be *sure* he wasn't burning.

His skin wasn't but part of his hair—that portion on which he always lavished the greatest care before leaving in the morning to go to work—was. Nothing serious; there wasn't even any evidence of fire. Not yet. His coal-black hair was merely smoking, inoffensively charring dozens of strands and emitting a stink that Sutor had never smelled before.

He'd have been all right, perhaps, except that the face looking back at him in horror was no longer *his* face. Not entirely. The nose, the eyes, the smoulder-ing dark hair were all Andy Sutor, but the mouth was an immense, animalistic gash in the lower portion of Andy's face. And despite the fact that he was simultan-eously shocked and terrified, the mouth was *grinning* with every evidence of toothy enjoyment. He'd never seen such teeth, such a ghastly smirk, but didn't even think to look or feel behind him to learn if anyone else was in the room. The breath, bouncing back at him, was sulfurous and foul, as if he hadn't fed it regularly the finest breath-sweetening mist he'd been able to buy.

By the time he'd stopped swiping at his new mouth and checking it in the mirror over the sink to see if it had become his former mouth, he felt dazed, half drugged, and was making whimpering sounds in the back of his throat. The front part of his washed-and-blow-dried-daily black hair was now red as flame—for a perfectly sound reason.

Pain was scheduled for another few seconds.

Making strangling noises, Sutor fumbled with the faucets in the wash basin, yearning to put his head under water. Nothing emerged, and *then* the pain began, along with a different kind of stench. He hurtled his body toward the shower—

Leaving the smile and the remainder of Billy Salvo's disagreeable face perfectly mirrored, and merry, his body visible as well if he'd let the TV exec see it.

Among the three or four things Andy Sutor believed in was the true conviction that what one saw with one's eyes were there. A second article of faith was that fire burned. Consumed.

So it did.

"He's tricked me off the *Evening News*, Grady," Tom wailed in the Irishman's ear—"and his memo says that if *Confab* loses even one rating point I'm gone from Channel 61!"

Grady felt stunned. "I spoke with Andy right after Bud and I returned from the astrologer's, Tommy—and he said he was rethinking everything."

"Not quite everything," the director said, and Grady could imagine the distraught expression his old friend was wearing. "Or not quite everybody."

"I know Sutor will never win any awards from the people who work for him," Calhoun said angrily, "but I thought he had enough guts to fire people to their faces! I hope he burns in hell for doing this to you, Tom."

"To cap everything, Judith began immediately to worry about the money angle—instead of how I feel about it—and we got into a huge screaming battle. Aw, Grade-A, I treated her like shit!"

"She's a fine woman, buddy," Calhoun said reassuringly. "It was just her concern for the baby on the way; Jean got like that sometimes. Judith'll come around." He looked at the mouthpiece of the phone and shook his head doubtfully.

"Not right away, she won't," the lanky director declared. "She packed a few things and took off for her stepmother's. I can't understand what came over me, man; I never talked like that to a woman before, *especially* my Judith." Tom began to cry. "I've never been so miserable in my whole life."

"Tom, knock if off!" Calhoun snapped. His heart was beating frantically and he'd stood, as if trying to achieve a more direct and persuasive connection with his oldest friend. "You have to snap out of it—right now. You *must not* allow yourself to experience the beginning of misery— d'you follow me?" Calhoun's mind raced, looking for something that would cheer, Tom. "I'll talk to Sutor again, all right? I'll do my best to get it ironed out, Tommy, I promise! *But don't let yourself get down!*"

A moment later, when the connection was broken, it occurred to Grady that he was asking Simincola to do the near impossible. Anything except unhappiness for Tom now amounted to mental instability! Rajelis had struck again—or so it would appear—and he was getting cleverer about it, harder to defeat with every fresh, emotion-annihilating measure he took.

The phone jangled so loudly Calhoun jumped. He answered it in a mixed mood of irritation and new terror. Who was being hurt now?

"Wayne Sojourner, Calhoun," the tenor voice rumbled. "Hope I didn't catch you at a bad time?"

"Of course not, Wayne," Grady answered. "At least, no one I know has *died* in the past hour—I think!"

"Look—I've dug up some damned interesting information. A living, breathing lead—for now, anyway!"

Sojourner could not conceal his excitement. "We've located somebody who knew William Salvo very, very well. It's not impossible that he can verify whether Salvo actually *is* dead!"

"Maybe this is the bastard who's been hitting on my people," Calhoun breathed, full of fresh hope. "Maybe it's some kind of crazy vengeance both for Salvo and Calvin Rajelis!"

"I suppose it could be," Sojourner said dubiously. "But I doubt it."

"Why?"

"Grady, you forget how long ago Salvo is supposed to have died. This old boy—according to our records—is pushing 80 years old! But he *was* Salvo's buddy, more than 30 years back. And sometimes his partner!"

"When will you see him?" Grady demanded. Progress, maybe they were finally making progress!

"That's the thing, Grade-A," Wayne said sadly; "I can't speak to that old SOB at all! Look, I've got his address and all that—but without a solid reason for me to investigate his ass, any conversation I had with him would amount to harassment! And don't tell me there's a lot of good reasons, because I understand how you feel."

"I'm the king of interviews in the midwest, *I'll* talk with him," Calhoun said, talking fast. "And don't *you* give *me* a hassle over it, Wayne—just give me his name and address!"

Sojourner sounded his tenor chuckle. "No hassle. I planned on giving you the poop. But you be nice to him, Calhoun, hear me? Remember, he's an old man!"

Grady promised to remember, trying not to sound impatient. then he scribbled down the information and said the old man's name aloud: "Duck Sommers, huh? I'm going there immediately, Lieutenant! The minute we hang up!"

"One thing more, friend." Wayne's voice reached Grady when the receiver was already half a foot from his ear. He replaced it, listening. "Do me a favor and don't let the old boy know how you got his address." A pause. "My wife and babies would appreciate it."

Calhoun smiled, assured him that the secret was safe between them. He was out of his apartment in moments.

Bud let the phone at Calhoun's place ring a long while. Where could he have gone at this hour?

Giving up, at last, Bud shook her head and, realizing it had developed an awful ache, went in quest of APF tablets.

After she had taken two it occurred to her that maybe it was good for Grady not to learn immediately about Andy Sutor. He'd gone through hell, and Freida Rehfeldt's participation in helping them had buoyed Grady. If he learned about Andy's death now, he'd probably attribute it to that crazy mindreader—and that wouldn't make a lick of sense.

After all, it looked as if Sutor had committed suicide. Taken off his garments, including his sports jacket, then thrown them and himself into a full tub of water, and drowned. It was overflowing when they found his body.

At least, however bizarre it sounded, that was what Bud had been told by a friend from personnel who'd been at the station when the police called. And what else could it have been except suicide?

There wasn't a mark—not a mark of any kind—either on Sutor's body or any of his clothes.

17

Tuesday Evening and Night.
April 19.

"Tricky driving this time of day," Gill said.

"Yes, it certainly is," the girl agreed.

"Of course, I'm on such a sweet high I could practically pick up these wheels and *float* to Chi-town!"

"You aren't on drugs, are you?" the girl asked anxiously.

Gill swiveled his head to look at his hitchhiker again, more apologetically than leeringly this time. "No, ma'am," he swore, shaking his head and realizing how his remark had sounded. He laughed briefly to relieved the tension. "Talking about a *personal* high. Gill Riffey don't

require any help from chemistry tonight."
He saw that she still didn't understand
and tried to be clearer. "All I'm saying is
that I'm happy, babe, and everything's
cool."

"Oh," the svelte hitchhiker said,
doubtfully. A pause. "So you're a
musician, right?"

"How'd you know that?" Startled, the
trumpet player's brows shot up. When he
glanced at the girl this time he had the
dim impression that he'd seen her before.

She laughed, pointed to a shiny,
pebbled black case on the backseat.
"Nothing mysterious, Mister. That is a
horn, isn't it?"

"That is a trum-*pet*, my dear," Gill
replied airily, giving the kid his grand
manner, and grinning. Girls this young
were surely too young to pitch, but they
made him feel good and inclined to come
on to them anyway. "You may have seen
them pictured in old flicks on the very-
very late show. And Old Dad here is on his
way to the Windy City for a recording
gig—to show the people it's still possible
for another Miles to make it quite *large!*"

She giggled and showed a little thigh.
Not much, but it was such a glimpse that
had caused Gill to brake sharply and
respond to her lifted thumb. "So that's
why you dress funny."

"Funny?" he repeated, amusingly in-
sulted. He gestured broadly to his
emerald-colored suit and gaudy yellow
vest with the huge black buttons. He

turned his head slightly to peer mock dis-
approvingly at her, again struck by the
feeling that he'd met her. But no, not *met*
her exactly; there was just something
about the girl that was familiar. "These
threads set me back plenty, child! Lord
knows how many silkworms sacrificed
their squirmy lives to make this suit
possible!"

She flashed snowy teeth at him. "I'm
glad you picked me up."

Gill paused, pondering. He almost had
it now—who or what she reminded him
of—and for some reason he didn't feel
right about it. Night was coming on like
Mandelay thunder and suddenly it seemed
chilly in the car; disturbingly chilly. "I'm
glad too," he said, wondering if he meant
it.

"I thought you would," the hitchhiker
said in an oddly expressionless tone of
voice. "You're a bachelor, right? But not
gay?"

"Right on both counts," Gill said,
nodding. How'd she known that? Without
saying anything, he reflected on the
objects he had in the car. But there was
nothing in sight that could conceivably
have told the girl that he'd never been
married. Of course, it was possible she
was intuitive, a born mind-reader—or perhaps it was simply something about his
manner that tipped off his marital status.
Any female could pick up on jazz like that.
Once more he took a hard, quick glance at
her. "Not to get too heavy, babe, but Old

Dad hasn't had a lot to be gay over until recently."

"I know," she said, surprisingly, and nodded. But nothing in her basically ordinary young face indicated that she gave the slightest damn whether he lived or died. Kids today were honest as ice, even in the slightest, newest relationships, give 'em that. Then, incongruously and for no apparent reason, she was grinning at him and sliding close. "Actually," she continued, "you've been miserable for a long while, haven't you?"

Was it that grin? Something . . . "Naw, can't say miserable." Gill shrugged. His gaze returned to the highway again and he had to blink to focus; it would be night before they'd covered another three miles—well before they even hit Gary—and now they'd hit a patch of swirling fog. That made it even harder to keep track of the center stripe in the road. "I do research and a little writing for Channel 61 in Indy, and the Man's a good joe. It's just that I'd rather be tooting my trum-*pet*." He winked at the girl.

" 'The Man?' " She looked puzzled. Then her head bobbed. "You mean your boss, right? Mr. Calhoun?"

"Right," he answered and saw her image in his mind's eye while he worked at honing in on what was familiar about her. He got it at just the moment he realized that she could not know Grady Calhoun—because he hadn't even told her his *own* name.

Gill's hands tightened on the wheel. What had been bugging him about her face was, indeed, that big, wide grin of hers—because it looked exactly like a *smile face*. Which was silly, even stupid, doubtlessly; nobody had ever posed for the simple line drawing that had appeared with as much regularity for years now as the face of ol' Kilroy, back when he was a tad. But if it wasn't for her perfectly brushed woman's hair and girlish figure and clothing, this hitchhiker sitting next to him—and suddenly putting her hand on the inside of his thigh—*could* have *been* the smile face in person. She had, he saw, breathing harder for two reasons, the same emotionless little dots for eyes, the snub of a nose, and the complete vacuity—the spiritual emptiness—of the face anyone could draw.

Above all, she had that smile. That mouth.

Gill stared fixedly ahead, feeling ice cold, and feeling fingers dig into the soft flesh before moving down, lower. Jesus, what was wrong with him? He should be digging this!

But he most certainly wasn't.

"What do you think you're doing?" The words were forced out as if they'd been stuck in his throat for decades. His own voice sounded to him as if it came from some other automobile, two miles ahead of them. The fog swirling before the windshield was like colorless cotton candy. When her fingers closed on him, hard, Gill couldn't remember ever having been that scared.

"Making you have an accident," she said, and squeezed harder and produced greater relentless pain than any girl could do.

He gasped. His face shot forward in a reflex of exquisite, perfect agony. Simultaneously her other hand clapped the back of his head, smashing his mouth against the top of the steering wheel. Then she did it a second time. He felt his upper lip split and a tooth slice through skin and mustache like a letter opener through paper. He mashed his foot down on the brake, but his eyes filled with blinding tears and he couldn't see a thing.

Then they were zapping across the center stripe, and crashing.

Consciousness hung on; he didn't lose that, or pain. Deep in the outraged cellar of his brain he didn't believe he was supposed to.

And when his vision cleared enough to see out of one eye, and to register the fact that the lower part of his face was a bloodied mess, *she* was still on the seat beside him, unharmed.

Smiling.

"Have a nice day," she whispered in a toneless baritone.

Duck Sommers dwelled just off Indiana Avenue, in decades past the unofficial Main Street of semi-segregated Indianapolis' black populace, in a brick-fronted old two-story that—in its time—had been a near mansion; a pleasant residential hotel; and what it was today: a building with apartments for a maximum number of renters.

It was very late now, and the yellow brick seemed uremic and ominous, as if it contained dark secrets unsuited to the white Calhoun. There'd been a time when Grady would have been fearful of entering the place, especially at night. He wasn't proud of that when he remembered it, however. Yet on some occasions, he sensed, his fear would have been justified. Not all those who are economically depressed, recessed, or suppressed are disposed to be forgiving and philosophical about it.

Now, with many more real terrors preying on his mind, when he elicited no response after persistently rapping on Duck Sommers's second-floor corner apartment for a full minute, Calhoun decided to remain in the place and phone Jean. While twilight was hours ago and, according to Calvin Rajelis's strange pattern, Grady's former family was secure until early morning, that didn't mean the kids—or Jean—had escaped that day's periods of cuspal illumination.

Calhoun remembered passing a phone booth in what surely had been the lobby of the building, and trotted back downstairs without apprehension in any sense of the word. His watch seemed to have stopped, but it was surely past three

A.M. and he hadn't caught sight of a living soul. It felt haunted but not uncomfortably so, there; haunted by all the old structure had allowed to seep into its faded walls instead of by the spirits of people.

Having dialed, Grady thought of hanging up. It was an ungodly hour, and the ring might frighten Jean. But now he felt driven by the need to check up, the need to hear his ex-wife's voice.

What he hadn't bargained for or wildly imagined was the terrible news she'd confided to him a minute after she'd said hello.

"—And I'll never know why I even agreed to go out with him, Grady, but I d-did—and he raped me. Raped and b-beat me."

"My God, Jeannie," he gasped, "I'm so sorry." His temper flared. "That bastard, that son of a *bitch*."

"Wait," Jean added, her voice pitched at a level Calhoun couldn't remember hearing, sounding strained, or dreamy, "there's more. After he k-kicked me out into the street, like garbage, I tried to see his license plate, get the number . . . and I *know* this will sound positively ridiculous, Grady, but—the car *disappeared*."

—Motion, seen from the corner of one eye, drew Calhoun's gaze. Spinning to stare out into the area leading to a flight of steps and a rickety elevator tenants operated themselves, he saw a hunch-shouldered, broad-backed old man with a black bullet of a head trudging toward the stairs. He clutched a brown paper sack tightly under one arm. *Sommers*, Grady realized; *that's Duck Sommers.*

"I can't blame you for not believing me," Jean continued, and he realized he'd fallen silent after her amazing statement—"but the car simply became a sort of distant point on the horizon, then it v-vanished. It *did*."

Grady nodded, and wondered that he'd reached a state of desensitization at which he calmly accepted the concept of disappearing automobiles. "I believe you, Jean," he said simply, warmly. "I wish to God I didn't, but I do."

"That's all I had to say to you."

Grady blinked. What the hell did that mean? She was ready to hang up now—dismissing him, as if she had fulfilled an obligation of some kind and was free to go to sleep. He also realized how dreadfully tired she sounded, and distantly sensed how much more hideous her experience must have been than it would have been at the hands of a normal brute. "Jean," he asked gently, "what did he look like?"

"Who?" She was starting to nod off. "Bill?" A note of surprise registered. "Grady, I can't even picture him now . . . except for his mouth." She was concentrating, Calhoun realized; focusing on the facial image before it was gone for good. "He had the biggest mouth I ever saw. Y-You could look into it a-and feel almost that he m-meant to bite your head off. . . ."

When they'd hung up Grady yearned for vengeance upon the rapist, on Rajelis and whatever in Christ's name "William Salvo" was—and realized how fond he remained of Jean Calhoun. He needed to see her soon; to try to help her back to herself, and—

She's told no one what happened but me, he perceived, closing the phone booth door behind him and pausing to grasp the rest of this newest nightmare,—*because she wasn't* supposed *to. Because the entire goddamned* attack *was for my benefit! To go on proving to me that my continued existence means more awful things will happen to everyone I love.*

He was hurrying up the dimly lit stairway toward Sommers's apartment—that old SOB was going to tell Calhoun everything there was to know about Salvo if Grady had to beat it out of him—when he also came to the realization that the nightmarish horrors that were being inflicted upon the people around him were getting *geometrically worse as each day passed.* True; Timothy Calhoun had lost his life, but that was, Grady perceived, an announcement, an early proof; and the truth was, he'd never felt that close to poor Timmy. Bud's sister had been arrested, half broken, her little boy severely injured—but they hadn't *died* because Grady didn't care *that much* about them! His son, Tim, whom Calhoun didn't understand but loved, was on the verge of making choices that could forever *isolate him* from Grady—a truly evil thing to happen to father and son. And, already, the other children had been ill, as if Rajelis were *advertising* what he could do and meant to do, taunting Calhoun with what was in store for them. His mother, not only frightened into premature senility but left in a condition of *perpetual depression*—for the first time Grady saw clearly the scope of the mentalist's sadistic plan.

Now, Jean. Rajelis was truly diabolical; that was the right word for the man. He had sacrificed her to his Salvo-thing—whatever it was—because Rajelis had known *before Grady had* how much he still cared for her! The anguish, the deep, abiding sorrow, would fester for months; years. If there *were* months and years left to anybody Calhoun knew, including himself.

By the time he was once more knocking on Duck Sommers's apartment door, Grady wondered if the aged black man might be the one person capable of furnishing a lead to the whereabouts of Salvo and Rajelis—without which he might literally be obliged, in the name of common decency, to take his own life.

One round, dark eye shone from the shadows as the apartment door opened an inch and a half. "What you want?"

"I must talk with you, Mr. Sommers." Calhoun couldn't recall an earlier moment when he had felt virtually bathed by suspicion. That, and some society-inflicted kinsman of hatred, poured out at him. "I'm not the police."

"Then why you mention 'em? Got a name?"

"Why, yes; I have a name." The question triggered an idea and, summoning what he required from years of experience, Grady gave the wary black eye an ingratiating smile. "Haven't you seen me on TV? I'm Grady Calhoun. From *Confab*."

It worked like one of Calvin Rajelis' tricks! The door creaked open and the muscular old man materalized, fumbling for a light switch just inside the apartment.

But Grady knew that second he'd never be able to extract the information he needed from this man; not by force. Because Duck Sommers looked like a man who'd invented the meaning of old age. Or it had been named for him. Once unquestionably formidable, the kind of partner a sometime hitman like Billy Salvo might have sought out, all the malicious or uncaring acts of Sommers' life were stenciled in his ashen face and form. A dark Dorian Grey, Duck was surely supported in standing erect by hard-won survival practice in prisons from coast to coast. Shrunken, the staves of his barrel chest broken and the chest sunken to an uneasy union with his belly, the old fellow was trying to hide the contents of the brown sack he'd brought in behind his bent back. It sloshed.

"You here 'bout that letter I sent?" Duck inquired. When Grady didn't know what to say, Sommers helped. "*You* know—'bout doing a *Confab* 'bout my life in crime?" He extended the bottle, waggled it as an invitation for Calhoun to enter the apartment. "Knew 'em all, I did—Capone, Dillinger, Pretty Boy Floyd. And *worked* with 'em too." He moved in a sort of waddling fashion that reminded Grady of an old burlesque comic named Scurvy, whom Calhoun had seen as a teenager sneaking into a long gone burly house. Grady lowered himself carefully into a chair with dubious longevity. " 'Course, I meant what m'letter *said*: Been a honest man for more'n 30 years. We talkin the *past* here."

More than thirty years, Calhoun thought. "The producers believe your idea has possibilities, Mr. Sommers, but they're particularly interested in an . . . associate . . . of yours named Salvo. William Salvo." Grady watched the old man closely. "Think he went by Billy."

The expression on the aged face made Grady wonder if he'd just killed an old man. Duck Sommers froze, the seat of his pants still inches away from his own chair, and it looked as if he'd been freeze-dried and might remain that way forever. "Where'd you hear about Billy Salvo?"

"Well," Grady said, worried, "there are records the authorities have, you know. We researched—"

"You researched *shit*!" Duck sat, sweating, took a long pull from his bottle. One foot twitched. Worse, his free hand was doubling and, for an instant, Calhoun wondered how much strength the old fellow still possessed. "Nobody knows what happened to Billy Salvo 'cept Duck Sommers." An expression of cunning glittered in the eyes like dark tombstones. "And I ain't tellin' it on the tube lest I get paid *right*!"

"How can I know if it's worth it until you tell me the details? It's not worth a nickel coming from anybody but you, you realize," Calhoun added hastily. "Why are you the only one who knows what happened to Billy?"

Duck leaned forward in his chair. " 'Cause we was alone t'gether when he died." The bullet head nodded. "I saw it, and I'll never forget it neither!"

Calhoun gave the old man his warmest, most attentive smile. "Tell me," he said, crossing his legs.

Very slowly, Duck nodded. Before beginning, however, he cast careful, covert glances into the poorly illumined shadows of his room, and it might have been amusing except for the look of fear on his gray features. "They were goin' to 'lectrocute Billy, and I didn't blame 'em much. Even when we partnered, he was a cold mother-fucker. Allus thought he liked t'kill people just to be killin' them. Anyways, Billy escaped with the po-lice right behind."

"Go on," Calhoun said.

"Stupid mother-fucker runs to *my* place, can you imagine that?" Duck scowled. "Gets my old ass in deep shit when he shoulda *knowed* the po-lice would look for him there!"

Grady was perspiring freely, breathing hard, but hoped that Duck was too drunk—or too old—to notice. "And did they?"

Duck nodded. "Came in quiet as mices; best I ever saw 'em do it. And I think. Billy mighta surrendered if they let him. But one ol' detective, he hated Billy Salvo real bad. Wanted his ass dead. So he fires at Billy, hits his arm, and both Billy and me, we hightail it for the window at the back of m'place." It was, Calhoun saw, as real to the old man as if it had happened last year. "Shot at us again, and I threw up my hands; quit runnin'. And with my back to that ol' detective I was lookin' straight at Billy when he reaches the window and glances back."

. . . *Being shot had not seemed to him a possibility, and being mortally wounded had never even occurred to Salvo as a thing that could happen to him. His eyes were filled with the blackness of night glimpsed through the window of his partner, Sommers, when something—a distant noise, a furtive motion—made him look back.*

Strangely, he saw the detective who had hunted him down again clearly—in the front room—and saw the man's finger squeeze the trigger. In the instant before the slug from the automatic caught him just above the bridge of the nose, Salvo also saw the brilliant flash of light — saw it and knew for a fact it was the last thing he'd ever see in his life.

Some people, some men particularly, live their lives so wantonly and fully that their own foreordained annihilation cannot and does not occur to them. Whatever risks they've taken, wounds they have suffered, the ultimate fact that they will truly die has been omitted from their intellectual contemplations as it is from the presumably less complex thinking of house pets.

What William Salvo took into his unexpected dying with him was a trio of images: black night, and the cozy comfort of an escape that was within a hair's breadth of being a reality; the sight of a man of law and order quite improperly shooting to kill; and a blaze of vivid light that instructed him that he was absolutely wrong in believing that he was free to do anything he pleased by virtue of disbelieving in his own mortality. Those things, and the smallest instant of shrieking terror.

Then his brains were shot all over the wall — the essence, the this-life personality of a man in the truest sense of the word. The part of William Salvo that most accurately had told what kind of person he was — splattered on a wall as if at the hands of a mad modernist who worked in the basics of blood.

And when the screams sounded simul-

*taneously with the fractional point of
death, the brain's ruined chambers,
opened in a shower of splintered bone,
gristle, and fire-red blood, parted
company, too, with the shocked and
delivered soul, and that soul fled . . .*

"Lucky fuckin' shot!" Duck said scorn-
fully. "That ol' detective, he never was
much, but he got fuckin'-A *lucky*!"

"The police records," Calhoun said
cautiously, "are sketchy—"

" 'Sketchy!" Duck Sommers glanced
up, amused and angry and, judging by the
underlying gleam in his circular eyes,
lingeringly frightened. "Shee-eet! They
never wrote down nothin' 'cause they
didn't *see* it!" He hauled himself to his
feet, not noticing the tilted bottle and how
it was dripping on the floor. "Man, Billy
Salvo's head 'sploded!"

"Exploded? You mean, when the
bullet struck it?"

Duck nodded, waving his arms for full
attentiveness. "That ain't the main part.
Anyone's head can 'splode!"

Grady swallowed delicately. "I
suppose."

"It's what I saw happen *next*, Mr.
Calhoun," Duck continued, teetering.
Furtive glances wriggled into the room's
corners as he edged forward with three,
small paces that were like a baby's first
steps. "It's what I *saw*."

"Go on," Grady prompted him.

"Mr. Calhoun," Duck said, eyes
immense, "I saw *his soul*."

Calhoun had no idea what to say.

"Saw that soul clear as *day*! Truth is," Duck edged nearer, one foot twitching, "I sometimes used to have 'bilities like that. I seen many a strange thing, Mr. Calhoun—but nothin' as strange as *this*!"

"There's more?"

The dark, round eyes were lowered until they were half a foot away. Now the old man was whispering. "Mr. Calhoun, Salvo's soul done shattered. Shot out like a hundred million tiny little lights, bright as fire—and they're called soul spots. Now," he pursed his lips, "*my* feelin' is that a part of Billy's soul found its way t'that great tunnel and went straight on home—to wherever the im-mortal soul returns." The eyes came still closer. "But *other parts* of his soul went . . . somewhere else. 'Cause they was scared, Mr. Calhoun, scared into dividin' and stayin' and just waitin' for a chance to re-u-nite somehow, someday, with the *rest*."

Salvo's soul had been split; sundered. Grady took it in steadily, nodding now himself, trying to understand it. According to this old, gray man who had seen Salvo die, some *part* of him had remained. "But Mr. Sommers, how could it hope to be . . . reunited?"

The old man, straightening, staring eerily at him, gave his answer at the same moment Grady imagined Freida Rehfeldt whispering an answer in his ear:

Through some unnatural form of rein-carnation.

18

Wednesday. Very Early. April 20.

By the time Grady found himself sitting in an almost deserted Grimelda's, ordering a second cup of coffee from a man who looked even more tired, he was on the verge of believing anything. He'd have been drinking ever since he arrived except for the local liquor laws, and imagined he wouldn't be much more confused if he had been.

Because, once he'd replayed mentally everything Duck Sommers said, he'd had to conclude that the old man was probably senile as shit and that, if not, the information was still fundamentally useless. Salvo, the Salvo whom Duck had known, at least, was just as dead as Wayne Sojourner's official reports stated. And if fragments of his warped soul were floating around town like confetti, the lieutenant was sure as hell not going to put out an APB to apprehend 'em!

So he had thanked Duck Sommers, said that Andy Sutor would probably be contacting him about his show idea, and meandered over to Grimelda's in the hope that Gill Riffey might be hanging around, noodling on his trum-*pet.*

Too late, Calhoun remembered that Gill was on his way to Chicago to cut a few sides. Grady hoped it worked out, but the way things were going, they'd probably sign Gill up as Doc Severinson's replacement, Carson'd finally retire, and Calhoun would simply be out one reliable old friend, writer, and researcher!

Maybe he would talk Andy into doing the show Duck proposed, Grady mused, ordering a breakfast roll and yawning at the window. The street and sidewalk beyond it were cemetery-still; it was still dark, but most of the night was gone and he might as well check into the station for a couple of hours, then beg off sick and get some sacktime during the afternoon. Grady grinned. Duck's idea might make interesting TV if he'd promise not to curse so colorfully!

Thinking of *Confab* brought an idea to mind and Calhoun munched his roll more quickly, practically wolfing it down. Nobody would be around Channel 61 at this hour but Kiefer, the night watchman, and Bernie was a big fan of *Confab*. Freida, the astrologer, needed Rajelis' birthdate to do his horoscope and someone on Andy's staff should have set up a file at the point the mentalist was firmly booked! The sooner Grady got the info, the sooner Freida could do her thing!

Throwing down a five to cover the tab, he hurried out of the place, relieved to take any action that might help him go on the offensive. Happily, it was a clear morning, slightly warmer, and the station was only blocks away.

The skeletal type who'd looked 40 in his twenties and still did in the late fifties posed no more of an obstacle then Grady had believed Bernie Kiefer would. It was strictly against the rules to admit employees at such an hour, but, even at the local level, being a star had its advantages. Bony Bernie unlocked Sutor's bank of offices, said to ring for him when Grady was finished, and, obligingly took the elevator back down to the lobby.

Grady stood, reflecting, in the center of the programming domain—a plush outer office where Andy's assistant, Clyde Barker, handled the administrative duties as if he loathed the world—and saw several filing cabinets ranged against one wall. The sole illumination was provided by an overhead, recessed light in the foyerlike entrance to the office, and what tenuous lighting wended its way in from outside. *What if the cabinets were locked?* Calhoun asked himself, starting slowly forward. *Easy,* he answered himself; *I'll smash the lock.* He could always try to blame it on the evil influence of crooked old Duck Sommers.

But the drawers slid open easily, noiselessly, and the only problem confronting Calhoun then was locating the "R" cabinet. He eased the first drawer shut, guessed at another—muttering to himself about inefficient people who couldn't find a few minutes to type up 26 cards bearing the letters of the alphabet— and found himself staring at the letter *P.*

"Getting hot," he whispered, opened the next file drawer, and saw the names

RANDALL and RANDI at once. He ran his
fingertips back through the folders in
search of RAJELIS. "Ah!" he exclaimed,
barely above a whisper. "There!" He
reached for the file.

"What are you doing?"

Shocked, Grady jumped involuntarily
and nearly dropped the Rajelis file.

"I'd put that down if I were you."

For a moment, in the office's early
morning shadows, Grady couldn't locate
the speaker. But he recognized the voice
and his heart began to pound.

The program manager was on the
other side of the bank of cabinets. He rose
above them as if he might have been
sitting on the floor, alone in the dark
office, waiting. "Andy!" said Calhoun,
nervously. "What are *you* doing here?"

Silence followed his question, and he
knew there ought to be some sound, if
only that of clothes rustling; or breathing.
"You'll only make it happen faster," Andy
Sutor said sadly, but laughed. The laugh
was hacked off as if decapitated, leaving a
strange menacing, rasping noise that
mocked breathing and hung on the unmoving air like a stain.

"Not sure I follow," Grady said. "You
mean, what's been happening to everyone
I know?" He glanced restively around,
aching to turn on lights. Maybe it was
done by buttons under desks. Why in
God's name didn't his boss come out from
behind the files? "Andy, how would you
know I might make it worse if I discovered

something about Calvin Rajelis? What does that mean?"

Andy moved around the cabinets. His black hair, traditionally so impeccably brushed, stood wildly on end. It looked smoky, almost prematurely gray. "Who would know better than I, oh-great-communicator?" he inquired mockingly. "I am Calvin Rajelis' newest victim." There was a glimmer of moonlight on the pile carpeting near Grady, and Andy stepped into it. He looked more than pale. "Grade-A, Rajelis *killed* me. I'm *dead.*"

The folder with Rajelis' name on it slipped through Grady's fingers. His gaze fastened upon the program manager's hard, remarkably shiny, ebony eyes. And he saw no reason whatever to doubt that the entity before him was speaking the truth. "You're not, not *really,*" Grady denied it—denied his own senses. But he backed off as the specter came a step closer. "You're . . . *on* something."

"Yes. Yes, I am. On borrowed time." Nodding, Andy's head wobbled; something dark, and ugly, showed in a flash. Then he held up both hands, but the gesture only for an instant seemed terribly, terrifyingly threatening. It was just show-and-tell time as the sleeves of his immaculate shirt and sports jacket fell back loosely. Revealed were arms like burnt sticks. Almost gagging, Calhoun finally noticed that Andy's clothes hung baggily on him, and it occurred to Grady that only Andy's head had not been incinerated. And the bones. The thing drew closer; it was changing in some incalculable manner—within the apparition—becoming less Andy Sutor and more nightmare. "I'm here for you, Grade-A," it wailed.

Without quite realizing it, Calhoun had moved backward till his back was to a window. He glanced over his shoulder, fast. The fall wasn't great. Just enough to kill him. "I don't know wh-what to say," he began, chattering. Maybe he could filibuster his way out of it; talk forever, if he could find the words.

"That's a novelty," the phantom quipped. And *it* was nearer, much nearer, and it *hadn't* moved. "A speechless Grady Calhoun! A talk show host who can think of nothing to say is *very* amusing." The shiny eyes grew shinier, the pupils like spinning little stars; the winter-twig wrists were fully exposed as the awful, black, clawing fingers lifted to a level with Grady Calhoun's face.

It began to laugh, though, as if finding the whole situation too full of merriment to be endured without relief. And as it laughed, the entity appeared to recede from Grady . . . except it wasn't *moving* from him, it was getting *smaller* now, the whole burnt-out wreck of a creature was beginning to diminish and disappear. Fallen to one shaking knee, Grady nearly put out a hand, God help him, to help it—

But: "You damned stupid imbecile!" It shrieked with laughter that bounded from

the office walls and made the pane in the
window vibrate. "We wouldn't harm a hair
of your head, Grade-A—because that's
your role in this production, remember?"

It vanished. Like the light on an old-
style TV set blinking out, it vanished.

Before it died for good, it gave off the
brightest light Calhoun had ever seen.

19

Wednesday. 7:09 A.M., April 20.

Filled with an urge to telephone everyone
he'd ever met and even remotely liked to
make sure they were well, aware of the
impossibility of that and feeling more
futile and powerless than ever before,
Calhoun had gone straight home and
gotten into bed.

He hadn't even removed his shoes.

When he closed his eyes and tried to
sleep, horrifying images cavorted for him
as if he'd rigged up a movie projector for
the inside of the lids. Faces he loved, liked,
knew distantly, and didn't much care
about one way or the other flitted into and
out of focus and then they began to be
swallowed up by a gigantic mouth that
devoured them whole and smacked its
lips. His knees were drawn up to his chest,
he was cold and sweating simultaneously,
his muscles felt like someone else's—
someone who had just undergone a series

of killingly grueling exercises—and he was dimly aware that his fists were knotted so tightly that the nails were drawing blood.

It didn't look like a good day.

Who's left, Calhoun asked himself, *who's fucking left unhurt?* But now, when he strove to recall only the faces he truly adored or valued, the images in his mind's eye fled as if a length of film had split or run off and for an aching, annihilative instant, he was under the impression that he knew *no* living soul.

The emotion of isolation, of being the last man alive on earth, was paralyzing, and he couldn't even cry. Just open his dry eyes and stare across the bedroom at another beige Indy A.M.

Bud, Grady thought. And winced. Except for what had happened to her sister and her nephew, Bud was unharmed—which could only mean that she was one of those Rajelis and Salvo—assuming they were two entities and not the same—were saving for last. God, what did they have in mind for her! Jean was alive, yes, but how much remained of her spirit, of her . . . Jeanness? Calhoun couldn't even think about their children; not that moment. Ol' Tom was still around, but more forlorn and anxious about the possibility of losing his wife and the child she carried, as well as his job, than Grady could remember. Mom was also among the living, and he knew he must go to her when he could . . . even if

she was a haunted shadow of her once unbending self.

The awareness came to Calhoun that
he felt *secure* about the idea of Rajelis
saving Bud and the kids for last when it
would be just *like* that all-knowing nightmare to single out one or more of them
now, while Grady believed they were safe
for a while! Sitting up, half standing in his
rumpled clothes, the horror of that
possibility mingled with the realization
that his own imaginative insight was
obviously paranoid—and it was the first
time Calhoun perceived that rather than
reaching the point that he'd have to take
his life, he might just go *mad* first. . . .

If either the mind-reader or Salvo
could be *located,* somehow *questioned,* if
only Grady or Wayne Sojourner could find
them and *reason* with them—threaten
them, try to buy them *off*—other options
might become feasible. He could plead to
be told what in God's name he had *done* to
Rajelis, apologize, even make a public
statement, or—

Where did I put that file folder?
Calhoun wondered, rising stiffly to look
for it. For a moment he couldn't remember
bringing it home.

But he had dropped it on a table inside
the door when he'd staggered in and not
even glanced at the contents. Sutor—or
Sutor's ghost; or, for all Grady knew, a dis-
guised Billy Salvo or some construct of
Rajelis—had scared him silly. Now,
perched on the edge of the bed beside his

telephone, he checked it out eagerly, desperately, with trembling hands.

He found promotional stuff, ads for Calvin Rajelis as a professional mentalist. And printed as well as photocopied reviews of his act; a list of all the different places Rajelis had performed. Mentions in articles and columns; the customary stuff.

—Including a clean, white bio sheet! Grady saw the madman's date of birth almost immediately and reached for the phone.

At the other end, answering the ring, Freida Rehfledt sounded strange, strained, slightly frightened or, at least, disconcerted. It took the caller a second to realize that it was still very early morning, and that the middle-aged astrologer had been asleep. *Early morning*; he looked toward a window, wondering how exact Rajelis had to have to be about the interface of night and day, day and night. Was it possible the bastard could somehow *listen in,* psychically—or was considering that as a possibility another example of how paranoid Grady Calhoun was becoming?

Freida listened to what had just happened to him without comment except for tense little "uh-huhs" interspersing his narrative of the events. "I have no idea whether it was Mr. Sutor's phantom you saw, or what," she admitted when he had asked. "The materialization of a spirit at this point seems anomalous, but it *is* clear that Mr. Rajelis is escalating his attacks.

And we must not underestimate his gifts or skills."

"I won't," Grady said passionately. Then he wondered if he was; how could he conceivably guess the extent of the man's powers? He told her Rajelis' birthdate, apologizing that the bio sheet didn't list his hour and place of birth.

"The lack of that data is the common-place anethma of any astrologer's life," Freida said, more or less soothingly. "I'm delighted you got the information."

"How long will it take to . . . do . . . his horoscope?" Grady asked.

"Give me until noon tomorrow."

". . . That long?"

Freida's voice laughed humorlessly in his ear. "You would be perfectly astounded, Mr. Calhoun, by how many otherwise ordinary human beings *rely* on astrologers. I have two clients who threaten, respectively, homicide and suicide if I do not provide them with answers today." She paused, apparently sensing his misery, his deep need. "Society at large makes fun of astrology, Grady; but during any week of my life I'm obliged to handle problems that might better be directed to clergymen, marriage counsellors, psychologists or psychia-trists—and to the men and women my clients cannot usually communicate with. You are not alone in danger."

"I'll just have to wait," Calhoun mumbled.

"Don't hang up," she said warmly, en-

couragingly. "Talk with me another
moment. We discussed the colorlessness
of glaring light, touched upon the color
white, when you and that charming Bud
Rocker visited me. I've been thinking . . .
researching the matter." She hesitated
and, in the background, at least one cat
meowed. It seemed as if the astrologer
might be clutching one of her feline
companions in that hand that did not
grasp her telephone. "I came across a
rather *intriguing term,* Mr. Calhoun—and
I'd like to know if it means anything to
you, or if any one of your circle of
associates have heard it mentioned."

"Go ahead," Grady said, listening
intently.

Freida cleared her throat. "When the
soul departs the body, particularly when it
is then discarnate—when it hasn't gone
anywhere, not been relocated or
'collected'—those who have the special
ability to see it are dazzled by a queer
effect it possesses. One of light and yet
one of shadow. It's called . . . *the white
darkness.*"

Calhoun tried to remember. "It
doesn't sound quite familiar to me," he
said regretfully.

"Well, it didn't hurt to ask," Freida
said cheerily. "I intend to be alert to use of
the term and I hope you will be, as well.
You see, Mr. Calhoun, metaphysicians
claim that those discarnate spirits that
have been mired in evil, but resist going
on, find it exceedingly painful. And

. . . disturbing." Then her tone of voice grew businesslike. "Maybe tomorrow, when you call, I will have learned enough from Mr. Rajelis' natal chart to enable you to mount an offensive. Or if not that, to prepare a final defensive."

For Tom Simincola, sleeping in his bed without Judith beside him felt abnormal, and he had known he wouldn't be able to sleep. So, last night, he'd downed a few doubles at Grimelda's, continued the onslaught on his system alone at home, and fallen into unhappy, restive sleep on a sofa in the living room.

He awakened there to noises; from the front door.

He sat up at once—too hastily, since a headache began immediately to pound in both temples—hoping it was Judith.

And a moment later, when he'd realized it had to be his wife, home from her stepmother's, since she had the other key to the house, Tom saw the long shadow of a man cross the entrance from the foyer.

Son of a gun, I've got me a burglar, the director thought, and froze in watchful silence.

A rattly, metallic sound clattered at or near the front closet, and then the closet door creaked open. The combination of a hangover and acute loneliness blended in Tom to produce a querulous and dogged kind of irritation verging upon anger. He didn't have *enough* to worry him—Judith, angry or hurt and carrying their last chance at parenthood; Andy Sutor threatening to can his ass after years at 61—he was supposed to tolerate some lowlife SOB who'd come to steal the *rest* of his life!

Not this time, pal, Tom resolved, slipping off the sofa on the balls of his feet and slowly, soundlessly, tiptoeing across the room.

He might have forgotten a lot of it, but he remembered *some* of the hand-to-hand he'd learned in 'Nam. And he'd taken about half a course in Tae Kwando last spring, specifically because crime rates were increasing in this part of the north-west side of town.

Now the burglar had fallen silent. For a split second, Tom wondered if he'd made some telltale noise of his own and alerted the SOB. He didn't really believe he had, but one could logically reason that no-goodnik types who broke-and-entered were similar to blind people who overcompensated with a functioning sense—*if* one didn't mind getting honest blind people pissed off!

The lanky director was suddenly full of second thoughts: A glimpse, that was all he'd gotten of the slimy bastard; one short glimpse while he himself was emerging from an alcoholic stupor. He'd heard in recent times about home-owners who took the law in their own hands and managed to do terrible things to innocent people. Before going after the SOB, Tom realized, he'd *have* to have another look.

So he looked. Craning his neck, he put the top part of his long, bespectacled head around the edge of the entrance way—

And despite the fact that it was barely daylight and the foyer was steeped in shadows, a man—a complete stranger— was going through the things in the Simincola front closet.

Which was when Tom spotted the knife gleaming dully from the floor where the Bad Guy had laid it, to have his hands free for the wholesome purpose of ransacking somebody else's things!

The man turned his head, langourously, to peer at Tom just as Tom rushed him with both arms raised above his head. There was a microsecond's sight of a somewhat drab masculine face uptilted in apparent surprise, a wide and vacuous mouth hanging dully agape.

Then Tom was atop him, long arms flailing, describing a dual arc as he chopped downward with the braced edges of both hands.

At once the burglar was flat on his back; he cried out, moaned in a voice more high pitched than Tom's own, said *Don't*. But at that moment in the director's life the crooked SOB handsomely represented all the lousy, unjust things that had gone wrong lately, and Tom hit him again; and again. Then, after pausing, he hit him again. Also kicked him, but not very hard, the solitary instance of savagery and lost control in Simincola's life ebbing out of him as fast as it had filled him up.

Whew, Tom said, arm-weary and surprised, a bit proud of himself and a bit more embarrassed by what he had done. He knuckled sweat from his eyes by raising his thick-lensed spectacles, let them drop back into place, and stared down in absolute absence of comprehension.

There on the floor where the male intruder should be, his wife Judith lay with glassy eyes, some blood, and the point of a bone showing under one ear. It looked somewhat like a tooth.

Two lives had been lost, but that did not immediately occur to the broken man.

Because it was devoid of sentience, of any purpose of its own design, it did not know that it had become a source of evil for many beings called "people" on a planet called "Earth."

In the essentially incomprehensible vastness of cold and arid space, it had assumed life of a kind, too, but the realization hadn't occurred to it. "It" was collective, nothing more, to any astronomers who chanced to gaze its way— a chance dependent not only upon the existence of beings with such an intellectual focus on a planet in range, but on such astronomers happening to peer in precisely the right place at precisely the right instant—but a once-in-millenia alignment, theoretically countable millions of miles across the universe.

The alignment had occurred not by chance, since all its immense segments were—theoretically—wholly predictable in their rate of motion. But calculating it would have required a lifespan on the part of astronomers abundantly greater than that of any sentient creatures dwelling within 1,000 light years of it, in any direction.

It also did not have the aesthetic judgment to perceive that its infinite number of connections created a pictorial ambience rather like that of a great, human, Earth-style brain.

Lifetimes of unbreachable distance from Earth yet unswervingly true to the old Earth tenet, "As above, so below," the configurations formed of stars, planets, and asteroids had always possessed the destiny to achieve such an alignment— and, in due time (an imponderable), a similitude of rational thought.

For now, however, its ancient obligation was to influence *some* toward replicating its own capacity for massive change, for personal growth, for unassailable progress toward the fulfillment of its destiny regardless of anything whatsoever standing in its way.

Others might be influenced toward a similar emulation of thinking life.

Others would interpret its influence in their own, narrower ways, and seldom pause to consider whether their course of choice represented good or evil. At its core, the cosmos was mechanism set in motion, its once planned purposes unalterable and impersonal, too sweeping to respect exception.

It was mortal, sentient life that possessed reason; compassion; the blessed wonder of choice; a soul.

20

Thursday Morning. April 21.

Yesterday—Wednesday, after conversing with the astrologer, Freida—Grady decided that phoning Jean wouldn't be enough. She had still seemed bewildered or in shock when he'd called her from old Duck Sommers' place and, besides, he grew even more concerned about the safety of the kids.

Dropping by, unannounced, Calhoun surprised himself by spending all day in the house that had once been his home—first alone with his ex-wife, later with the children, as they arrived home one by one. At first, he'd had the notion that Jean welcomed him simply because he was the one person to whom she had confided her frightening story, and needed to get the rest of it out. He didn't mind; when Jean was relaxed and not uptight he still enjoyed her company.

As the hours passed, however—and even before Jean got Petey up from one of the interminable little naps she went on foisting upon him—Grady came to realize that she was truly happy to be with him. And when she broke down, in tears, and he consoled her, he sensed that he was able to touch her without a swift upsurge of desire. *It's either a sign of maturity,* Calhoun mused, sympathetically patting her back—*or male menopause!*

To Grady's further surprise and pleasure, Jean was even willing to let him tell her *his* story, to bring her up to date on the growing number of people both of them knew who, in one fashion or another, had been under attack. Jean did not appear ready to concede that the string of nightmarish miseries was anything more than bizarre coincidence until he had told her of that morning's conversation with the Rehfeldt woman. "She asked me a funny question," Grady said lightly, sipping a beer and wondering if it was one he'd left behind. If Jean, who detested beer, had purchased more, the implications were highly intriguing.

"Funny, ha-ha?" Jean asked.

Grady sighed. "Gill Riffey's the only guy I know who can make me laugh, these days," he admitted. "No, she asked me if anybody I knew had mentioned—or heard the Salvo character mention—the expression 'white darkness.' "

Jean had been sipping hot tea. Her eyes rose above the rim of the cup and, if she hadn't lifted the saucer along with the cup, she might have burned herself.

"*Yes.*" It was a whisper. Her gaze fixed upon Grady's eyes and face as if something told her she must not prolong such a conversation—but she'd already admitted it. With an effort, clearly, of strong will, she lowered her cup and saucer to the coffee table between them. "Before he . . . kicked me out into the st-street . . . he looked at the sky, stared at it as if it hurt, but as if he—had to. And that was what he said, Grady. 'The *white darkness* . . .' "

"Evil souls," Calhoun said softly, "find . . . it . . . painful. Freida said that those that haven't, um, gone on, are half blinded by it. 'One of light and yet one of shadow,' Freida said."

"I'm not surprised to—" Jean blurted.

"What?" Surprised by the tone in her voice, Grady stared at her.

She twisted her head, appeared to be trying to shake away a series of awful thoughts. She looked, he thought, in some pain. "Can we not talk about it?" Jean asked finally, trying to smile at him. It was a ghastly grimace, instead, and she'd turned pale.

He told her of course, and changed the subject.

But he'd also made a mental note to tell Freida Rehfeldt: At least *one* of the Rajelis-Salvo victims had heard a reference to the enigmatic term. What was that other thing Freida had said? But no; no, it was Duck Sommers who'd described what happened when Billy Salvo—the first, the truly-he-lived William Salvo

—died: "His soul shattered. Shot out like a hundred million tiny little lights . . . and they're called soul spots." Calhoun thought about the old man's remarks again today, Thursday, and wondered if he'd dismissed them prematurely. "Other parts of his soul were scared into *dividin'*—just waitin' for a chance to *reunite*." Reunite when? With what? How?

During the afternoon there had been Calhoun's own reunion with his children—and Jean's promise that he could see them again on weekends—and, after uncountable kisses and hugs, he'd felt relaxed for the first time in weeks. Jean had offered him his old bed—*their* bed—for a nap, and he'd taken both the offer and the nap.

And last night, eating a late sandwich and devouring Orville Redebacher popcorn with his family, Grady had been more content and experienced more peace of mind than he had in a very long while.

This morning, Thursday, he hadn't been able to make himself go to Channel 61. He knew that all hell must be breaking loose at the station, and cared—distantly. With Andy Sutor dead, an unsought and unplanned-for state of flux was upon them all, they could use his input, and he also knew that nobody's job was safe under such circumstances. Not in TV. He also knew that it put his buddy, Tom, in a helluva position, since it was conceivable that no one knew Andy's intention to can the director *except* Tom—and Grady, of course, who wasn't about to mention it.

But once he went in, Calhoun figured, he'd need to be 110 percent committed, maybe stuck at 61 until dark. And even while he was concerned about Bud and the pressure on her at a time like this, he didn't *dare* allow his job to consume that much of his time and attention.

Not until he'd spoken with Freida Rehfeldt, at noon.

What really made him feel like a chunky piece of garrulous shit was the fact that he hadn't even phoned the station from Jean's and told them where he was. What Bud would think, or believe—she definitely would never believe that he hadn't slept with Jean—Calhoun couldn't imagine.

What was even worse, he thought with a sigh, glancing at a wall clock and waiting for the hour-plus to pass until it was noon, was that he'd discovered he and Jean could be together without practicing the Number One Hobby of the American Couple: working fiendishly hard at finding something *really* nasty, to top the other one.

I still love Jean, Calhoun admitted to himself; *probably*.

And a moment later, popping the tab of his day's first Bud, *Bud too*.

Most of the hour had passed before, aloud, he added: "Probably."

It wasn't like wrestling a bear to get

home. Nobody zip-locked you into an emergency ward for a short set of chops. No one wrote it up for the papers or issued spot reports. They just sewed you up, recommended plastic surgery, and side-stepped every one of the frantic frigging notes you wrote asking them if you'd ever make a sound on a trum-*pet* again. Side-stepped them with really cool evasions while their shiny-red eyes said, "No, Mr. Riffey, dude, no way, has-been and never was. You'll be lucky if you can pucker up to whistle."

It was the end of the set and the variety of aches and pains in Gill's body were so goddamned insignificant in comparison to what had happened to his *embouchure*—the proper application of the lips and tongue, if one wishes to play any wind instrument professionally—that he literally didn't notice them. Not during the lonesome ride home in the cab, or when he unlocked the door and went into his dark bachelor flat, alone.

People said they understood why a trum-*pet* man protected his chops, why he was the guy who, when a fucking building began to fall on his head, didn't shield either his eyes or the top of his skull—but his mouth. They didn't, though. They understood athletes who insured their pitching arms or their running knees, they understood dancers who fretted about their legs and also the regular guys who, if a maniac was shooting or kicking crap around, cupped the ol' family jewels—but they didn't dig cats too dumb to play guitar, to make the rock scene, who wouldn't give a passionate kiss to Cher's left booby if it popped out right in front of their faces.

At 19, Gill Riffey'd had one date—one date only—with a homecoming queen. She'd told everybody she knew he was a faggot because he wouldn't French kiss or go down on her. "Foreign saliva makes the mute sound funny, and when hair gets stuck in my teeth, it makes the high notes wobble," he'd explained to her, reasonably enough. "Besides that stuff screws up your wind."

It still might have been all right, but she'd been the first girl who wanted to blow into his trum-*pet*. He'd wrested it firmly away from her; Gill Riffey never got *that* high. "I," he informed her, "I wouldn't let Gabriel blow in my horn!" And when she started putting on her clothes to bug out he'd shouted a clarification: "Not *God*, either! Ziggy or Miles, maybe."

His instrument's case was where he always kept it when he stretched out on the couch, wondering idly if any of the sawbones would try to haul him back. The case was on the coffee table, within easy reach. Because you never knew when you had to play, it might happen at any hour of day or night, you had to have your trum-*pet* handy.

But when he'd opened the case, wondering who the good Sam was who'd retrieved it from his wrecked car and hauled it home, Gill froze in horror. He didn't swear, throw anything, want to make a phone call to the White House; that wasn't Gill's style, so he simply stared at the ruined companion of all his years without touching it, knowing he would never touch it again. It was an obscenity now.

The entire business end of the horn—the mouthpiece, hell, the first three inches of his old trum-*pet*—looked as if it had been especially designed to be played by a large-mouth bass. More likely, he realized when his brain resumed minimal operation, someone had taken it by the bell—hard—and methodically beat on it, and beat on it, 'til the horn's mouth was split open like Gill's lip and big enough around to contain a baby's fist.

Goodnight, sweetheart, he heard the old lyric in his mind while he walked deliberately toward the kitchenette. *Sleep will banish sorrow* . . .

He tipped the black pebbly adored case upside down, emptied, without touching the demolished trumpet into a trash can. Something smallish and shiny clattered to the linoleum floor. For a second he just looked at it, reminded of how much the clattering sound had been like the crashing of his automobile. Then Gill picked up the nickel-plated pistol that had been secreted in the trumpet case.

He felt pretty sure it was loaded. That was something, anyway.

"If I had any doubts before, Grade-A," Wayne Sojourner's tenor growled in Calhoun's ear, clearly apologetic, "I am 100 percent in your corner now. Man, I am convinced."

Grady's eyelashes fluttered. He yearned to hang up the phone without speaking a word into it. He couldn't, even though logic informed him something terrible—something *else*—had happened. Something Wayne felt he couldn't shrug off this time.

"You just got the report about Andy Sutor yourself?" Grady remained essentially hopeful.

"Naw, that's not it." Sojourner seemed somewhat aggrieved. "I knew about that. But you weren't each other's number-one fans exactly. Correct?"

"Just tell me who," Calhoun rasped. He closed his eyes for it.

Sojourner said it was Tom Simincola. "Now, hold on—he isn't dead. Boys got there in response to some goddam anonymous call. Just in time t'stop him from—well, anyway, it seems his wife came home and Simincola had been sleeping, and he thought it was a burglar." He paused. "Tom hit her too hard. Too often."

Grady believed he said some such things as "*No*," or "Dear *God*," but wasn't certain. The baby . . . And Tommy adored Judith. "Uh-uh," Grady did say, finally. "Oh dear God, *no*." He had no idea he had begun to cry.

"Look, I'll come right over," Wayne continued, soft but quick. "Give me half an hour and I'll just—"

"*Don't come* near *me*," Calhoun shrilled. "I'm a leper, Wayne! Don't you *dare* come over here! Stay *away*!"

"Man, I believe your friend, all right? Too many coincidences, too many accidents and errors." Now he *did* growl in helpless anger and frustration. "I believe somebody else was in Simincola's house— and I have a theory working its way out, Calhoun. It's drugs, babe." The big cop sounded solemn; enormously earnest. One could picture his great head, nodding, selling it to himself. "Somehow Rajelis is using drugs to make your people hallucinate. Hell, maybe it is an hallucinogen, right? 'Kay? It could also be that—"

Without speaking again, Grady hung up.

21

Thursday, Noon. April 21.

By the time he could call Freida Rehfledt and learned what she'd discovered, Calhoun had pulled himself together from his newest surfeiting sorrow precisely to this extent: He'd relocated his cheery, casual, boyish public personality and was ready to inundate the astrologer's cat-cluttered house with cleansing bubbles of Welkian exuberance.

Because Grady believed that if he attempted to tell Freida what else had gone stunningly wrong since Bud and he visited her, he would break down and the bubbles would become endless tears.

"Mr. Calhoun, I've begun researching curses and jinxes since we spoke last," she began without further preamble. "Some of what I have learned seems, well, rather promising."

I want to know about Rajelis' horoscope, Grady thought, miffed; *if the skinny SOB was actually born.* But aloud he said, "Go on."

"The movie actor, James Dean," Freida began. "His sports car seems to have borne a jinx. The mechanic of a man who purchased it had both legs broken; its engine was put in another automobile that crashed and killed the driver; the chassis, which was on display, fell from its mounting and broke a spectator's hip. Other persons were killed and nearly killed by that Porsche, or parts of it—including incidents involving the handbrake slipping, the tires from it simultaneously exploding, and a most bizarre and peculiar instant when—while it was again mounted—it simply fell apart. Into eleven parts, representing the late Mr. Dean's sun sign, Aquarius—which is the eleventh zodiacal sign."

"Is there more?" Calhoun's lips were compressed. What did this have to do with anything?

"Patience, Mr. Calhoun," Freida trilled in his ear. "There are more curses and jinxes than you'll allow me to report! Another involves a Lockhead mechanic who was hideously killed when he strolled into the plane's propeller. Afterward, tragedy after tragedy occurred until the aircraft crashed, in Chicago—killing all those aboard her. And there's the positively amazing nineteenth-century ship, *Great Eastern,* the world's largest until then: A man and his son disappeared and were presumed killed during the ship's construction. Following that accident, the *Great Eastern*'s engineer died of a stroke, and it appeared to exist only to take further lives. Firemen were burned to death and the captain drowned. Oh, there were *dozens* of abominable incidents, Mr. Calhoun, until the ship was abandoned to rust." Freida lowered her voice, conspiratorially. "When it was demolished for scrap, both the skeletons of the father—a riveter—and his son were discovered, trapped in the great double hull."

"Freida, m'love," Grady said as airly as he was able, "what do these fascinating little misadventures have to do with Calvin Rajelis, Billy Salvo, and yours unruly?"

"Maybe a lot," she replied. "In almost all the cases of jinxes and apparent curses, Mr. Calhoun, the series of calamities *begin* with a single tragedy."

"Don't follow you, Freed," Grady confessed.

"It's obvious, I think," the woman at the other end said with a sniff. She sounded just as airy. "Mr. Calhoun, I think that your Mr. Rajelis is occultist enough to perceive the nature of a curse—and to understand that if a tragedy occurred in *his* life, it paves the way for him to implement it—in ways neither you nor I can comprehend."

"Did you do his horoscope?" Grady asked. Sometimes the astrologer gave him a first-class case of the willies.

"My, yes, and an adventure it was! There is a Grand Cross in his chart, Mr. Calhoun—a perfect one involving all the cardinal points."

"Really?" Grady frowned and wondered what *that* meant.

"Mr. Rajelis is all water and fire elements, creating a constant conflict so well balanced that his flame is never extinguished. And the *aspects,* Mr. Calhoun! Mars squaring Neptune, which, of course, indicates a life of rebellion."

"Of course," Grady mumbled, and felt not only out of his depth but more hopeless by the moment. "But—"

"Don't let me forget to mention his Uranus, afflicted and strongly separative when he was only a boy!"

"I'd never let you forget *that*," said Calhoun. He glanced at his watch.

"None of that—not even his Saturn in the Eighth House—means a *thing* to *you*, I understand," Freida continued, regaining Calhoun's attention. "but it means a great deal to *me*."

"Then, how does it help us to—"

"Mr. Calhoun," the astrologer interrupted, "certain occultists and metaphysicians subscribe to the belief that there is a cycle of *evil* in a man's life. It occurs every nine years. You need to stop to think about multiples of nine—and multiples of 11, as well."

Sweating, Calhoun nodded and squeezed his eyelids together. "I will, I will," he promised. Then he stared at the phone. "Why eleven?"

"Because there is some scientific evidence of that pattern, sir," Freida fired back. "Soviet science; they're far more open-minded about such things than we are—or than we pretend to be. They believe that the 11-year arc produces an upsurge of unease and even disease, of potential revolutionary movements."

Salvo was shot to death just 33 years ago, Calhoun calculated without mentioning it. Which was three times 11. *A guy could go completely bugs messing with shit like this*, he mused.

"I'm almost finished," Freida promised, as if clearly sensing both his impatience and his disappointment. "I've been giving you food for thought—somewhat exotic thought, given your customary diet, I imagine."

"Those conflicting nine- and 11-year cycles can be a bit rugged to swallow," Grady admitted. "Without ketchup or Lea and Perrin's."

Then even before the middle-aged woman formed her next syllable, a muted chorus of wailing sound poured from her old house through the connection to Calhoun's ear. It seemed diabolic; soulless, chilling. It took a moment before the volume went up and he was able to identify the strange noise as that of Freida's cats, their feline voices raised in distant, plaintive, eerie song.

"I am not formally religious," she said quietly, matter-of-factly. "But I am a believer and I suspect that one of the relatively few realms in which Christian fundamentalists may possess a strand of the truth lies in their belief in 'end days'—of a period of time not far in our future when many features of our known, daily life on the spinning world called Earth will be expunged. Eradicated."

He caught his breath. "The end of the world?"

"Of course not!" she exclaimed. "There's no end to anything! And most of what we're familiar with can be taken from us without the world ending. Really, I know few persons who truly believe that the *planet* is scheduled to end; it's too disruptive to God's much more important, overall scheme."

"I don't—"

"Only the lives of numerous people and—this lies at the core of my conviction, Mr. Calhoun—those eradicated

and drastically modified features I just
mentioned."

He made himself consider that. "For a
lot of folks," he offered, less "public" of
manner now, "complete change like that
amounts to the same. To the world's end."

"Surely," she agreed, unperturbed. "A
new broom and all that. But for such modifications to happen, when one is an astrologer who subscribes to belief in a
Creative Primal Energy, it *must* mean
massive changes in the skies *first*—in the
configurations of those planets in our
system that influence us."

"Why?" Grady asked simply.

"God very rarely destroys that which
He made for our use," she answered.
"Whether this tiny instant of time finds
ignorant human beings too narrow to
acknowledge the influence of planets,
they go on providing it—just as God
remains accessible to prayer whether anyone chooses to contact Him or not." He
paused and, when the cats abruptly cut
short their lament, her voice was over-
powering in its authority and intensity.
"So long as there is life of any kind on
Earth, it will continue being subtly guided
by planetary activity—even should we
elect not to be among those beings who go
on experiencing it. Therefore, Mr. Calhoun, if 'end days' are coming—if we are
to be forever altered—it must start in
Heaven, and the heavens."

"The times," Calhoun murmured
reflectively, "they are a-changing."

"Not," Freida gently corrected, "until

the ceaseless formations and formulations of the planets are altered. Not 'til they provide influences we have never known before, Mr. Calhoun. And *one* person who knew how to interpret them might also seem to *control* them. If he were able to do so, he would effectively control the affairs of all sentient life on this globe. He would, in a word, rule the Earth."

"How can we defend ourselves?" He asked it point blank—swiftly—before he changed his mind, and his heart was pounding.

"I erected his chart; now I must study the ephemerides before *new* configurations form and render them invalid." She seemed to half pause, and Grady heard a contented purr near the receiver. "Now comes the *major* step, because I must discover *when* Mr. Rajelis is most vulnerable."

22

Friday; Very Early. April 22.

"Man, we could *kill* ourselves with shit like that if we use it wrong."

The second boy neither spoke nor changed expression but stayed where he was; beside a stump of a tree near the middle of the old vacant lot, two blocks or so from school. The tree was a tight-knotted, gnarled fist with a couple of blackened branches sticking up like fingers indicating something sinister. They worked a tentative dark shadow on the second boy's impressive face. Minimally, he shrugged.

Tim was incredulous. "I never *ever* thought I'd fool around with such crap, Billy. and I sort of promised my mother and father I wouldn't."

"It's not like you got to." The slightly older boy seemed noncommital, as if he didn't really care. "But I thought we were friends. Best friends."

"Oh, we are!" Tim assured him, impulsively reaching out to punch Billy's biceps. It was like striking rock. "And I guess you went to a lotta trouble to get the stuff too."

"It's called dope, Tim." The wide, bear trap mouth scarcely opened. "Coke; cocaine."

"Yeah, right." Tim Calhoun nodded his understanding. "See, that's the thing. I've never even smoked pot before." That realization seemed to afford a potential out, and Tim stepped nearer his friend, unable to conceal his enthusiasm. "I mean, you *should* begin with marijuana, right—not with the real stuff, right? Maybe if you had some grass we could—"

"Tim, we made *plans*, remember?" Billy's eyelids fluttered nervously, as if he was working at getting it straight, almost as if he was listening to someone prompting him. "To spend some time to-

gether. Tell jokes. Talk about people we
know . . . like girls, right? But especially
to tell each other all about our secrets;
what parents do to us, how they just don't
understand that we're almost grown up or
how much we need to have somebody our
own age to rap with."

"Yeah, I hear that," Tim agreed
slangily, bobbing his head. "But I didn't
really think you'd connect, Billy. I thought
you were just bullshitting, you know?"

For one instant it was apparent that
young Billy had lost his temper. A queer
expression twisted his features so badly
that he no longer looked young or even
boyish. The shadows from the lightning-
struck tree lay against his sallow cheeks
like black martial arts blades, drawn and
held at the ready.

"I do what I say I will, Tim," the older
boy said flatly, decisively. He inhaled, held
it a moment, and briefly closed his eyes as
if the sun were shining into them. But it
wasn't. "And it cost me a lot of bread to
make the deal. A lot, Tim. I don't think I
want any friends who won't hang out with
me or who can't believe in me. And who
break dates at the last second."

To Tim's dismay and a surge of awful
loss, he saw Billy Salvo start away. "Hold
on, man!" he called, grabbing one
muscular arm. "We don't have to free-
base, just . . . just snort some. Right?"

Billy, back turned, said nothing.

"Well, what I mean is, we don't have to
use—*do*—all your stuff—your coke—that

night. Okay?" He knew he was grinning foolishly but patted his one friend's broad shoulder and felt the sweat break out on his forehead even though it was early morning, and chilly. "A newcomer like me, shit, I probably won't *need* more'n a line or two to get really high!"

For another moment Billy held his pose. It was the craziest thing but, despite how well-built and hard the guy felt, with the still-rising sun at just this angle, Tim had the impression that he could almost look *through* Billy. See the rows of neighboring houses across the lot, or the American flag rising over the high school roof, right through ol' Billy!

When he turned back to Tim there was the lifeless look in the pitiless eyes and the familiar, somewhat sad and vacuous smile. "You've got it, Tim. Main thing is us, together down at the cottage; the cool times we're gonna enjoy together." His voice faded away and he blinked so badly it was as if he had to concentrate to remember where he was and what he was doing. Maybe Billy already used drugs, but Tim didn't think that was what it was. "You and me . . . using your father's cottage . . ."

"All *right*!" Tim stuck out a hand, palm ready for the high-five. But Billy just stared at it so Tim locked their hands together in a clasp of camaraderie; of need. In his best Duke Wayne imitation, he declared, " 'A man's gotta do what a man's gotta do.' "

Billy's gaze settled fixedly, then, on Tim's eyes. "One thing." He raised his index finger.

"Shoot. Anything, man."

"You said we could kill ourselves with shit like mine—remember? Well, maybe we just will, kid. What Wayne said, y'know? When your number finally comes up you don't whine about it like a little baby, you read me?" Billy's smile widened. "I know about jazz like that. And sometimes the dope *is* bad. So if it kills your ass, well, it kills your ass. All right?" The smile widened, but the dull eyes bored into Tim's, and, automatically, he nodded. "Great. So I want you to hold some of my stash till our party. Got it?"

Fear had surged inside Tim. Now it deepened as Billy handed him a small, clear-plastic sack. But Tim did not close his hand around it, didn't quite accept it. Knowing a guy like Bill was seeing a side of reality that had been concealed, and that made him special. Different from all the fiction Tim had read, all the stories his mother and father had told him about life. And parents had to like you; other guys didn't. Billy actually *wanted* him as a friend, a companion, was even willing to see him when he might be at his very worst. "Got it," he whispered, and took the sack.

He saw his friend slowly nod, eyelashes batting like a young girl's, no words wasted. So Tim Calhoun just went on gazing with some awe and lots of

wonder as Billy stalked across the vacant
lot. Alone and, just then, clearly liking it.

Tim even refrained from calling after
him when he noticed that Billy wasn't
headed toward school at all, but starting
to weave aimlessly in the vacant lot before
settling upon a course that took him
directly toward the slowly surfacing sun.
When he had reached the sidewalk and
appeared to wander past a high fence
from which rose the antic cries of small
children at play, Tim's friend was simply
no longer there to be seen at all.

He shared William's memories only at
the unconscious, unidentifiable level, but
he wondered about them frequently and
how they motivated him. Because it was
clear they did; he hated daytime as much
as William and, while it had something to
do with the magical instant when he'd
been accepted by the Forces, he knew it
went far deeper than that.

Surely it wasn't Salvo who awoke me,
Rajelis thought, opening his eyes and,
despite a morning's glare through the
undraped windows, blinking owlishly in
William's direction. *When he is coming or
going, he doesn't need to use doors . . .*

Sometimes having Salvo around
turned Rajelis more irritable than usual.
Even, he confessed with some reluctance
to himself as he tugged a blanket higher
on his thin chest, remotely fearful. There
was no reason for the latter since they
were less consciously aware of one

another than either was aware of any other being. Occasionally, since they could not communicate with speech, Calvin Rajelis had to focus his remarkable energies just to sense William's return from a given errand, and he felt certain that Salvo was often unaware of his own presence. Which also tended to annoy Calvin, who was perfectly real—entirely flesh and blood and brilliant, purposive brain-power—regardless of the intentional lack of integration.

It might be sleeping in yet another unfamiliar place that was making him edgy, thought Rajelis. Except that that wouldn't wash considering his ceaseless string of one-nighters as a professional mentalist. But it surely didn't hold up, either, that he felt nervous today because he was occupying surroundings familiar to the bastard, Calhoun. All was going according to plan, so there was no ascertainable reason to experience the slightest concern.

But he did. *Maybe,* he thought, trying not to glance at William where he sat in the corner of the room like a child being punished, *maybe it's only that Mother is looking in on me again.* To track the course of his vengeance.

And it dawned on Calvin that he was able to picture her on that imbecile's first New York program more clearly, with greater detail, then he had in ages. See her at an instant when the aspects and the omens were intolerable—when Seera was so badly afflicted that it was impossible

for her, or anyone, to perform. If Grady
Calhoun had done even the most minute
amount of research, he'd have perceived
that no sensitive person could perform
expertly, unfailingly, upon demand! Had
the young fool not been so filled with his
own egotistical lust for success that he
was blind to Seera's human problems,
he'd have understood a psychic's need to
improvise and to embroider under
dreadful planetary conditions—

—Because people *expected* it—*insisted* on it, unfeelingly—and people were
required as clients if the sensitive desired
to go on eating! And the same people had
to be *impressed.*

Rajelis tossed and turned on the front
room sofa, perspiring now. The young
Calhoun had taunted Seera, teased and
goaded her mercilessly—he had *hit* at her
and *hit* at her, *forced* her to make the sort
of unequivocal, declarative statements
that inevitably *destroyed* even the most
gifted occultists. And he, the still younger
Calvin Rajelis, not even in his teens yet,
had been obliged to sit in his broken-down
chair at home and *see* it happen,
incapable of helping Mother—staring at
the black-and-white screen of their eight-
year-old TV set while that son-of-a-bitch
pushed the great Seera farther out on a
limb until he could *ruin* her, destroy her
spirit and her business!

And what was left of little Calvin's
boyhood.

So he'd welcomed the Forces of Suffering even before Mother gave herself to them forever. Vowed that he would never be subservient to the whims of those sightless neurotic normals who'd bled his mother dry, sworn that he would not be poor when *he* grew up but powerful—always in command of any situation . . . able through his own youthful commitment to learn any scrap of information he needed, and always both able and willing to mete out the same destruction Grady Calhoun had visited upon Mother. Calhoun, trying to follow in the same path as the CBS newsman, Mike Wallace, who also started with interview shows—happy to *crucify* little Calvin's mother, and then *forget* about it as if it had never happened! And that was what made it ultimately unforgivable to the adult Rajelis. Because he understood perfectly how it was to strike out and go on striking in order to make progress or to achieve revenge, but the Calhouns of stinking society—they didn't even *revel* in the people they hurt, the careers they destroyed! They struck like scorpions before audiences of hundreds of thousands who cheered their destruction, *laughed* at it—and didn't even remember the names of their victims. *That* cold and calloused an attitude chilled Calvin Rajelis to the marrow.

He hadn't set out to discover that humankind had entered a new, cosmic age other than the innovative, peace- and freedom-loving Aquarian Age that seers had anticipated; running across it was a gratifying bonus for Rajelis' single-mindedness. How it had been created, twisted from what should have been, he had no idea, but theorized it had to do with nuclear testing. Whatever the source of the Age, he'd predicted its coming years ago, started to experiment with somewhat modified planetary transits, and found that this solar system's heavens were—warped. Altered, but susceptible to apprehension and comprehension, as well, once a dedicated mage—supported by the privileges granted by the Forces of Suffering—perceived the central fact: that there were, now, periods of time when *anything* was possible if it were done in conformation with proper astrological principles. What remained of the long-desired Aquarian Age was the ruthless license of an independent, experiment-oriented man and his drive to move to the top—overnight.

Calvin Rajelis had owned the right genes. And Seera had, all unknowingly, perfectly cultivated them.

The next move had been honing in on his objectives and pinpointing the right moments. What he was doing to avenge Seera was only the inception, his moral payback to she who—just as selflessly, as ruthlessly—had paved the way for his own acceptance by the Forces. Soon he'd complete his plan for Calhoun-the-bastard, who would watch his loved ones die and, ultimately, take his own pointless but energy-bestowing life. That was one of the pluses.

Then Rajelis would be ready to shape, to guide, and to control the lives of all people. He'd begin with those in the leadership of Calhoun's own profession, people who already shaped, guided, and controlled the communications and information industries. There were relatively few of them; politicians and law-makers would fall quickly into lock step.

Sighing in anticipation, still drowsy but too excited to drift back to sleep, he revolved his head on the arm of the sofa and slowly glanced at the sleepless entity sitting quietly in the corner. Staring at nothing.

Inside, of course, William Salvo was in torment. A nonstop confusing crisis of identity, perpetually pursued by the specter of white darkness from which he, Rajelis, had plucked him. Calvin knew what it was, but he hadn't experienced it, wouldn't experience it until, and unless, he himself perished. And Calvin did not intend to do that. His nose wrinkled in disgust. He had no compassion, no sympathy, for Salvo; in a very real manner, William was not there at all. What portions of him existed lingered exclusively to fulfill an old destiny of evil and corruption, and the destiny Calvin had selected for himself and humankind. The part that existed in the present obeyed few physical laws of space, or distance; at an instant's notice, Calvin's Billy would be wherever he wished him to be and do whatever Calvin told him to do—so long as it was corrupt; evil.

And the bonus for *this* achievement was that those things Salvo did, Calvin Rajelis experienced—visually, and with all his senses. With impunity. William could not die if he was obeying Calvin's injunctions, because he was little more than a remnant or relic—a half-living, quite minor footnote in the yellowing pages of time. A soul spot.

And Rajelis couldn't die while he merely experienced William's shape-changing forays, because he wasn't present. He just ordered them.

Calvin sat up. Studied a long list. Made a selection; thought a name, an exact location—with clarity. With telepathic projection. He thought of others. He thought of deception; dialogue, and plans. And death; bloody, murderous death. Plural: deaths.

In revulsed fascination he stared as his William stood, the mouth agape like some consuming star-eater in deep space.

Salvo vanished.

BOOK III

"Heat not a furnace for your foe so hot/That it singe yourself."

—Shakespeare
King Henry VIII

23

Tuesday. April 26.

When he had finally finished reading the horror in the morning *Star* Grady lowered the newspaper to his desk at Channel 61 with trembling hands and left the obituary page face up.

Yesterday, it had seemed a coincidence. A ghastly series of coincidences. Well, no; it hadn't, really, but he'd striven for all he was worth to see it that way.

Decent people didn't really accept the premise that they'd been personally responsible for so many deaths.

A long moment later—realizing both that he could not possibly pay visits to all those mortuaries, and that the number of human beings suddenly expiring could not conceivably be explained by coincidence—Grady turned the newspaper back to the front page and scanned it with feelings of unreality and consternation.

Nothing in the national or international headlines was nearly as hideous, certainly not as personally devastating, as the nature of the death toll reported—in clinical newspaperese—yesterday and, now, this morning. After one peaceful day, Sunday, with his family and Bud, later, he'd awakened to what was meant to be a quick glance at the *Star,* at the obits—

And after weeping, buying more

280

flowers, and paying his respects more times than during any previous day of his whole life. Hour following hour of signing his name in pure-white keepsake books and staring at human remains. And today's obituaries were three times as shocking, hideous, and devastatingly saddening.

What made it worse was realizing there was no point in phoning the police; not even Wayne, his friend. They'd never have been able to believe he'd *really known*—had as *Confab* guests; met them as neighbors, dates, merchants, schoolmates (well-known persons dying elsewhere in America were featured in local obits); done business with—*all* the reported dead. *Every* man and woman whose demise was recorded for the span of the weekend plus Monday. He'd have been certified as paranoid by the end of the day.

And what made it impossible to tell anyone about it but Bud, maybe, was the terrifying *implication*: Rajelis and William Salvo had clearly stolen life from literally dozens of innocent people, persons whose only crime was coming into infrequent contact with an Irishman from the east—*and they'd kept all* other *dying people alive . . .*

Bud won't accept it either, Grady moaned to himself, and tossed the horrifying newspaper into his wastebasket. *And I'm mad as a hatter if I believe it and probably responsible for another*

30 or 40 deaths if I don't.

Despite the *Star*'s banishment, Grady saw the names parading before his inner eye, some of them accompanied by vivid pictures; because close friends, loved ones weren't the only people you remembered with clarity. It wasn't noon yet, but he finished another pack of cigarettes and groped in his pocket with a shaking hand for the second pack he'd thought to put there. You met, wherever you lived and worked, dozens—no, hundreds; maybe thousands—of others whom you knew could become intimate chums if there was an excuse for it. And needing an excuse to form relationships that would bring sunshine into at least two lives was a sorry goddam commentary on humankind! But it was the truth; you experienced brief encounters weekly, sometimes daily, with women and girls you sensed that you would freaking *love,* if you gave them a chance; and some of them would have shared with you the most exciting and fulfilling sex you ever knew! In drugstores, restaurants, and bars, over at the barbershop or buying a new sports jacket, or interviewing a man or answering a letter, you sensed you'd just spoken with guys you might lay down your *life* for, under certain circumstances! It began in grade school, for chrissakes, continued into high school or college and well beyond that—the endless string of human life with all its quirks and twists, its very special individual idiosyncrasies; and though you also shook hands with men you knew you might shoot, or sue, if things went bad, the overwhelming total of persons you simply *enjoyed*—felt fondness for, however passing—was gigantic.

Those were the men and women Rajelis and Salvo were murdering now, to make Grady Calhoun commit suicide. He knew not one of those folks reported in the obituaries an iota better—and, in a queer fashion that made Calhoun feel acutely, hideously guilty because he'd never taken the time to make them part of his personal A-team, he grieved more for them than any others.

What he could not consider at all was the ingenuity it had taken, and the tireless, space-devouring energy, to make so many deaths credible as "natural," "accidental," and "suicidal." It astonished and nearly brought shivering admiration from Calhoun to observe the cool, mathematical increase in the latter category: just enough more suicides than usual to avoid detection, and an inquiry. The bastards had spread them around the map; three or four life-takings in Indy over a three-day period, a baker's dozen more scattered over the United States with no obvious connection of any kind.

Grady Calhoun was the sole connection.

Sooner or later, he thought darkly, privately, *I'm going to have to do it*. And, *What in God's name am I waiting for?*

He'd told Bud on their date that it

seemed to be easing off, even dared express the lunatic, optimistic hope that Calvin Rajelis had called off his psychic dog. Young Tim, scaring Grady silly by stating his new friend's name was Billy, had also handed over to his father a clear plastic packet of cocaine he'd been "holding" for Billy. Although Calhoun had not been able to force Tim to agree never to see Billy again or reveal his address, and Calhoun had not then persuaded himself that William Salvo could turn himself into a teenage boy, Tim had reaffirmed his pledge never to use illegal drugs. There'd been a tender moment for Grady and all his children, even laughs, when little Petey, asked to choose their Sunday dining place, suggested the hotdog stand at the local Indians baseball park.

Now, Calhoun forced himself to check in at the station for reasons other than hosting *Confab*—the studio had been packed Friday night, the show had gone great—and the absence of Andy Sutor and Tom Simincola were only the tip of the enormous iceberg Calhoun encountered. *Iceberg* was the right word, because most of Grady's colleagues were cool about his recent absences and more than a few were jockeying into position for a race at Andy's or Tom's jobs.

Calhoun was surprised when Bud strolled in at half-past twelve, ashen-faced beneath her makeup. "What are you doing here at this hour?" he asked her after glancing at his watch. "The evening news is—"

"Trudy Ellaire has some kind of blood condition and I pinch-hit for her." Bud averted her gaze, but might as well have met Grady's. Trudy was the female anchor for the noon news and both of them liked her. A lot. "Nick Wolfsey—who lives with her—phoned in. Said it might be fairly serious."

"Sit." Grady motioned to the chair on the other side of his desk, always embarrassed by the need for friends to assume such a formal seating arrangement. *But Bud's not a friend of mine,* he thought, trying to believe it, *and I don't like her and I sure as hell do* not *love her.* Something in Bud's wide-spaced eyes, the extent of her pallor, alarmed him. "What else is it?"

"Susan." She shrugged. Still did not look at him; toyed with the lapel of her jacket. "Little Ernie too."

Calhoun's heart sank. "Say."

Again the shrug; preceded by standing tears. "My sister's had a b-breakdown. She's at St. Vincent's." Then she raised her head to look at Calhoun at last and he wished she hadn't. "There's a chance Ernie may be made a w-ward of the court."

"Hell," Calhoun said, and broke the gaze they'd shared, telling himself there was no sign of accusation, of blame, in her lovely face.

When he could he told Bud about "the victory." Their one, slim victory: Tim's decision to turn over the drugs, and not use them. He hoped he hadn't imagined it when he saw infinitesimal gladness, or relief, in her eyes. "Buddy," he said softly, "I think Tim's friend was—I hope to God it's 'was'—Salvo. And I think Rajelis was getting at me from still another crazy goddam angle by trying to get my first-born hooked on drugs."

Bud didn't immediately reply. "That," she said at last, her tone level but not challenging, "would mean he can turn himself into . . . practically anything; or anyone." Calhoun gave her a nod. "Then—what *is* he?"

Now Calhoun shrugged. "Dunno."

"No-no, wait." Bud waggled her raised palm and shook her head. "I'm not asking precisely *what* he is . . . I mean, is he even *real* or not?" Head up, she started to cry. She was looking right at Grady, but quite possibly did not see him or anything except the phantoms of death and merci-less loss. "How can we fight him—*how*? Will you tell me that, Grady—how can we stop a *ghost*?" Leaning forward in her chair, Bud began pounding her doubled fists on the surface of Calhoun's desk. "How? How? How? *How*?"

"Shhh-h-h!" he coaxed her, crying too, racing round the desk to Bud and kneeling, fingertips caressing her cheeks. "Hey . . . hey . . ."

Despite herself, Bud gave him a wan smile. " 'Hey, hey?' What kind of cheering up is 'hey, hey'?"

Grinning goofily, patting her hand, he wanted to kiss her but adored some minuscule element of the moment too much to break it. "Same kind as saying I love you. Did I ever tell you that?"

"Never." Her wet eyes opened wide, makeup destroyed. She was infinitely beautiful to Grady then. "I guess this proves even the worst of times may have something good to them."

Wishing he didn't even like her, he did kiss her.

And the telephone on the desk raged at them.

But Freida made Calhoun's worried scowl vanish with her first remark: "Your Mr. Rajelis—he's most vulnerable *this Friday*!" she exclaimed. "Three days from now."

With Bud listening on an extension in the office adjacent to his, Calhoun found his heartbeat—and his hope—accelerating.

Only for a brief period. "But Freida, how is that going to help us if we don't know where he is?"

"Or if we can't even get a line on Salvo?"

"Patience, people," the astrologer said soothingly. "It's perfectly obvious now that he's nearer, geographically, than he has been since his appearance on *Confab*."

"How do you know that?" Grady asked.

Freida's sigh was like a wistful breeze in his ear. "Do you really want me to teach you all the principles of astrology at a time like this?" she demanded. "Despite lacking the hour of birth and the resultant rising sign—which would permit me to place his planets in their houses and *really* get to know that madman—my study of transiting aspects to his natal chart made everything about him much clearer."

"Transiting aspects?" Bud asked. "You mean the *current* influences in relation to the positions he had at birth?"

"Excellent, Ms. Rocker!" Freida praised her. But she quickly sobered. "Mr. Rajelis's horoscope is very ambivalent in terms of positive/negative signs—by which I mean that he is psychologically divided between masculine and feminine motivations. If anything, I've underrated the scope of his occult studies—and his psychosis."

"Have you found *anything* that we can use against him?" Calhoun asked. They were, he felt, getting nowhere fast.

"I have." She said it so matter-of-factly that, momentarily, neither Grady nor the listening Bud registered their understanding and anticipation. "In a way, I believe that your Mr. Rajelis—"

"He's not 'my' Mr. Rajelis!" Calhoun interjected.

"But you're *his*, Mr. Calhoun," Freida remarked. She let it sink in, and they heard several cats play-fighting, hissing in the background. "When the soul returns to earth, people, a phase of it continues to possess the same emotions or mental turn; they are carried over into the new life, although they are expressed differently. I won't get into a discussion of *karma*, one of the few eastern terms to become familiar or established in this society; but it might be said that we're all haunted by what we have been in the past—because we carry along not only our feelings but the rewards and obligations accrued in previous existences. Do you follow me?"

Bud and Grady said they did.

"Your policeman friend with the strange name . . . Mr. Sojourner? He established that William Salvo definitely did live, correct? And died 33 years ago?" She waited till they confirmed her impressions. Neither of them was remotely prepared for what she said next. "I believe it is obvious that Calvin Rajelis is the *reincarnation* of William Salvo."

In sharp intakes of air, Calhoun and Bud asked how that was possible.

Freida Rehfledt was ready with her answers. "Rajelis clearly did not live a normal childhood. His mother, according to his chart, brought him up by a mixture of metaphysics, superstition, quite possibly child abuse, and something rather like *wicca*. Witchcraft, but with bizarre, advanced distinctions I cannot fully place or identify." She paused again and, in the late-morning bustle of their TV station, they imagined the woman doing all manner of offputting, arcane things.

"As a boy, Calvin was emotionally re-
tarted, I'm sure. But in his way he was
remarkably mature intellectually. I feel
sure that he learned to trace each of his
former lives—possibly with the aid of
hypnotic regression, whether at his
mother's hands or, even after her demise,
by—"

"She's dead?" Bud asked. "You're
sure?"

"Quite sure," Freida declared. "Even
with only solar fourth house influences
afflicted by Saturn in transit, one may be
sure that the loss of a maternal figure has
occurred . . . and in young Calvin's case,
it would have altered and totally mal-
adjusted his moral and psychic growth, as
well. Growth, in realms other than
knowledge."

Grady wanted to believe they were
close to something worthwhile but was
reluctant to make progress and risk losing
it. "I don't get what you're saying," he
argued. "If you are reincarnated, then the
person you used to be—all those persons
—are dead, right?"

"Ordinarily. But not," she said softly,
"if the presently corporeal soul has
learned how to *separate* from the essential
personality of the prior life. Separate from
it, and, by summoning it—*use* it. Which is,
I think, exactly what your Mr. Rajelis is
doing. And he's involved in much more
than that, I can tell you."

"Wait," Bud interposed. "Use it . . .
how?"

"Magically, of course. Selfishly. With enormous destruction." The older woman's answer had been instant; decisive. "You see, Ms. Rocker, the recalled personality would be comprised of distorted yet vaguely remembered substance of what was real. It isn't 'spiritual' at all in the way that an earthbound ghost may merely house a lost, bewildered soul. Because it has not gone on, either to the plane of existence between lives or to the next corporeal existence, it's bound to be badly limited. To behave erratically, or stupidly; and to be indecisive and brute-like. Until it's either commanded or encounters conditions in which it may react in the most common ways it reacted in its past life."

"Billy," Calhoun said, barely audible, "reacted by killing people."

"You do follow my reasoning. Mr. Calhoun, if my assumptions and research prove out, Mr. Rajelis is directly commanding those reactions and actions of Salvo. Using that poor, partial spirit as his tool of revenge. Mr. Rajelis' will has mastered an apparitional entity, and sees what Salvo sees, any time he's attuned to its feeble telepathic vibrations." When she paused Grady jumped, and turned, sensing a presence. But it was only a shift on sunlight through the office window. "If Mr. Rajelis and Mr. Salvo were integrated as nature intended, they would think as one—save that the Salvo mindset of the past would be unconsciously known. It would be muted, subliminal, important but never compelling."

"The way it is now," Bud murmured. "In a way."

"How can Rajelis be stopped?" Grady asked, point blank.

Freida, to their surprise, laughed ruefully. "When I paused, Mr. Calhoun, I inadvertantly placed that thought in your mind. I wish I had controlled it better."

"Why?"

"Because Mr. Rajelis's vulnerability ceases after Friday. Just as it is with biorhythms, he will immediately begin an upswing." She cleared her throat. "My experience tells me it is essential we locate them by then—unless, of course, they locate *you*."

24

Thursday, April 28. High Noon.

There had been a matter to clear up at his eldest son's school before Wayne could head for work, and then Mrs. Sojourner had wanted to talk it out. It was one thing, she said, to neglect a wife because of the press of police business. It was another to neglect your children, and she wanted to go on record as telling Wayne that she wouldn't tolerate it.

"Duly noted," he'd said somberly, and even before he'd started the engine of his car, he'd known that only Der Bingle could save him today.

It didn't occur to the lieutenant that Bing Crosby only existed now on records and film, and had never been a really big man anyway.

Heading for work this particular sunny morning when, at last, spring seemed to have bloomed in Indianapolis, meant trying to think of Grady Calhoun's reaction to the most recent bad news. And also trying not to go on thinking of Calvin Rajelis' hit man as a ghost of some kind.

"How are things in Glocca Morra?" Crosby's lilting voice inquired from Wayne's tape deck.

"Shitty, Bing," Wayne told him. "Pretty shit-tee."

Because Calhoun's pal, Gill Riffey, had hung on awhile after trying to kill himself, but he hadn't hung on forever. Getting the report at home, Wayne Sojourner had manfully tried to reach Calhoun—he didn't even think of phoning the station since Grady had only been there long enough lately to do his program—but had found him neither at home nor at Bud Rocker's.

So he'd left the message of another death with Grade-A's ex-wife, Jean, and now he felt crap-pee because, in a way, he'd shirked his duty. Something police-man like Wayne Sojourner did not do.

And it wouldn't be that way if it wasn't for Wayne's inability to learn the where-abouts of either the crazy mothering

Rajelis or the whatever-the-fuck-it-was pretending to be the late William Salvo. On his own, without informing Calhoun, he'd called in favors with half a dozen homicide departments around the country, practically wornout a handful of computers and *definitely* worn out his welcome, trying to get a lead on either suspect. But Rajelis, his agent said, and the SOB was really pissed off, had dropped off his tour without telling anyone about it.

Later in the day, Wayne thought ponderously, gloomily, punching up another Crosby tune and not even disposed to sing along, he'd have to go find Calhoun and retrieve the coke his kid, Tim, had surrendered. That disturbed Sojourner a helluva a lot, too, because he knew Grady's kids well and he'd really thought Tim was one teenage boy who might never get *that* close to dope.

"Which goes to show what a sentimental turkey I am," Wayne muttered, aloud, and tried to concentrate on Crosby's mellifluous accents.

"Would you like to swing on a star?" Bing posed the musical question.

"I'd like to swing Calvin Rajelis from one," Wayne grumbled. "By his skinny honky neck." Carry his geedee guts home in a jar.

What was the matter with him this morning? He was behaving like some rookie whose old lady had just bawled him out the first time. Hell, he was even sweating out a new shirt and the temperature couldn't be hotter than 70 or so. But he had been in a crummy fucking mood before he even met that uppity teacher and then got his ass chewed out by the lit-tul woman, and he didn't know why. Male menopause, maybe; even Crosby wasn't helping.

He was trying to find Bing's *High Society* album with Frank and ol' Stachmo, sure that "Now You Has Jazz" or "Did You Evah?" would chase away his growing feeling of dark apprehension, when the police radio overrode his favorite vocalist's soothing voice.

A B&E not two blocks distant, and right on Wayne's route to headquarters. Maybe action was what he needed! Loosening his tie and collar, Sojourner informed the dispatcher that he'd take the call and began immediately checking out addresses on the buildings he was passing.

Then it dawned on him that he didn't need the address. He remembered the liquor store—Dwight's—from his prowl car days, was momentarily astonished that he had ever forgotten it. Because his first partner, Edwin "Whitey" Sallee, had been gunned down; shot and killed. For a while afterward, Wayne recalled, he'd halfway faulted himself for Whitey buying it. Not that he had. Not for a minute. But you got better at what you did if you were any good as a man, whatever the hell you did for your bread, and there'd come a time when he had known what to do to protect

Sallee. He supposed his superiors had known it, too, at the time, but they hadn't expected a rook to know the ropes that well.

Sojourner braked as soundlessly as he could at the entrance to a bleak, rundown alley; got out with deliberation. The spot hadn't gotten any worse with time; the one thing about total deterioration was that it couldn't get worse unless it just disappeared. And the constant crime in this neighborhood invested in it a sort of skitterish vitality. In a way, it haunted itself, Sojourner reflected, drawing his piece and entering the maw of the alley silently. Areas like this ate their own tail, barfed it up and chased it again, always claiming a few new victims in the process.

This is a two-man job, really, Wayne realized, looking toward the rear entrance of the liquor store. He considered calling for a backup, but there probably wasn't much danger except, of course, the risk of the perpetrator scooting out the front door. He'd grooved on that word, "perpetrator;" part of it, mispelled, was "traitor" and Wayne Sojourner genuinely believed that people who hit on other people to survive *were* traitors. To society; their race; their Mama and their nation.

Drawing near, Wayne distinctly heard the sound of footsteps inside the store. Heavy ones, making no effort toward silence. At the door, he saw that it was open; ajar. Yelling for the mother to come out would only chase him toward the front, and escape. Probably the best thing was to go inside, after him, except—

The per-pe-traitor was *coming out!* The footsteps louder. Wayne retreated several feet to the left of the open door, basically out of sight, braced himself, and, clasping his piece firmly, aimed it at what would be approximate chest level.

For any human being that had exited the store instead of the monstrosity that did.

What it was was a titanic white mountainous mass with huge glittering claws and just a psychic impression of red-hot eyes deepset at head level—but the head (if that was what it was) had to duck to precede the rest of it out of the alley door. When it straightened the ambient bulk of the abominable white creature took up the vertical space of a two-story building. The claws, *man,* the claws alone were a foot in length, curved like bird talons, pointed as daggers at the tips. He saw wings; and fur—

Not human, Sojourner thought; said aloud, *"Stop!"* and waited for a second to be noticed, and to follow procedure.

It looked down a long way, and certainly noticed him.

It gave off the instant impression of delight. As if it were greeting a friend it'd yearned to see for millenia. Or delicious food.

Sojourner got out of its way, or it would have run over him—at best. He slipped awkwardly to one knee without losing his aim, more full of wonder or awe now than that initial surprise and terror. He perceived, with its back turned to him, that the thing had a discernible skull. The snowy rear of the head was better defined this way and presented a target that bullets might, in theory, penetrate.

That was when Wayne saw the creature's friend—or keeper. Or maybe the guy was merely a passerby. Except that the young black man staring at Wayne was smirking, as if enjoying this. By the time Sojourner was ready again to fire, the enormous white mass had relocated him, and turned—and Wayne squeezed off two fast rounds. They seemed to pierce the massive skull somewhere in the vicinity of the red-hot eyes, without fazing it, and he understood then that cannons wouldn't bring the thing down. Nothing else occurred to him at all except hurling his piece at it as hard as he was able, then trying to escape from the back of the store, the young, grinning black, the alley, the monster—.

But somebody *fired* Wayne's own gun at Wayne from behind. He sensed at the moment the searing pain caught fire in his crushed spine that this would be the last time he ever had to fall down. . . .

One foot, nudging at his side; rolling him over on his paralyzed back. Not gently.

The smoking gun in the black hand of the youth, who looked incuriously down at him, stony dark eyes like photographic

lenses merely recording the killing of a
police lieutenant; for posterity. And
nowhere, *nowhere* above the youth or
beyond him—because it would have been
impossible for it to hide such bulk so
fast—was the white monster with the
glittering claws.

"You're . . ." said Wayne, not easily.

"I used to like Bing Crosby too," said
the youth conversationally, features
swarming, melting, no longer black or
white or definitely anything. He did a
perfect vocal imitation of the Groaner
singing "When the Blue of the Night Meets
the Gold of the Day," displayed a feature-
less pale blob of a face and next a mouth
that might have swallowed Sojourner
alive.

Except the blue had met the gold and
Wayne wasn't.

Grady's office phone rang.

Mom was dead in the nursing home.

The phone rang.

When he managed to answer it a cop
named Alberts said that Lieutenant Wayne
Sojourner had been shot to death in an
alley. That someone from vice would stop
by to pick up Mr. Calhoun's drugs. And,
oh, did Mr. Calhoun know Lieutenant Sojourner personally, was that what was
wrong with him?

The phone rang.

Grady ran.

Ran, tears streaming down his
cheeks, shrieking *"Nonono"* inside his

head, to the men's.

Pushed his way inside and leaned against the door when it had shooshed to. *It isn't real, none of it's REAL,* the words spoke to him—

And cunningly, grinning to himself, Grady pushed himself off the rest room door and almost daintily tripped to the urinals and, choosing one merrily, unzipped.

Of course! "Of course," he said aloud, agreeing. The answer was not *letting* it become real.

And it *wouldn't* be real *until he* got *the news!*

Aw. God, it was so *simple,* so *easy* . . . why hadn't he thought of it before? Maybe it was even retroactive—because he hadn't *acknowledged* his own mother's sudden *death,* he had just hung *up.* He hadn't cried, said "I'm sorry," he hadn't *told* anyone or—

Or about who? whom? Who *was* that *other* one the cop had just mentioned, minutes ago? Dammit, *who else died?*

But the name wouldn't come and he peed all over the toe of one shoe. He began rocking, shifting from side to side as he squirted aimlessly and felt it burn and thought he might never *stop* urinating, by God *wouldn't,* until—

Then he got it, beamed with relief because he hadn't lost his memory or his mind, after all—he'd remembered who just died:

Wayne Sojourner, sure *that* was it!

This time it was ol' *Wayne*—but he'd blanked out and forgotten it! He had fucking failed to remember for six or eight or a thousand minutes the report of a friend who'd been *murdered,* and—

But that was *it,* that was what you had to do, *uh*-huh . . . you kept *off* the goddam phone—you spoke to *nobody* who called or came up to you *with that look*—you were *out,* you *stayed out* and you sure as Christ did not *call BACK*—

And then none of it turned *real!* NONE!

Grady whistled tunelessly. Pretended to muse. "Funny, nobody's called me at all today," he observed brightly, and whistled another note. He zipped up haphazardly, lurched over to the washbasin with his cuffs shot. He allowed a slight stream of water to fall on his hands and failed to dry them at all with a paper towel he plucked airily from its container, tossed the partly wadded-up mess at the wastebasket and missed it by five feet. He began whistling in earnest, then. *Got to think,* he told himself, firmly—*about tomorrow night's show. Yeah, THAT'S the topic.* He rolled away from the basin area and needed a second shove to get through the men's room door, tottering. It wasn't too late to line up *somebody.* The show did have to go on, that was the Eleventh Commandment.

Dripping water from his damp hands, still crying and not quite zipped, he went on blowing air between his lips, down the hall to his office. Working at jauntiness, gnostly pale, he strode with staring eyes inside and promptly lost the melody of the song he'd tried to whistle and found it unbearably, abjectly sad.

The phone rang, sending Calhoun banging off the wall as if struck by titanic sound waves. Making small sounds that were part mutter, part sobbing, he sank to his bottom on the floor, seeing nothing but an adamant princess telephone on the desk: calling him. Insisting he answer it.

"Don't think so, no," said the grinning Grady, cunning and coy. Turning his back on it, he got up; in segments. His limbs were assembled all wrong now and it took awhile to stand erect, arms thrust awkwardly like someone robotic. "Nobody in," he told the phone, pursing his lips and shaking his head. Again the phone bell jangled, so he glanced over at it with a judicious look and found his feet taking two steps toward it. "*Naaaah*, I don't think so," he told it. "No thanks."

But modern people do what their machinery tells them, and he was kneeling in front of his desk, shaking terribly as he scooped up the phone and rested it clumsily, roughly, on the surface of the desk. "Hullo," Grady said. The word came out a mile long and shook like a hosed-down terrier.

"Are you there, Grady?" Jean's voice, tinny and tiny from where it emerged from the phone. It seemed a good question, but still he wouldn't touch the instrument, just nod. "Calhoun, damn you—it's about *the kids*!"

He sprung up at once. In the same motion Grady strove to hang up and found the receiver pressed tightly against his ear while he breathed into it like an obscene caller. He managed another, marginally human-adult sound.

"It's David," Jean wept, "and P-Petey." Jean stopped for a second, almost stopping Calhoun's heart before she continued. The room was spinning. "They got into a squabble out at the curb; over Petey's trike. I guess D-David wanted to ride it. Aaaaaaand *they fell,* Grady—into a lot of broken glass. I *know* it wasn't out there this morning, Grady, I swear to God, but they're—pretty badly cut. They . . . *rolled* in it."

"Where are they?" he got out. Major effort expended.

"St. Vincent's," Jean mumbled. "Ambulance came. Grady, I couldn't take them 'cause *Tim's disappeared* . . . in *my* car. And I had to stay with Cathy." Then her composure broke and she began to make the worst sounds Calhoun had ever heard. Most of them were unintelligible; but not all ". . . Wayne called . . . morning . . . he—"

But Wayne's dead, Calhoun's mind replied. The day was a pinwheel, a mandala with madness and murder at the center.

"He said . . . friend Gill Riffey died . . ." Choking cries covered the rest.

Mom. Wayne. Gill. Kids all cut up. Tim *gone.* He had no words to speak so he put the phone back on the desk. Stared at it.

What Jean said next would have been audible across the Channel 61 office. Because of her intensity. How she screamed it: *"Do* it, Grady! For all our sakes, while *anybody's left*—please—kill yourself. Grady, please—*DO* IT!"

He nodded quite a bit. He stooped down finally to speak into the mouthpiece of the princess telephone, quite distinctly. "I will," he said. And whispered good-bye, darling.

25

Thursday, April 28. 12:49 P.M.

"My car broke down not far from here," he said, check-faced through the ratty screen door, "and I simply *must* get to the campus of Indiana University by one-thirty!"

The middle-aged woman saw the way her cats—those who were presently sunning or playing on the front porch—took to him, and didn't automatically shut the door. Ging and Matilda, particularly, had commandeered a leg apiece and were rubbing and purring like crazy.

And that butterball Matilda didn't take to anyone!

"What's going on at IU?" Freida demanded.

A   card   with   small   printing

materialized in a hand with manicured, pink nails. She hated the notion of allowing a stranger into the place, considering how far she lived from the nearest neighbors. But this man seemed very proper. "I'm Dr. Charles L. Cross; from St. John's, in the east? My dear, I'm a guest lecturer in Professor David W. Tyler's senior theology class and—"

"You're a priest?" Freida interrupted.

"My, no!" His pale face crimsoned slightly, but he went on poking the hand with the business card at the screen door, eager for her to verify what he was saying. "Alas, I'm merely a humble instructor." Brow raised, he glanced at a costly but tasteful watch and looked more flustered by the second. "If I could just borrow your telephone for a tiny moment, I'd be ever so—"

"Let me see your card then," she sighed, unlatching the door and opening it a fraction.

His burst of furious motion sent Matlida and Ging flying from his feet and he was within the house before Freida knew it.

And when he smiled at her from ear to ear, and she finally peered directly into his lifeless little eyes, she remembered with a start that she hadn't considered her own horoscope for days.

—Knew, too, who—or what—he was. Wondering why it had never occurred to her that a man who'd go to positively cosmic lengths to wreak vengeance upon one person would hesitate to do it again.

He headed for her and, when she glanced at the business card, it bore an address in the east and a single name: *SEERA*.

"If you shoot yourself with my gun, Calhoun," Bud said coolly, quietly stepping into the Irishman's office and showing no surprise over his kneeling posture behind his desk, the revolver barrel between his parted lips, "they'll have me up on a murder rap."

Grady blinked till his eyelids were dry and he'd begun thinking again. Unhesitatingly, he pulled the gun out of his mouth. He didn't try to stand yet. "You said the one thing that would stop me."

"Stole it out of my handbag, huh?" Bud put out her palm, rather maternally; took the weapon. Rested her hands on her hips and looked down at Calhoun quizzically. "How can you shoot yourself, Grade-A? You don't have a license!"

The laugh didn't come fast, but it came, sounding rusty, unpracticed. Grady hauled himself to his feet on rubbery legs, avoiding her eyes.

Both of them knew he was safe now.

"Mom's—gone." He gazed at her, working at keeping his stare fixed and sensing that he wouldn't cry so long as he held the gaze. "Wayne. And G-Gill." He saw her take a step toward him, arms upraised, and gestured to her to stop. "Stay *there*. I'll catch you up on it, then I want you to—to go somewhere. *Anywhere,* so long as you no longer know me." He felt his self-control begin to crumble and began to blink.

"That wasn't the only line that would make you stop," she said. And went nearer anyway. "Not with you on your knees with a gun stuck in your silly mouth."

His head ached; he couldn't think straight. "What was your other line?"

Bud smiled. "That's the only time I ever saw anybody give head to a revolver." Then, smiling, she embraced him. "It's not grade-A material, Grade-A, but I'm trying."

"You're the most trying person I know," he managed, hugging back.

And, when he could, he told her about Tim taking Jean's car; about Petey and David in the hospital, "Cut up pretty bad if I read Jean right." His bottled-up fury showed for the first time. "If my ex-wife says there wasn't anything broken out by the curb—no glass at all—then there wasn't any. Which means Rajelis *put* it there—meant my little boys to *fall* in it, cut themselves up! What kind of man—"

"Salvo could have killed them, for Rajelis, already," Bud said softly.

Grady gasped. "You're right. I never thought of that."

"He's still *saving* some of us, Calhoun." Her expression was intense; her on-camera training, her readiness to handle fast-breaking news, had her in complete control of her emotions. And,

Grady saw, something unbending Bud had been born with. "He's maintaining his plan. Come on." She reached for his hand. "Rajelis obviously figures you'll either kill yourself or head straight for the hospital, and the boys."

"Well, aren't I?" he demanded. But gave her his hand, let Bud tow him toward the office door. "Shouldn't I be with them?"

"Absolutely not. These aren't normal circumstances, and you're forgetting someone."

He paused at the door. "I'm not forgetting about Jean," he argued, struggling to shake off his depression. "If anything happens to her children—"

"One of whom is apparently still in the house with Jean," said Bud, close in front of him and trying, he realized, to impart some of her poised courage. "Your daughter. You can't leave Cathy in that house if Rajelis has sent Salvo after Jean."

He went through the doorway at a run. "I was behaving like a selfish bastard." He led the way down the corridor, dashed to the elevator, and jabbed a button. "I was opting out and simply *leaving* everyone to that crazy bastard!"

"Right," Bud said, bobbing her head. "Because you can't trust him to *stop* killing even if you *are* dead!" She caught a glimpse of Andy Sutor's assistant program manager rushing toward them, lowered her voice. "Life doesn't get better for people when someone in trouble commits suicide, Grady. He just leaves a mess for other people to clean up."

"Where are you going, Rocker?" Untidy, red-faced, not yet 35 and already somehow deep in middle-age, Andy's assistant wanted to be boss and everyone at 61 knew it. "With Trudy ill, we need all hands on deck to prepare the evening news."

"Tell you what you do," Bud snapped as the elevator doors opened. "Why not edit a *Best of the Evening News* for tonight? Include clips about a crisis in the Middle East, a terrorist bombing or two, dissension between the White House and State, throw in a local rape, a new shop opening at Union Station, and a tax increase and no one will ever notice the difference!"

She and Calhoun jumped inside and the elevator doors closed.

"D'you realize what we're doing?" Grady asked, incredulous. "Between the two of us, we're probably blowing a couple of careers in television to kingdom come! *Us!*"

She was racing toward car in the parking lot before she answered Grady: "Either that—and ask me if I care!—or we wind up with a story that'll take us straight to the networks!"

She only caught the quickest glimpse of him, while he was strapping her to her own bed, but she assumed that was how William Salvo looked whenever Rajelis had not ordered another guise, and she hoped she'd never see him clearly again.

He had lowered all her blinds, drawn all her bedroom curtains, and, completely abandoning all trace of "Dr. Charles L. Cross," almost appeared to have forgotten her. She'd have hoped he would simply go away, leave her to starve; except Freida, on her own, had procured his birth facts.

And knew that, living or dead or occupying the strange limbo of the white darkness, Billy Salvo was a homicidal psychopath who existed to torture and to kill.

He was going to murder her now and the only question that remained was how.

He reopened the bedroom door and, silently, motionless as a corpse, stood framed in it for a matter of moments. Freida craned her neck from her pillow to stare at him, more frightened by the lunatic's methodology than by the accepted fact of her own demise. Everybody died; it had often seemed silly, to Freida, that people tended to wait until they were old before, one way or the other, making their peace; preparing for it. As if they lived charmed lives that guaranteed they'd reach the so-called golden years! Because of astrology she'd known this was a crucial year in her life, but had not allowed the knowledge to prevent her from doing the simple, orderly things that pleased her. She had no regrets about never marrying, having no children or grandchildren, nothing, really, except the cats she cherished, and Lord knows she'd made an accommodation with her Creator years ago.

But she was only human, at the last, and it did seem less than right to be trussed up like a Thanksgiving turkey on her own bed, obliged to gape at a not-quite-real stealer of life who lacked the simple humanity to wring her neck and get it over with!

Never, Freida thought, feeling the muscles in her neck start to hurt from straining to watch Billy Salvo's silent and motionless form, had she seen anything to compare with the raw *power* he exuded. In real life, more than 30 years ago, he wouldn't have seemed inordinately tall, more muscular than many other men his size. When his features had been more or less normal, he wouldn't have drawn stares, or shudders—unless, of course, one had been exposed for 30 minutes or so to his stolid, uncommunicative, totally self-possessed ways. Then it would have become clear to almost anybody that a quality other men had was curiously absent from his makeup, that *other*, stealthy, definitely evil attributes were there instead. . . .

Without making a sound, Freida realized that instant, without moving, Billy Salvo had summoned them. From all around the rickety old place they came, virtually as silently as Billy. She had no idea of how many of them there were because she had never attempted to count them; she'd just let them make their babies, and opened her door—and her heart—to them, without ever turning one away.

Perhaps they were born to be familiars, companions of evil; Freida had considered that, in the past, without asking a thing of them. Except tolerating her, eating the food she supplied; now and then brushing with a phantom's touch against her ankle or arm, pretending in that rare moment of time to love her too.

Salvo stepped aside. Unhurriedly. Even in the act of tumbling over one another to get inside the bedroom, filling the doorway with a massing of muted colors and scurrying across the floor toward the bed, they made little sound. Even when, effortlessly, they clambered up the legs of the bed and poured across the white sheet like an ocean of soft fur, they did his bidding noiselessly, with neither fuss nor passion.

Matilda was first to reach her, followed by one she had never named, then Ging, her other favorite. For a moment Freida imagined that they paused. She looked into a growing circlet of alien eyes with her tired human ones and tried not to blame them.

Then, through a single gap in the dozens upon dozens of muscular little shapes starting to dig into her chest, she saw Salvo smile.

And they covered her face in a growing, feline tower, and snuggled down.

26

Still Thursday. 1:17 P.M.

She didn't know for sure she was going to kill herself that day until Cathy said how awful she felt and begged to skip school that afternoon. Cathy was the conscientious one, and the ten-year-old knew that staying home from school also meant going to bed. Not playing.

Which meant that either Cathy was more upset over what had happened to her brothers, with the broken glass, or Cathy's time had come too. And if that was the case, why, then, so had Jean's.

Or so she told herself as she shuffled out to the kitchen in bedroom slippers and robe. It no longer mattered much that she'd let herself and her appearance go, since the rape, and she wasn't sure whether she really felt depressed enough to commit suicide, but something told her it was the thing to do. True; the boys had cut only their hands and arms, were already sewn up, and Dr. Gregory, returning her frantic calls from St. Vincent's, had said he'd "seen a lot worse." It was also true that young Tim could have taken her car for some utterly harmless joy-riding, or because of an errand that only seemed urgent to a 15-year-old boy.

But Jean could sense Tim slipping away from them, had known for weeks, now, how changed he had become. Even when he'd turned the drugs over to his father Tim had avoided Grady's eyes and wouldn't even say where his friend, Billy lived. He'd had the gall to say he didn't know, that he'd never even been in Billy's house or met his parents!

Cathy getting sick is the final straw, the words formed in Jean's mind and she stretched up into the kitchen cabinet for the sleeping pills. It was a considerable reach because she and Grady had always put the riskier medicines on a top shelf, out of harm's way—or, as Calhoun had put it after Tim, age four then, had rigged up a makeshift ladder and eaten enough St. Joseph's aspirin to oopse, "so high up that nobody *but* little kids can get 'em down."

Jean got them down, new tears standing in her eyes like motionless pools. *What a truly terrible thing I said to him,* she thought, beginning a struggle with the childproof cap on the prescription bottle. *If he does it, too, that will be two of us as black marks on my soul.* The cap came away suddenly, several gaily decorated little sleep-makers scattering into the sink like spraying bullets. Instantly, frantically, she picked one up and gulped it down without water; then she stopped, distantly aware of having gone mechanical, automatonlike. For one brief instant she wondered if this was really what she wanted to do, if it was actually her decision, and sensed at the fraying,

tattered fringes of her volitional consciousness that another moment of
rational thought would produce a range of
countering arguments—reasons why this
final action should definitely not be taken.

Her attention, however, was drawn by
a *soupcon* of motion at the window
opening upon the driveway. Whether she
imagined it or not, Jean couldn't tell.
When she seemed to see on the other side
of the pane a man standing quietly on the
paved driveway, exposed, the remote
chance of realizing that she was being
motivated—a victim of the ultimate
rape—was forever lost. *He's back,* her
mind gasped. *He wants to hurt me again.*

And those portions of her body that
remembered as if it were yesterday the
revulsion and shock, the brutalizing pain,
the humiliation, and all those dark
feelings he'd put into her to carry like a
malformed fetus for the remainder of her
life, created a reflex action in her arms,
hands, and fingers. First, frantic to do it,
she snatched up all the pills that were
beginning to make pretty, miniature
rainbows in her sink, and ate them,
smearing her lips and turning most of her
gaze inward.

Then she upended the ones that were
left in the bottle into her mouth,
swallowed hard, then swallowed harder,
and turned back to the window on the
driveway with a face of violent triumph.

He was a shimmering, drab miasma,
all but colorless radiation with an up-

turned slash of curving blackness where a mouth should be . . . a six-foot tower of nothing much, except for a grinning gap of midnight that remained when the rest of it had dwindled away.

She made it to the couch in the front room by thinking about the cheshire cat, rabbit holes, and wonderland.

In a way, he decided, standing and dressing, it was just as well he could not order his William to go anywhere except at noon and on those fringes of light and darkness, darkness and light, which both of them preferred. Not when some fugitive remnant of Salvo's essence sensed that the slightest chance existed for him to be trapped, outside, by either true daylight or full nighttime. Had it not been so, logic would have demanded that he send Billy.

And Rajelis would have been denied the delight of killing Grady Calhoun's youngest boys himself.

Not that it would be without misery, even psychic agony, to drive all the way from here to the hospital where Calhoun's offspring had been taken after William's little stage setting with the broken glass. Rajelis had assumed that the ambulance summoned by Jean Calhoun's frantic phone call would come from a closer hospital; Community. It was his first mis-calculation—a valuable reminder of the adverse aspects to which he would be increasingly exposed, this day—and he would pay for it by driving farther than planned, washed in spring sunshine. There would be no more assumptions. No more miscalculations.

Unlike William, of course, yet partly because of that clumsy idiot who had preceded him in life, Calvin Rajelis was entirely able to function physically under any conditions. He was, after all, a real, a *complete* man. It was only that he felt uncomfortable under the extremes of nature, and sudden outbursts of illumination or obsidian night. All men of incomparable greatness possessed their quirks, their minor idiosyncrancies, even eccentricities. Only common mankind and ludicrous, mindless *constructs* such as the thing he had summoned, now returned once more from an errand and lolling in a corner like a lifeless puppet, gave in to their frailties.

For the hundredth time anger and bile rose in Calvin as he examined his appearance in a convenient mirror. If he hadn't recalled William himself, he would never have imagined it possible for nature to achieve such a quantum leap in intellect, ability, and overall *worthwhileness* from one incarnation—one life—to the next. Other than their mutual willingness to take life from others, Rajelis could not imagine what earthly ties were shared by their same soul.' And that did not appear to Calvin a particularly exceptional quality.

Perhaps the distinctions, he mused, affixing an artificial flower to his jacket lapel, *are solely the superior genetics of Seera—and the cooperation of the Forces of Suffering.*

Rajelis paused at the door, relieved to be leaving there. He did not like the cozy, laid-back restfulness of the place or how obviously it had been built for recreation, relaxation. Ignoring William, he adjusted his sunglasses before stepping outside and locking the door after him; then he ventured his first cautious look at the sky in many days.

With a shudder, he ducked into the rented car, pulled down the visor. He needed to center upon his objectives of the day, his one direct experience of murder so far. Starting the motor, he thought briefly about how surprised he'd been when the bastard Grady Calhoun had refused again today to commit suicide. Part of it, of course, was the interfering work of the bitch with the absurd name. Well, she would begin her suffering on schedule, his William would see to that.

In the meanwhile, there lay ahead the ecstasy of seeing Calhoun's face at the instant his precious "little Petey" and the other brat expired. *That,* Rajelis reflected, allowing a thin smile and heading out onto the highway, *should do it. That will make Seera's revenge complete.*

Seeing those little guys hurt and bleeding had just been too much. Mom and Dad thought he was such a jerk, always hiding him from what was coming down, refusing to confide in him even now, when he was almost a man. God, it had hurt badly, so badly. Deep inside, he knew it was why he'd turned to somebody like Billy—

And why Tim, today, had taken Mom's car in order to bolt for the cottage where ol' Billy'd be waiting.

Tim tried not to cry, he really did. He knew he was a mess, mentally, now, yet he couldn't care—not so long as he could quit bawling before his buddy saw him. It was just too much to fight hard for grades and like to do things with words when his own father didn't give a damn, and then, when evidently the whole family and everyone they knew were in some kind of deep shit, to be shut *out* . . .

Billy would be happy to see him. A guy could rap with someone cool like Billy. Not that Tim had any intention of snorting coke while they were down at the cottage; he'd really handed it all over to Dad and what he needed was only somebody who'd hear him out, treat him like he counted for something.

He blinked and almost let Mom's big Buick wander across the center strip. The possibility had hit him like a ton of bricks.

What would he do if Billy had *more* coke with him?

27

Grady didn't think for a moment that she was sleeping.

Bud drew him away from his ex-wife's body, an easy feat because the Irishman was rubber-legged. She even had to press herself against him with one arm supporting his torso, the other round his waist, to keep from knocking him to the floor. If she could have done it, she'd have nestled his dazed face in the hollow of her shoulder and kept him from continuing to gape, open-mouthed and making heartrending sounds at the root of his soul, at Jean's crumpled form.

Apparently, she had tried to rise at some point during her dying, possibly with a change of mind; one slipper-clad foot was flat on the floor while her back and shoulders were slumped against the couch's stiff arm. Oddly, Bud noticed, Jean's head and neck were erect—further argument that she had fought to shake off the effects of the sleeping pills—and, had her eyes been open, Jean might have been staring directly at whatever came next.

When Bud felt she could leave Calhoun she went in search of a blanket, or sheet, and, upon returning, draped the dead woman's body. Grady had stopped making audible sounds of grief and, she observed, appeared to be supplanting his sorrow with outrage, even fury. *He'll be okay,* she thought, relieved but still anxious. *I don't think Calvin Rajelis is the only one hungering for revenge now.*

It occurred to Bud to fix Grady coffee, or a drink, and she started toward the kitchen when something far more urgent crossed her mind. Heart racing, saying nothing whatsoever to Calhoun, she rushed to the stairs and raced to the second floor as quietly as she was able.

Calhoun, moments later, heard her shout and was so shocked he literally leaped to his feet. "Grady!" she'd called from the landing. "Get up here—*quick*!"

Before he was halfway up the steps he had a clear idea of why Bud was shouting and, sick at heart and fearing the worst, stopped short in his daughter's room, trying to peer around Bud's impeding form. "Cathy . . ."

Bud's eyes were solemn, cautionary. "I don't *think* she's dead." She put up a small hand, not so much to prevent him from entering the bedroom as to hold back his panic and delay the possibility of the worst. "Eaaaaaasy," she whispered.

They advanced together to the ten-year-old, apprehensive beyond anything they'd experienced before. Cathy, motionless and pale, was on her back with all four limbs sprawled proportionally from the center of the mattress. Unbidden, as Calhoun knelt at the side of the small bed, the storybook image of Sleeping Beauty suffused him with a terrible mixture of hope and dread, fantasy and reality. *"Hey, Princess,"* he called gently, taking one hand and caressing it. *It's warm. She's alive!* "Naptime's over . . ."

Bud's hand squeezed his shoulder. "Check her pupils." He glanced up and blanched. The possibility that Jean had given pills to Cathy, too, was stark and paralyzing in her pretty features. When Bud stooped beside him and gently retracted one gossamer eyelid, it also occurred to both of them that Calvin Rajelis had many ways to kill. Perhaps she was alive but would remain this way forever, healthy and breathing, even growing, but lost to any real life.

With Bud's careful fingers holding back the little girl's left eyelid, both Grady and Bud saw with wonder the sweet illumination of alert intelligence dawn in it anew like the rising sun.

"Had a bad dream, Daddy," Cathy said sleepily, hazily, paying no heed to Bud's presence and groping with her round arms for Calhoun's neck. Her breath was clean, healthy; like spring flowers. Surfacing from the unknowable realm of the unconscious, all brittle pretense of being self-assured and independent had fallen away. "A real bad dream . . ."

And it's not over, thought Calhoun, remembering with anxiety and fresh panic that his daughter's mother lay dead in the front room downstairs. "It's over now," he lied, and patted her.

"Someone died," Cathy said in a complaining tone. She used that inflection when she couldn't understand what had happened, and Grady'd always believed it was an index to her thirst for knowledge. This time he froze, wondering what she had seen. "A lady . . ."

"It was only a dream, darling," Bud said. "A nightmare." Her gaze met his above the child's tangled mop of hair.

"She doesn't live near us," Cathy murmured, insisting upon being heard. "And she's old . . . and she has *lots* of cats . . ."

"Do you think she picked them up psychically," Bud asked from the passenger seat, "and that Freida is really dead?"

"I'd bet a thousand big ones on it," Grady snarled, trying not to take it out on the car. Or on Bud. He glanced briefly into the backseat at Cathy, who'd fallen asleep again in the sunny, springtime breeze. They hadn't told her yet about her mother, but he'd called Alberts, Wayne Sojourner's man, and reported it. With any luck, Jean would be out of the house before they brought Cathy back. "And I don't think it was to shut her up, either."

"How do you figure?"

"If 'our Mr. Rajelis,' as Freida called him, knew about her and dispatched that slimeball, Salvo, he must've also known that she already helped me out." He stared studiedly out the windshield at the road, blared his horn, and passed a pickup truck. "So now I'm responsible for one more good person getting it in the neck."

"*Us,* Grade-A," Bud argued, gently. "Not you alone. She was helping us, and . . ." Bud's voice trailed off.

"And everybody who's left." Calhoun's knuckles were like ice frozen to the wheel. "I'm going to stop him before he gets to you, Cathy, or Tim, Buddy. If it's the last thing I do." His laugh was sardonic. "Which it very probably will be."

"Where are you headed?" she inquired. He hadn't said. He'd just rushed them into the car and driven away. Although he was used up, almost certainly permanently scarred by all that had happened, there was nothing suicidal, nothing aimless, about his driving.

"I won't say it aloud," Grady declared after a pause. "No one, not even poor Freida, knows how Rajelis does what he does. How he learns where to send Billy Saliva. So I'm keeping our destination to myself." He glanced quickly toward Bud, sensing her apprehension. "But I'm taking you and my little girl where you will be safe. I think." Grady blinked. "I pray."

She turned fretfully to him. "I noticed you didn't say 'us.' " You're going where you think they are, aren't you?"

"I'm not telling you that, either," he said shortly.

But he had answered her anyway.

Neither of them spoke again until another couple of miles, south of Indianapolis, had been covered.

Then something peculiar happened. It

was neither Bobby Knight basketball nor Bill Mallory football time at Indiana University and this was midafternoon on a Thursday; traffic was light. Calhoun, absorbed by his grief and his driving, striving to formulate plans that might enable him to get past the creature called Salvo and, in the protection of Petey and David, combat Calvin Rajelis directly, did not experience it.

Bud, on the other hand, felt surfeited by queer tension even before the late-model Cadillac began to draw abreast to them from the opposite direction. She could not have described her feelings, couldn't make herself draw the speeding Caddy to Grady's attention.

Nevertheless, just as the other vehicle roared past, she felt dismaying waves of fright and revulsion wash over her and turned sharply in the passenger seat in an effort to see around Grady and catch a glimpse of the other driver.

She didn't—both automobiles were on a divided, four-lane highway—but Bud shuddered from head to toe and went on trembling. She felt, overwhelmingly, that she had just come closer to the physical incarnation of evil than she had ever desired to come. It left her not only fearful, nervous, and shaken but feeling dirty—unclean.

She knew, without the ability to mention it at all, that they had just passed Calvin Rajelis.

A moment later thunder growled

beastlike, seemingly from all around them, and the rain spattering upon the road was at once hot, bizarrely furtive, and uremic.

Suddenly it was dark enough that Grady Calhoun switched on the headlights.

He admitted himself with his own key, promptly surprised and slightly disturbed by the fact that the place was steeped in shadows. All the way down Tim had been grudgingly cheered by the apparent arrival of real spring and, while he heard thunder boom to the north, it was still glaringly bright outside.

In the long main room, near the unlit fireplace, light flashed and Tim, going nearer, thought he detected a male figure crouching above the coffee table. For a second he froze, imagining it was an intruder.

But it was only his friend Billy, smiling in greeting.

And several lines of white, powdery substance carefully columned off on the table like the inviting and wide-open gates of hell. "What kept you, Tim?" the other boy asked, nostrils flaring. "I've been waiting."

28

"Hold on a minute before you try to go inside or you'll drown out there." Grady addressed Bud and Cathy, the latter now apparently entirely free from her drug-like sleep. She perched with an unknowing, expectant smile on the edge of the backseat, satisfied with the explanation that Bud was her father's friend. She had always enjoyed going to the cottage—nearly as much as her big brother, Tim—but it was generally summer before they made it down. Grady glanced out his car window at the tumultuous rainfall. "Boy, that came up suddenly!"

Suddenly enough, thought Bud, *to have been caused.* Privately, she felt the storm, the darker skies, were the product of Calvin Rajelis's ultimately unguessable range of magickal abilities, but wasn't about to say so—especially with a ten-year-old sitting in the backseat. Cathy had enough genuine heartaches coming without being exposed to her own frightening theories. Bud looked questioningly at Calhoun. "Aren't you coming in?"

"No way." He shook his head. "I have to drive back to Indianapolis and St. Vincent's Hospital as fast as possible if I'm going to make sure those crazies don't get near Petey and David." He reached out to take her hand. "This is where Jean and the kids and I used to come for a week or so on vacation. It should be safe because, since Jean and I"—he hesitated, conscious that Cathy was listening—"agreed to disagree, none of us have been here. Meaning that Rajelis probably doesn't know about it and, even if he does, there's no reason for him to believe we'd come down. Not . . . at a time like this." When, he wondered, would he have to tell Cathy and the others about their mother? And how?

Bud had turned on her seat to peer through the hard, slanting rain. Although the Calhoun cottage would not make those magazines that liked to picture dream houses, even with a storm that conjured neurotic fears the place had a cozy "family" look. As nearly as Bud could tell, the cottage was unlit inside—the way it should be—wide, one-story with a stone front, constructed on the fringe of a thick woods. The latter was foreboding, somehow, ominous in the bleak downpour.

When the rain began to subside Bud sighed and glanced reluctantly back at Calhoun. "You might as well give me the key now." She wasn't quite able to conceal a persistent impression that he'd made a mistake bringing them there, nor hide it from itself. Her coffee-with-cream complexion both looked and felt pale; drawn. "We'll have to make a run for it."

How petite, how small she was. "Look," Grady began emotionally, and reached over the backseat to lock his arm round Cathy's neck and include her in his remarks. "It's nearly over. And I'm . . . my-self again. Bud, I mean to put a stop to this nightmare." Impulsively, he craned his neck to kiss the child's soft cheek and then rumple her hair. "There are good times for us right over the horizon, gang. Will you remember I promised you that?"

"I know, Daddy," Cathy nodded in perfect faith. She gave him a quick kiss back.

He handed Bud the key to the cottage. When she'd gotten out of the car and Cathy was running through weeds and puddles to the front door, Bud put her head back into the car. What she had to say to Grady sounded hopelessly inadequate. "Good luck, Grade-A. See ya."

"Maybe you can get a blaze going in the ol' fireplace." Grady had to shout above the drumming of raindrops on the car roof. "Hey, Buddy . . . I love you."

"Yeah; me too." She began to straighten—to let him go—but stopped, suddenly filled with a dread that they might never meet again. "Wait." She stretched across the passenger seat to him for a kiss. "Hey—I love you too."

"Naturally," he joked. Then he grabbed her wrist, smiling, with very bright eyes. "I'm glad you do. Let's do something about that. Sometime."

Bud saw his surprise, recognized his joy. And with a wave that was almost cavalier, swashbuckling, Calhoun was pulling the door to, gunning the motor, and squealing back out on the highway.

Off, she thought, to do valiant battle against the evil sorcerer from the east. Her sweet, foolish knight templar.

Confident in his restored courage and resolve, Bud was still smiling at Grady's boyish image when she had unlocked the cottage door and—prompting Cathy ahead of her—passed through a short hallway to the main room.

It seemed dark. Not as dark, perhaps, as it should have been with none of the lights on. After pausing to put her purse on a table inside the entryway, she and the child edged further into the deep room—

And became instantly aware of a subtle, almost indiscernible illumination. A second later, eyes adjusting to the gloom, Bud made out two figures kneeling at the far end of the main room. They were so engrossed in what they were doing that neither seemed to have heard Bud and Cathy's entrance. For another moment the newswoman was unable to detect the reason for their furtive activity.

Actually, only one of the two males was behaving furtively, she realized. The second, his back turned, was lighting old newspapers in the fireplace and attempting to ignite some older logs. He looked queerly familiar.

The furtive one—it was the impression he gave at once—was snorting cocaine. On his knees before a coffee table, he had apparently used up a number of brightly colored straws, which, Bud saw with disgust, came from a gaily decorated box depicting Donald Duck, Mickey Mouse, and other Disney characters. The perversion of using drugs with straws manufactured for little children brought Bud another swift, curious step toward the two males—

And she recognized the one at the fireplace as young Tim Calhoun, realized that the one languidly pulling a straw from his reddened nostril was staring at her. Directly; as if he'd known all along she and Cathy were there. He grinned.

"You're Calhoun's woman," he said in a high-pitched voice.

Despite his seeming youth, the armless tanktop and frayed jeans, he was *no boy.* Bud sensed that with a certainty accompanied by rising apprehension. Because she was almost certain that she knew who, and what, he was.

Tim pivoted, startled, guilty-faced. And—"*Hi*, bro!" Cathy called to her big brother, and skipped toward him.

Avid between the child and Tim Calhoun was the kneeling murder machine called Billy Salvo.

Children's wards weren't heavily guarded realms, and saying he was the boys' Uncle Cal admitted Rajelis to their room without difficulty. The kind of tall, slender man who carried himself both proudly and with a performer's aura of dramatic intensity, he was also young and knew how to exert his quite fictive charm.

He'd known he would have no need for

his hypnotic or more rarefied gifts. All was on course; he was sure he'd made no further miscalculations, and he entered the double room where David and Peter Calhoun slept under sedation with an air exactly like that of a worried relative. In separate beds with a chair set between them, along with a table bearing tissues, a styrofoam water pitcher, and two glasses, the seven- and three-year-olds seemed tiny. They could have been slain with consumate ease in seconds, and the thought cheered Rajelis.

But that event to which the mentalist anxiously looked forward would have to wait for the arrival of the boys' father.

Calvin lowered himself into the chair between the beds dapperly, warily, and beamed in turn upon each unconscious boy. Beyond the single window on David's side of the hospital room, the storm Rajelis had thought to create—in order to moderate the light and make his trip from the Lake Monroe area soothing—continued to rage. It was neither twilight nor dawn, but he rather enjoyed an occasional makeshift version, and never tired of utilizing his powers—and the favors of the committed and supportive Forces of Suffering.

Rajelis, at a thought, scowled. Thunder clapped.

All that was wrong was his recent realization that his own negative planetary aspects required him to end the game between Grady Calhoun and him a few days early. In all probability, nothing would have gone astray if he had elected to sustain his plan for a theatrical climax on the second of May. But staying with his William in the Irishman's own cottage, waiting until the bastard finally had the idea of taking members of his family where they'd be "safe," had made Calvin ill at ease. Too close. He had no need to fear any physical action of a fool such as Calhoun, but the *emotions* in that place . . .

What had gone amiss—what had forced Rajelis's hand, obliged him to take expedient steps—was his William's telepathic discovery that Calhoun had prematurely learned about his ex-wife's "suicide." There had been certain exquisite plans for the child, Cathy, much more tantalizing designs than merely placing her in a deep sleep. The bastard's interference had *ruined* that! It was William's finding that Calhoun had rushed with the Rocker bitch to his former family home as much out of concern for Jean, the ex-wife, as from anxious personal interest in his female offspring. Rajelis hadn't anticipated that for the very sound reason that he imagined divorce finished and forever banished any regard between the people involved. Since he did not believe in love at all, the actions of Calhoun had been incomprehensible; unpredictable. Why did one marry, except *believing* in love; why did one divorce, except for hatred? All life was black and white to him; affection, even ordinary interest in the safety of another human being, was repugnant, enigmatic, anethma to the performer.

Well, the precise timing might not be everything he could have desired, but the circumstances most definitely were: While Jean-the-bitch had sent her injured boys to a hospital other than what Calvin had expected, she *had* dispatched them . . . and effectively divided the brood. His William had Rajelis' instructions for how to dispose of the Rocker woman and the girlchild, Cathy, and—after he had been forced to observe those dyings—the boy, Tim Calhoun. Unless, of course, young Tim was easily addicted to the drug and did not seem to mind too much. Should he pass that test, Rajelis had other plans for him; ways that Tim could be of interesting, personal use.

Calvin permitted himself a smug smile of contentment and glanced at the small boys on either side of him. *This* was an element he had planned from the start, knowing the bastard Calhoun's obvious preference for the three-year-old, the "baby." What was soon to happen was ineffably delectable, a culmination of Seera's revenge that was gloriously appropriate. Through the long, lonesome nights when he'd had no company but that of the oaf, William, looking forward to the perfect suffering planned for Grady Calhoun had sustained Rajelis, made him sometimes merry and jovial of spirit. It would be an experience to look back upon glee-fully forever.

First, the bastard would burst into the room, ready for a confrontation and willing to do anything whatsoever to save his offspring. Then Calvin would pretend to ask the insensitive mother-killer which of his boys he would like to go on living a while longer—*show* Calhoun his sons in peril of losing their lives . . . and *force* him to choose between them! He would, of course, select his precious Petey, thereby implanting the memory of that dreadful choice in his tortured brain for so long as he lived!

And at *that* exact point, he, Calvin Rajelis, would slaughter *both sons*—right in front of the helpless Calhoun's staring eyes!

Whereupon he, Rajelis, would simply . . . *leave*. He'd *let* Calhoun live with what he'd done—make the conscious choice of which son lived, which son died, instantly followed by his abject and unmanly failure to save *either!*—

Until William Salvo perceived that the true microsecond of occult magick had come . . . and Grady Calhoun was at the moment of suicide. Then he, Rajelis, would *see* it happen, in perfect safety!

And some people said there was no justice and no beauty left in the modern world!

Eyes bright, breathing an exhalation of purely pleasurable anticipation, Calvin settled back in the chair between the two beds, took the hand of each medicated child as befitting a worried uncle, and waited breathlessly for the bastard to arrive.

29

3:44 P.M.

Calhoun had never driven so fast in his life.

Once, he slowed to a speed in the broad vicinity of 70; but after he'd gone another seven or eight miles, his foot had flattened on the accelerator again.

When it occurred to him a short and hectic while later that Petey and David might depend upon his getting there in one piece to stay alive—and the impossibility of attempting to explain himself to a motorcycle cop or sheriff (There's this mentalist who's trying to get *me* by making my little guys cut themselves so he can attack them *again* in the hospital, and . . .) arose dismally in Grady's mind—he trimmed his speed to the low sixties, and kept it there. Gritting his teeth and waging a war to control his own right foot.

Dear, sweet Lord, he hoped and prayed he'd done the right thing in taking Bud and Cathy to the cottage! It made sense in a logical way; yet in the country of the irrational, maybe the wholly illogical was king.

But *where* was Tim? What could account for the way that kid had changed in such a short period of time? Did all boys these days reach a certain age—a teen-for-between-age—and feel more comfortable dwelling in the country of the insane? He'd left his mother *alone* with his bleeding little brothers . . . hell's bells, it'd be easy to *blame Tim* for what had happened to Jean.

And the way it was, *none* of the children knew about that. Not a one of them knew—unless poor little Cathy did and was blanking it out—their mother was gone. God almighty, if he *did* save David and Petey, he'd have to try to *explain* Jean's suicide to them . . . try to make them understand that, in a very real way, it was no suicide at all—that she hadn't abandoned them or cared less about them, but was terrified *for* them . . . simply incapable of waiting until the next hideous bad news swept over her.

But, *They drove her to it,* Calhoun thought, nodding his head in grim certainty. He might never be able to prove it, but he knew he'd known Jean well enough to be sure that she *hadn't* taken those goddam pills entirely on her own! *When Salvo raped and beat her, he left more than his seed . . . he left a means of getting to her later, of telling her—through Rajelis—what to do.* Grady was certain of it.

—Just as certain as he was that he

could die a halfway contented man if he
not only stopped Rajelis and Salvo once
and for all, but took them with him.

  —Except that, Grady realized as he
approached the south side of Indianapolis, a part of him—even now—was the
laid-back, good-humored, fast-talking TV
host on the way up . . . a part of him was
still Mr. Ordinary With a Television Show;
and that part could not quite assimi-
late—make real—the terrible things that
had happened in such a short stretch of
time. How long was it, now? He made himself think, concentrate, almost missing a
right turn onto 465 that became a hair-
rising adventure without slackening his
speed. It'd begun March 18; this was April
28. Grady gasped: *41 days!* In 41 days, a
skinny madman mind-reader he hadn't
even met 42 days ago had murdered or
arranged for the deaths of most of the
people Calhoun had known in his entire
life! All his friends; half his business
associates; his only brother; his mother;
now, his wife.

  Oddly the term *ex-wife* wouldn't stick
when Grady tried to go back and use it as
an exercise in accuracy. Maybe he'd marry
Bud if everything worked out, *probably*
he'd do it—flashing through Calhoun's exhausted and harried mind was the realization that he hadn't lied when he told
Bud he loved her—but he knew he was just
old-fashioned and stubborn enough that
Jean, in a manner he couldn't conceivably
define, would always be his wife.

Because he'd never, really, stopped loving her. Either.

He began to cry, and the tears clouding his vision matched the wash of raindrops on the windshield, and Grady told himself to *stop* it, now. Because he'd never use them all up before he reached St. Vincent's, or, for that matter, before he died.

Especially if that was scheduled for today.

Traffic started picking up as plant employees quitting for the day at four o'clock or 4:15 flooded onto the road. It was impossible to exceed 55 miles per hour now, and live; with greater frequency, Calhoun was having to brake sharply or slow for 40-mile speed limits near shopping centers and other exits. And the hospital was on the west side of town . . .

One satisfaction brought a tight, grim smile to Calhoun's lips. Rajelis had planned for him to be dead, a suicide, in 45 days. That was still four days away and there was no chance in hell Grady'd be taking his own life now—not with the little guys to save, and both Bud and Cathy dependent upon him to get back to the cottage alive. If Calvin Rajelis forced him to die to save Petey and David, that would be no suicide; not in Grady's book, nor in God's. Which made Rajelis and his freak Salvo the losers; it meant the SOB's plan for vengeance—which Calhoun still did not understand in the least—had fallen short.

At the point he was at last turning left—west—and knew he'd reach St. Vincent's in another eight to ten minutes, it occurred to Grady that the rain was coming down harder, almost purposefully . . . the nearer he got to his destination. For an instant he wondered if the mentalist had learned the boys' whereabouts and pursued them, the storm following his route like a dark cloud trailing a cartoon jinx.

And when he made out the hospital complex in the distance—just south of hectic West 86th Street—and the storm was firing thunderbursts and lightning flashes as if locked in combat with the renewal of spring, he found himself beginning to tremble—and wondering how sure he dared to be that only a brave man's life or death awaited him.

"I'm Tim's friend." Scarcely taller than Tim, more muscular but not as filled out as most men are, he pushed himself to his feet unhurriedly, lips twitching in an artificial smile. "I'm—"

"I know who you are," Bud said. Cathy had safely reached her brother without Billy Salvo even looking at her. "But I really don't think Tim does." She poised on the balls of her small feet, ready to run. But Salvo wasn't moved.

"Sure, I do," Tim said softly, disagreeing. "Bill's a friend of mine. Like he said." The boy dusted his hands, stood away from the fireplace, and grinned briefly at his sister. "What's going on? What'd Billy mean about you being Dad's woman?"

Not now, Bud thought; *not here.* "I work at 61 with your father." She only glanced at Tom, unwilling to remove her gaze from Salvo for any length of time. He was some 14 or 15 feet away; Tim and Cathy were to his right, farther. "We date." Somehow she had to get the kids closer— get them all *out* of the place while Billy Salvo stayed put.

"Well, hi," Tim said doubtfully. Child- like, he kept his own eyes from the lines of powder on the coffee table; he gave the impression that if she mentioned them, he might pretend not to have known they were there. Yet he looked clear eyed; his pupils weren't dilated. "I guess Dad sent you. Well, we're okay here; no sweat."

You're farther away from okay than you've ever been, Bud reflected. And that portion of her mind that remained a news- woman's, that never stopped asking questions, was intensely curious about the . . . thing . . . between the kids and her. Those eyes, they lacked malice but not menace. Deadly menace. Bud had seen creatures with eyes like that; they swam in water and ate almost anything.

Needing a plan of action, it occurred to her then that Calvin Rajelis directed Salvo's actions. What he'd told Billy to do, he'd done. But where Rajelis was intellect- ually active, wily, this mock boy or man—assuming Freida Rehfeldt had been

correct—was more a remnant, a motivated memory, than human. She had an
idea. "How old are you, Billy?"

Nothing of the bland features moved.
But he'd hesitated. "A year older'n Tim."
He didn't know!

"It's nice of you to befriend someone
younger." She managed a smile. "Do you
go to the same high school Tim attends?"

"Uh-huh." The head bobbed.

Bud glanced at Tim. He was listening,
if frowning, looking bewildered and increasingly irritated. She seemed to be
picking on his only friend, but he wasn't
sure of that yet. "You're a big, strapping
guy, Billy. Like sports?" A second pause
and then he nodded. "What do they call
your school team, Billy?"

Silence. He was stumped! That much
had to be obvious, even to Tim. Yet Salvo
showed no sign of anger, cunning, or
deception. "Baseball?" he asked at last.

"I see." Bud's gaze found both Tim
and Cathy in turn. Returning it to Salvo's
vacuous features, she held her hand at her
side and wriggled her fingers; *come,* they
said. *Over here.* "What's your principal's
name, son?" The *son* almost caught in her
throat. "Who's your favorite teacher?"

The faintest blinking of the eyelids.
Behind him, Cathy, and Tim, the fire
suddenly blazed up and Billy's slack-jawed
face was red-ringed through the shadowed
interior of the cottage. "Don't know . . ."

"That was a hard one," Bud said. Her
heart soared; young Cathy, puzzled but

unafraid, had begun walking toward her.
Tim's eyes had widened in embryonic
amazement. "Do you have a favorite
subject?"

No answer at once. Bud studied Salvo
with excitement and realization too.
Rajelis had programmed Billy just enough
to deceive and lure people. That had been
sufficient. By the time they had figured it
out, they were dead.

"Hey, what is this bullshit?" Tim
clearly wanted to defend a friend. Yet,
when he took a step, it was motivated unconsciously by some instinct for survival.
It was closer to Bud. "Let's not have—"

"Yeahhh," Billy breathed. They looked
at him. He'd come up with an answer.
Light from a mental bulb left decades ago
in a musty attic gleamed in the witless
eyes like a snout protruding from a dark
corner. Meaningless to the kids, his reply
was a joke from the long-dead past.
"Recess!" he bawled. And giggled.
Shuffling his feet spastically, he stared
back and made noises of horrid amusement that started as snuffling sounds.

They all lapsed into stunned silence.
With shock, Bud saw that the "boy" before
her, however impossible it appeared, was
quite literally from another time. All his
points of reference had been established
years before they were born. Thoroughly
aware of their danger now, Bud perceived
that she was conversing with—interviewing—a sort of ghost. "Tim," she said
softly, easily, "would you come over here a

minute, please?" Cathy, she rejoiced to see, had, as any child might have, lost interest; she was poking into things at the entrance way.

And when young Tim headed toward her she thought he'd pieced it together and miraculously understood. But clearly, questions—the wrong, dangerous ones— were leaping to his lips.

She thought faster. "Billy . . . who is the president of this country?" It was the first thing to occur to her. She needed something—anything—that would make Grady's son grasp an inkling of the truth. She had to have his aid. Laughing sweetly, lightly, she added, "I think Tim's forgotten."

It was too broad even for Billy Salvo. "You makin' fun of me," he accused her, looking pained, aggrieved.

Tim made it worse. "Knock if off, okay?" he begged. But he was beside her now. Spinning, he pleaded with his friend. "*Tell* her, Bill—show her how smart you are . . . please?"

"Smart?"

"Yes, go on, son." Bud folded her arms. Nodded. "Show me."

Salvo rubbed his wide mouth and, dragging the hand down his face, he felt a glistening trail of moisture on his chin. He wiped the palm on his chest, and anger drew his almost colorless brows together. "Anyone knows what a president is." Upset, he shifted clumsily from foot to foot.

"Of course!" Bud agreed brightly. She tried using her hand to manipulate the teenager toward his sister, and the door.

Instead, Tim glared incredulously at Billy. Comprehension formed in his line-less features, along with disappointment, and anger. "Aw, man, you don't even know *that*! Do you?"

Existing solely to obey Rajelis and kill, yet out of touch with Calvin until the slaughter began, the Slavo entity wanted out. That was clear. The transformation began as the product of intellectual failure and embarrassment. The legs of the jeans grew muscled; the shoulders broadened, the chest filled out until the tanktop was taut—and *it grew.* Swinging knuckles brushed the cocaine away in a snowy cloudburst. And when the real people in the cottage's main room raised their disbelieving gazes to the face, the mouth widened till it seemed the skin must rip.

But—it wasn't smiling. It was remembering the right answer, a mind divided by the passage of time struggling for teacher's approval. And—"*Eisenhower!*" it declared in a voice that boomed. Now it did smile, a shark's black grimace of smug satisfaction. "I . . . I *like* Ike!"

Cathy, at the entrance way, saw the transformation and shrieked. Tim, Bud sensed, was backing toward the door in speechless awe and horror. But she was still a matter of yards from the mature, vindictive apparition.

"You thought I didn't 'member," Billy said, giggling and groping for her.

30

4:08 P.M.

"The Calhoun children—where are they?" Grady, dimly aware that he'd ventured into a land where cartoon characters bedecked the walls and Walt Disney or Charles Schulz had replaced great surgeons as the beacons of hope, was breathless after his dash from the hospital parking lot. "I'm their father."

"One moment." Younger and more agreeable than nurses Calhoun remembered from his own bout with a bad-tempered appendix, she paused to munch on a pencil and consult a clipboard. Why, he wondered, didn't they have cartoons by Gahan Wilson and Charles Addams stuck to the walls of grown-up hospital wards? Smiling, she gave him a number, adding, "Their uncle is already with the boys."

"Thanks," Grady murmured.

And was already following arrows painted beneath cartoons before the young nurse's information sank in.

The uncle of little Petey and David Calhoun, Grady's brother Timothy, was dead and buried.

And the madman who had ordered Timmy's execution—having beaten Calhoun to the children's bedside—was surely *sitting* with them that minute.

Rooted to the center of the corridor, not because of fear for himself but in a desperate attempt to decide his best course, Grady longed to get the attractive nurse to call security—to see strong-armed men in uniform physically throw Rajelis from the room. Better, to phone Wayne's man and have the mentalist arrested—or shot on sight. But each plan, in turn, Grady rejected. Rajelis would not have shown himself in public in this city if he wasn't positive he could dispose of any uniformed opposition. At best, seeking and winning official help meant that young Calvin would merely exert his performer's charm and, appearing offended, quietly leave . . . disappearing before Grady could keep him from taking his next murderous step.

But if the son of a bitch was able to *lie* and just *walk in* to St. Vincent's children's ward—with no concern for any kind of help Calhoun enlisted—what earthly chance *did* he have against the madman? Being blasted into the cartoon wallpaper or zapped away in a puff of smoke wouldn't help David or Petey.

The one bright spot, Calhoun thought, was that—

"Aren't you going to come inside, dear brother?"

Rajelis! Dapper, outwardly concerned only for his nephews, wearing a smile that shared his apparent anxiety with the boy's father, the rail-thin mentalist had popped his head out of a zoom up the corridor like a rabbit materializing from a hat.

Lips pressed together, nodding but not speaking, Calhoun headed toward "Uncle" Calvin. Briskly. *The one bright spot is that she didn't say anything about a second man.* "If you've done anything to my little guys—"

Nonchalant of manner, graceful as a dancer, Rajelis preceded Grady into the room. "All's well," he murmured with a glance over one fleshless shoulder—"that ends well."

Heart pounding furiously, Grady brushed by the embodiment of all his suffering and stopped short at the foot of the beds, gaping down at David and Petey. He lacked the courage to go nearer.

But he saw, then, that each boy was obviously sedated; unharmed. The three-year-old's thumb—thoughtfully allowed to protrude from the bandages—was firmly caught between his lips. That endearing and familiar pose touched Calhoun but enabled him to start breathing again.

Rajelis, to Grady's amazement and a rush of revulsion, clapped him lightly on the arm! With a shake of his long head and the air of a man who has been misunderstood too long, he slipped round Calhoun and lowered himself, casually, to the chair between the boys' beds. He removed his dark glasses, pocketed them. "It's time we talked."

"Talk!" Grady gazed in disbelief at the

younger man. His hands fisted, the Irishman sought even a trace of his customary aplomb but found himself incapable, that second, of believing he was staring down at a man who'd arranged for the misery and murders of most of the human beings he knew. "I should be attacking you . . . *strangling* you!"

"But understandably, you can no longer accept the premise that I am responsible for bringing so much suffering to those you care about." Calvin raised a hand and an unopened pack of Camel cigarettes materialized between thumb and index. "Come; let's be civil. I believe this is your brand?" Deftly, he tossed it to Grady. "Would you care for coffee?"

Calhoun, automatically, caught the cigarettes. At once he dropped them to the floor. "Are you?" he demanded.

"Am I what?" inquired Rajelis. Leaning back in his chair, he extended his long arms, draped them. His expression stopped just short of defiance. "Responsible for all that suffering?"

Calhoun nodded. Was he really an expert telepath or merely a master psychologist? Because, if Grady could get him out of that chair and away from the boys, the man was not physically intimidating. That very fact, coupled with the nonchalance, the disarming manner, continued to make it easy to believe that it was all—

All what, Calhoun? Grady asked himself. A hundred or more dead in 41 days

350 J. N. Williamson

counting the acquaintances Grady had read
about in the obituaries twisted the word
coincidence into the realm of impossibility.

"Let us discuss the question of responsibility, Mr. Calhoun." Rajelis, for the
first time, could not keep intensity—the
razor's edge of hatred—from his voice. His
eyes were hard, shining diamonds someone had cursed. "You have never remembered the name *Seera* have you?"

"Never," Calhoun admitted. Carefully,
he sat on the edge of David's bed, at the
foot, but an inch or two closer to Rajelis.
Then he blinked his blue eyes as something clicked for him. "But it sounds like
the name of a woman in your line of
work—the vocational line, that is; I
imagine slaughtering people is your
hobby." Grady peered at Rajelis with fresh
curiosity. "Your wife . . . or . . . your
mother?"

"Think back to the start of your
career, Mr. Calhoun," Rajelis urged. The
burning eyes sought to hold his, but Grady
glanced briefly away, alarmed. "See if it
isn't possible to summon from your
memory one of the first innocents you *destroyed* to advance your childish
ambitions. Think of someone quite pretty,
a vivacious conversationalist, a brilliantly
knowledgeable, charming woman"—
Rajelis dangled his arms, the manicured
nails of his long fingers grazing the sheets
of the sedated children's beds—"whom
you *forced* to perform—to exceed her

momentary capabilities—against her will!"

"Come on!" Calhoun snapped. "How could I conceivably—"

"Don't deny it, you ignoramus!" Rajelis exploded, fingers clawing the sheets. "You *raped* her beautiful *soul*! Why, you're typical of the unevolved majority that has always meddled in and villified whatever you can't grasp in your woeful little sphere of experience. Worse, you're one of the *new* kind—the kind that attacks and plunders before an applauding audience of tens of thousands . . . that sacrifices *anybody* to advance another rung up your ridiculous ladder! Well, your shallowness and stupidity is no longer condoned!"

"Look, Cal," Grady began, truly upset. For the first time it occurred to him that getting things out in the open could mean a less than bloody end to the nightmare—but he was deeply shocked to hear that he'd done such harm to anyone's mother in the name of achieving an interesting interview. Much worse, the notion that even a man like Rajelis had a side of his own contradicted still more of Grady's bland, lifelong assumptions. "If I hurt Seera because of some tough questions, man, I apologize. Sincerely."

"It's far too late for that."

"See, Mr. Rajelis, folks who appear on TV aren't *forced* to do it, they're—"

"You still don't get it!" Rajelis exclaimed. The first tender emotion Grady'd seen in the mentalist surfaced in the not-unpleasant features and Rajelis's body began to jerk. "My Seera was exquisite: vital . . . a *goddess!*" His arms and legs twitched violently as Rajelis leaned up from the chair, face like flame. "She was the one I could *love!*"

He jumped up, then, each hand clutching the wrist of a sedated child. Before Grady could move, the tall man was clambering across David's bed, dragging both boys with him to the window. They were only on the second floor, but it was high enough. Rajelis's motion had been lithe beyond Calhoun's belief, apparently effortless. Groggily, David had opened his eyes. Petey cried out in pain, and Calhoun saw that the bandages on the wrists Rajelis clutched were turning red. Grady muttered a threat and started forward.

"Stay *there,* Calhoun!" Rajelis hoisted the children into the air until his arms were fully extended. Now he was smiling and Grady, who had not seen Billy Salvo, could never have believed that Salvo's smile displayed greater evil. Rajelis inclined his head to indicate the curtained windows at his back. "The windows are closed—but I promise you I have the strength to throw these spawn of yours through the pane!"

Spontaneously, with no thought at all, Calhoun half-turned and raised his voice to the shout of a lifetime. "*Help* us, for God's sake! Security—*help!*"

Each word bounced back at him like

stinging pellets. *Help us*—as if alive, the
simple syllables caromed off an unsee-
able wall of silence between Calhoun and
the corridor beyond the open door—*for
God's sake*—and Grady threw up his hands
to protect his face from their sting—*security help*—Calhoun winced with pain, spun
back to face the occultist.

What he saw simultaneously amazed
and paralyzed him.

Still holding Grady's children high,
swinging them to and fro, Rajelis had
created a world of his own liking. He stood
upon the pinnacle of a towering,
mountainous growth the color of decaying
human skin. Petey and David, clutching at
Rajelis in terror, no longer were
threatened by a fall of two stories to the
city street but were dangled over a pit of
unfathomable depth . . . a pit with
immense, ebon lips that moved hungrily
like the mouth of some monstrously
sucking beast.

Even that did not bring the greatest
horror to Grady.

Rajelis and Calhoun's youngest sons
existed now, apart from him, in an atmos-
phere of abject hopelessness . . . a world
of off-white bleak nothingness akin to the
confines of a tomb sealed for centuries—
a wholly lifeless universe comprised of
inverted shadows . . . shadows, perhaps,
cast by the shades of the first men and
women to die on the planet earth.

"This is how I have existed, Calhoun,"
Rajelis whispered; "it is the world into

which you plunged *me* at the hour you chose to destroy my mother." Squeezing his fingers, he jerked Petey and David from side to side until they howled. "*Choose!* One shall be permitted to live—for a while." Rajelis's dark brows raised and his features were radiant against the backdrop of his perpetual gloom. "The other goes into the pit . . . to serve the Forces of Suffering forever."

"It's a trick, an illusion!" Swallowing hard, Grady took a step toward them . . . and nullity. But he froze when the mentalist braced himself and suddenly stopped swinging the children. His gaze defied Calhoun to come closer. "You crazy son of a bitch, this isn't *real!*"

Calvin's face turned to unmoving gray stone and Grady instantly regretted his invective. That instant, Rajelis became one with the fleshy promontory upon which he and the boys teetered. " 'Son of . . . a *bitch*?' "

"It's only an expression," Grady moaned. "Please—"

"Too late!" Rajelis snapped. His eyes were like jewels. "Time for you to choose, Calhoun . . . which one lives." In turn, he shook each terrified boy like a terrier shakes a rat. Portions of the mountain that resembled body parts crumbled and fell forever. "And which offspring lives *forever*—in Suffering?"

Bud had a split-second to realize that her gun was in her purse, and the purse was on the table by the entrance way—

Then Salvo had her in his arms. His strength, like everything else about him when it had revealed itself, was astonishing. If Bud had momentarily hoped that his life and death decades ago had rendered him insubstantial or frail, her hopes were instantly dashed. Simply the dismaying force of his crushing arms, dragging over her and trying to bring her to the floor, tore the front and one sleeve of her jacket and left the cloth hanging.

Worse was Billy's touch as he pawed at her, and the sudden, mind-reeling press of his mouth to the side of her neck. His hands were dew-damp and clammy, sending shivers down her spine; the moist lips were rough and scaly.

And when he wrestled Bud to her knees, still witlessly hugging her to him, his chest was flush to hers and, for one quick tick of a moment, Bud tried harder to feel a heartbeat than to get away from him.

"I 'member everything!" Billy boasted. With no warning, his pawlike hand reached beneath Bud and caught her heel, her foot. He yanked and she sprawled on her back. He was atop her at once.

"Tim!" she screamed, and tried to wrist her head to see the boy. "In my purse! Please—*get it*! Help me!"

Then she realized Cathy's shrieks of fright made it impossible for Tim to hear.

She strove with all her might to get Salvo off her, make him stop what he was doing. How had this creature ever deceived anyone? But of course, Rajelis had fed him what to say, telepathically.

When Billy cuffed her, bearlike, and straddled her, and she saw his awful smirking face painted by reflection from the fire, she gave up and almost went under.

Her solitary hope was that Tim and Cathy would get away.

"Or is there the slightest doubt in your mind whom you will select, Mr. Calhoun?"

Grady gasped his self-revulsion, his feeling of unforgivable betrayal. His gaze *had* been centered on three-year-old Petey, his "baby." Had poor David caught it? Would he take such an abandonment with him to hell? Grady sucked in a deep breath.

"Your mother, Cal." His own voice sounded tinny, distant to Grady. "She was *one person.* Right? You've taken the lives of *dozens.*"

"She," Rajelis said sententiously, "was worth the world . . ."

"Uh-uh. You're wrong." The accumulated shock to Grady's sensibilities was now so overwhelming that he realized distantly that his emotional facility for reacting normally was stunted; only aspects of his mental capacity remained. Rajelis had inadvertently put him in touch with his own deepest individuality but, to do it, he had stripped Grady of all he had hoped or attempted to believe, everything he'd ever wanted to consider his own, his most precious personal view of "the world." In a bleak, alarming way, Calhoun had now reached either the exact root-center of his brain's capacity for empathy, compassion, the will to love—or he was reacting by rote. No longer could he be sure he loved anybody enough to complete this dreadful game. But he knew that his own horror would be sufficient to prevent Rajelis from winning it. Any other outcome was gross, indecent, and meant that Calvin's view of life from a tower of flesh made dead because he willed it so was the *real* view. Grady inhaled. "Nobody is."

"Come on, Calhoun—get it over with!" Rajelis held out Petey's wriggling body, the young face ashen and the eyes enormous, almost within arm's reach of his father. "You know *this* is the one you prefer. *Take* him, Calhoun, so I can pitch the other one into immortality!"

Immortality, the madman was saying, was the pit . . . was hell! Calhoun shook his head, dizzied by contradiction—and an amazing thing came over him. He sensed it happening, knew at once what it meant: that he'd either become mature, whole, valuable in the scheme of things—or irremediably insane.

Because he didn't hate Rajelis any longer and he didn't fear him. He didn't even fear what the son of a bitch could do to his children.

"There isn't any choice," he said. And

began, inch by inch, stalking the man on the mountain. Carefully; because risk-taking was not courage. A pace, and he felt the inverted shadows cling like cob-webs to him; but the lifeless ambience was a construct as so very much was in Rajelis's period on the planet. "I am going to save my children," Grady announced, "or all of us are going to die. Including you."

The illusion shimmered, and shattered. Vanished. There was no pinnacle, the mountain was imaginary; there was no cosmos of drab meaningless-ness. Whatever was, was. That was all. Nullity was merely the choice Rajelis himself had made years ago, and it thrived in his mind, but nowhere else.

Calhoun looked straight ahead. What was left was an ultimately pitiable lunatic who, without question, was both willing and able to throw either of Grady's kids through a plate-glass window. He *wanted* to. There was a difference between experiencing fear and simply under-standing the foe.

"Give me the little guys," he said calmly, putting out his arms. Expectantly. "Or I'm going to tackle you and we'll go through the window together."

Ambivalence constituted of surprise and doubt appeared on the tall youth's lantern face. Petey and David squealed; the baby cried, "*No, Daddy!*" Rajelis didn't appear to hear them. While he'd known a vulnerable period had begun for him, he clearly had not expected this kind of opposition from Grady Calhoun.

For one moment the Irishman thought he'd won. He held his arms steadily, patiently, waiting to collect his children.

But while the madman nodded, seemed to reflect slowly on his options, he also began unhurriedly elbowing and nudging the curtains behind him until they began to part. A strange glint appeared in his eyes.

Then he smiled and beamed at the Irishman, who gradually understood that the expression was not, in fact, directed at him. Grady shivered. Rajelis no longer saw him *at all*—his vision had reached beyond St. Vincent's Hospital, extended itself until it saw with another's eyes . . . "My William," Rajelis said. "He's raping *your* woman."

"No!"

"Well, not exactly in the technical sense of entry as yet," Rajelis murmured. His cheeks were flushed with excitement. His far-off eyes were like the bottoms of two switched-on flashlights and they might have glowed in the dark. "But William *has* . . . initiated contact."

I forgot about Salvo! Grady thought, heartbroken. Incredibly, he had also, somehow, underestimated Rajelis—who might not win the insane contest but could well become the one who left it with a smile. "Stop him," Grady pleaded. "Cal, you have to *stop* him."

"Come now." Rajelis looked disapproving. "When he has killed the news-person, as well, he'll do the same to each of your children with him: Cathy, the girl. Tim, the boy. William has your level of acuity, Mr. Calhoun . . . but he senses that a new world is beginning and knows who's in charge."

"*Please . . .*"

"Ah, you realize, then, that they are all beyond your protection now?" Calvin smiled. His full attention returned to the hospital room; he licked his lips and again lifted the boys into the air. "The failure is all yours, sir. You drove Tim away. Quite literally, you drove Ms. Rocker and your daughter into my William's waiting arms. *Think* of it, Mr. Calhoun: all your brood, dead . . . because of *you*."

"You can still stop him." Grady fell to his knees. Tears welled into his eyes. "Please do. I *beg* of you . . ."

"I'm teaching you certain lessons that will be engraved upon your soul. I am teaching you to respect my Seera. Calvin Rajelis. Magick. That the exquisite suffering of nothingness is quite real. And that evil is never to be taken lightly . . . that one must run from it, always—or serve it." Calvin was onstage and per-forming, but he played, primarily, to his deceased mother and Calhoun, who was also a performer, sensed it. Rajelis's arms were moving; he was rocking and sweeping Petey and David back and forth, back and forth, hypnotically—gathering the leverage required to send both little boys completely through the pane. His smile at Grady was almost tender. "You know, Mr. Calhoun, when they find our bloody bodies . . . when the so-called authorities make the vital connection between so many ruined lives, and *you* . . . I should not be surprised if they prove that Grady Calhoun went mad and murdered us all!"

With his last effort of defiance, Grady roared, drove up from his knees toward Rajelis—desperately trying to reach his youngest sons before they were gone for all time.

31

4:44 P.M.

He was biting her on the neck, breasts, wherever he could, the huge mouth seeming to devour wide areas of Bud's skin. Mostly, he sucked at her, fishlike. He had yet to close his jaws with their full, rending strength, but Bud knew he would and that he was playing with her—that Billy would, in all probability, eat a portion of her flesh before finishing with her.

Because the worst pain hadn't begun yet; other monstrous things kept trying to shove Bud's keen mind off center, send her thoughts spinning in a sort of erratic spiral until she veered dangerously near the actual desire for this to be ended. His prying fingers, the press of his naked chest against hers—he had ripped away his tanktop as if it had been made of toilet tissue—were lizardy, maybe froglike. And, even when he hugged her clumsily against him from time to time, his hands fawning, Bud felt no heartbeat.

They'd scrabbled close to the far wall—as distant from the petrified kids as Bud's presence of mind and personal valor could take them—and she had held him off from the opportunity to pin and to penetrate her. It was at the painful cost of countless splinters in her bare back and upper thighs; she felt painted by bruises. At one point she had begun a droning wail of misery; at some other point she'd stopped it and started simply fighting him, any way she was able. She'd clawed at his dumb face and hairless arms, constantly striven to raise her knee sharply into his groin, but he'd flopped like a fish, giggling.

Now he had her; she had no space left in which to scoot away from him, and Bud realized her strength was spent, or close to it. With a leg on either side of her squirming body, a pale meaty hand holding her down, Billy was sitting up and working at undoing his zipper. She wondered dully if they'd had zippers when he was really alive. When it stuck Billy wrenched at it with his entire strength and the thing came away from the cloth of his ragged jeans. He displayed it for her, dangled it in her face like the smile of a sideways shark—

Then showed her something else.

Bud gagged in disgust, turned her head to choke back bile. Billy's regeneration had not been whole; even his private parts were not quite normal. When he undoubtedly functioned—she could not question that, didn't dare hope after what had happened to poor Jean Calhoun—it wasn't right. The thing was corrupt, unclean. It observed ancient, malodorous midnights. Lightning flashed at a window above the fireplace and Billy paused, fleetingly, with a wince.

Then he'd regained his composure—remembered his instructions—and was attacking her undergarments like a frenzied beast unearthing bones. Bud dimly recalled a childhood prayer.

As Grady leaped, seven-year-old David Calhoun caught Rajelis's arm with his bandaged little hands and yanked—hard! It threw the mentalist off balance. Astounded, he turned his head to glance down quickly at the boy.

Grady tackled the man waist-high, driving both of them—and the children—sickeningly forward.

But young David's surprising action had pulled the thin man out of line, and the four of them collided against the wall instead of the windows. *My little David did it!* rejoiced Calhoun—

But the heavy curtains were entangled with Rajelis and came down with a rush like Niagara, the rod hitting Grady, dizzingly, in the temple.

Stunned and blinking, he made himself keep his eyes open, look up. Rajelis had maintained his rough hold on Petey—

And he was spinning toward the window with a feral and purposive growl.

Her face averted to prevent him, at least, from kissing her lips, Bud's heart soared with hope. Tim *had* heard her, after all! He'd snatched up her handbag and plunged his hand inside! Buoyed, Bud clamped her legs together with the rest of her waning energy. Now Tim *had* it, he'd *found the gun—*

But he was looking questioningly from it to Bud and Billy, to his sister Cathy, and back at the gun. "Tim . . . please!" Bud shouted. "Shoot him!" Thunder boomed; lightning crackled at the windows.

At that moment, Cathy broke and ran, further distracting Tim. Bud heard the little girl's footsteps as she rushed frantically through the entrance way and toward the cottage door.

Salvo seemed to notice none of it. Poised above Bud, reaching down with his hands to paw at and pry her legs apart, he was in his element. Rajelis' guidance was not needed. The wide mouth was open, drooling. His nails dug at her soft flesh, scratching deeply. She freed one arm, struck the thing in the jaw as hard as she could and, laughing, he seemed to like it.

Distantly, Bud realized, the front door was being tugged open. She looked again toward Tim, yearningly. Awkwardly, he'd raised the pistol and was aiming it, taking forever.

The storm ended. The interior of the cottage filled with light. It was as if Bud, the children, and Billy Salvo had stood in the center of the Indianapolis Motor Speedway at the running of the fastest 500-Mile race ever.

It was bright as noon.

Tim Calhoun's finger squeezed, and most of Billy's skull separated from the lower half. What remained was a twitch of one nostril and a gaping mouth frozen in a lustful smirk. One bullet had penetrated his brain just as one bullet had more factually "killed" William Salvo more than three decades before and, to Bud's horror, she watched as droplets of oozing dark blood splattered against the wall behind the all but headless body. Other substances emerged, as well, glimmering faintly like dying fireflies.

Then the body fell away from her and thudded against the fireplace. Beyond it—beside Tim—Bud thought momentarily she saw the uncertain, pale form of a burly man in a double-breasted pinstripe suit and snap-brim fedora, a smoking police automatic clutched in both hands.

But she must have been wrong. Because, as it was with the incomplete, ultimately insubstantial Salvo when she glanced back at where he'd been, the eerie shape had vanished.

In his soul, Grady yelled *NO!*

Rajelis's arms shot out, murderously, thrusting Petey against the window—and time seemed to stop. Where the world had been streaked with rain and oncoming dusk, *brilliant light* flooded the hospital room. Calhoun threw up his hands to the glare, instinctively, saw with relief and amazement that his smallest son had not gone through the glass . . . thought perversely, *Sun's out*—but nothing about it resembled twilight time. Nothing about it was the wan luminosity of the period between night and day or that between day and night.

He caught Petey when Rajelis dropped him to fumble frantically in his pockets for the omnipresent dark glasses. Without hesitation, Grady tucked a son under each arm and backed off, staring fearfully at the mentalist. Not for a second did he remove his gaze from Rajelis, who got the dark glasses up to his face before, strangely, letting them merely slip from his fingers. Yet he had neither spoken nor turned back to them.

Instead—while Calhoun deposited both boys in the hallway, strove to decide whether to follow them at a run, Rajelis was very slowly straightening . . . stretching to his full height. He'd never seemed so thin, almost emaciated. Again, back still turned, he began lifting his arms with infinite   deliberation . . . to   the   inexplicably dazzling, almost scalding sunlight.

He turned, at last, expression still beseeching. But the silent plea wasn't, Calhoun thought, intended for him. Grady tensed himself, expected to be charged. But Rajelis simply stood there, immobile. Behind him . . . beyond the windows . . . the sunstream abruptly dimmed, faded out. There came one microsecond when Calhoun, seeing past the tall man, imagined the sky had grown *darker* than he'd ever seen it in his life. But that was only an instant—and then it was late afternoon . . . evening . . . over the city; nothing more.

Still, Rajelis did not move. His arms remained raised but he did not speak. His lean face was unreadable.

Carefully, but not with hesitation, Grady advanced toward him, knowing only that he had to. Something was wrong.

Rajelis slumped to his knees then, silently. When he finally mumbled syllables that could have been a woman's name, it dawned on Calhoun that he was looking down at a grown man with the mind of a child.

"What is it?" Grady whispered, bending lower. "Cal?"

The expression was readable now. It was one of bewilderment. And hopelessness. One upraised hand was shaking. "Do you know where my mother is?" he asked.

Calhoun drew in a breath. "No," he admitted. "I don't know, really. I'm sorry."

Trembling fingers touched his cheek. "Would you find her for me and tell her something?"

Grady nodded. But only until it occurred to him that nodding wasn't enough. That Rajelis was blind. "If I . . . find her . . . I will."

"Tell her," Calvin said, haltingly, "tell her I love her. Okay?" He began to weep. His shoulders worked, his slender back spasmed. "And please . . . *don't* make me go back in that closet, okay?" Rajelis shuddered the length of his six-foot body and Grady knew he had never seen such fright in a human face—not even the face reflected to him by his own mirror. "Please? 'Cause . . . 'cause *something's in there!*"

"Take heed therefore that the light which is in thee be not darkness."

—*Luke* 11:35